IS STACEY PREGNANT?
Notes from the Irish Dystopia

Tomás Mac Síomóin

Originally published in Irish Gaelic.
Translated by the author.

Irish Gaelic edition, *An bhfuil Stacey ag iompar?*, published by Coiscéim, 2011.
Irish Gaelic text ©Tomás Mac Síomóin, 2011.
English text ©Tomás Mac Síomóin, 2014.

All rights reserved.

No part of this book may be reproduced in any form or by any means including electronic or mechanical photography, filming, recording or by any information storage and retrieval or video systems without prior permission from the publishers, Nuascéalta Teoranta.

www.nuascealta.com • info@nuascealta.com

Cover Illustration and Design: © Karen Dietrich.

Photo of Tomás Mac Síomóin: Máire Uí Mhaicín.

Typesetting: Nuascéalta Teoranta.

ISBN-13: 978-1499213546

ISBN-10: 1499213549

ALSO BY TOMÁS MAC SÍOMÓIN

NOVELS

An bhfuil Stacey ag iompar? (Coiscéim, 2011)

Ceallaigh (Coiscéim, 2009)

An Tionscadal (Coiscéim, 2007)

In inmhe (Coiscéim, 2004)

*Ag altóir an diabhail:
striptease spioradálta Bheartla B* (Coiscéim, 2003)

SHORT STORIES

Diary of an Ant (Nuascéalta, 2013)
English translation of *Cín Lae Seangáin agus Scéalta Eile*

Cín Lae Seangáin agus Scéalta Eile (Coiscéim, 2005)

For Karen, con mucho cariño.

You want to know something?
The Dark Ages—they haven't ended yet.
Kurt Vonnegut-Deadeye Dick

BOOK ONE

ERA OF THE GULLS

GLIDING SMOOTHLY along the twisting country lane between Killnad and Dunveaty, grassy townlands west of the Shannon waking up now from the long winter sleep, goeth The Citroën. Hawthorn is in heavy flower, the blossoms lying like snow on the branches of hedgerows that come down to meet the road. Crows, woodpigeons, even the occasional grouse, strut the deserted dawn roads. Spring scents waft in through the half-open driver's window. How great it is to be alive, says The Citroën to himself, as he drives along, basking in the luxury of what some might call "a banal sentiment".

The stone walls of Poulnalackan, Cloughgun and Tullybrack have now been left well and truly behind. However, his concern is now more with the time of the day rather than the etymology of the ancient townlands through which he is driving. He makes constant comparisons between the time indicated by the dial of the Rolex watch on his left wrist and that announced every half-hour on his car radio. He half-listens to *Josie Thornton's Morning Show*, Ireland's favorite phone-in program. Listeners' problems are discussed by the host, the "one and only" Josie Thornton, Ireland's Agony Uncle. "The only man in the country who really understands the minds of women" as Josie himself is wont to boast.

That god-awful yapping windbag is at it again, says The Citroën under his breath. But no denying the fact that although the same smarmy cokehead may well blabber through his arse, he does have his finger clamped to the pulse of the real Ireland.

Worse shaggin' luck!

+++++

ARE YOU STILL THERE, *Sheila? asks Josie.*

Of course I am, Josie! And why wouldn't I be?

True for you, love! A fine spring morning and the whole country on tenterhooks, wanting to find out if Stacey is pregnant or not! And is Doug the "naughty one", as Sister Mary might have put it? Or could it be Howard? Now there's a thought. But, anyhow, that is the mega-mega-question that is exercising all of the keen minds of Ireland this blessed morning. And everyone is sure to have their own answer to that question, except those who have yet to make their minds up. But, one way or another, all of us will get the answer to that question tonight. Tonight is the night, as the fella says. However, be that as it may, tell us this, Sheila: what neck of the woods do you hail from, Sheila, I love that name... can't say it often enough...

Get outa that, Josie! From Glenawney, would you believe! It's not likely that you ever heard of the place, Josie. Not every Dick and...

Fabulous, Sheila! Sheila from Glenawney! You'll have to fill me in on that one, love! For strange as it may seem, that is one glen I have never been to. Never ever! But, if you say so, Sheila, I'm sure it is a by-oo-tiful place. A by-oo-tiful name on a by-oo-tiful place, without doubt, folks. Even if every Dick, ahem, 'n Harry doesn't know it! And your accent tells me loud and clear that this Glenawney of yours, by-oo-tiful name, is less than a thousand miles from Galway fair city of the tribes?

Aren't you the sharp one, Josie! You never lost it, fair play to you! No flies on you, Josie! But I'm not livin' any longer in Glenawney, in Glenawney so far away, as the song says. I left...

Ah, Sheila, sure I remember that song very well. Didn't I often hear it being sung by Dirty Dan and The Drifters; they were probably a while before your time, love. And that tells you how old I am, folks. And a great singing group they were who never got the recognition they should have got. But that's the way it is in this vale of tears. In Glenawney those summer morning / With my true love I would stray / Down by the potato gardens / In Glenawney so far away. A great song, folks; they don't make them like that anymore. And a great place, Glenawney! What ever possessed you to leave such a great place Sheila? Why, now? Don't be afraid to tell Josie and all the folks out there. Shyness is banned on Josie's Morning Show! Oh, what a by-oo-tiful mornin'...

Well, who'd ever believe that Josie Thornton had the national anthem of Glenawney off by heart? That bates Banagher, as they say. Fair play to you! I love the Glen, I really do. But, unfortunately, Josie, there's no life left there at all. That's the way it is. Divil a bit! For young people, you know what I mean.

Of course I know what you mean, Sheila. All the crack is in Cricklewood, as the fella says. Even if there was a discotheque in the place! So you headed for the bright lights, Sheila, fair dues to you. And why wouldn't you and no life at all left for young people left in the Glen? But so much for that, folks! Sheila is here, folks, because she has a personal problem that is causing her to lose sleep. A personal problem that we are going to discuss here this blessed spring morning, isn't that right, Sheila? And isn't that why we are here every blessed morning except Sundays, Good Friday and Christmas Day. To discuss your problems and, with the help of our listeners out there, to find solutions!

I hear what you're sayin', Josie. I have a bit of a problem, all right.

(A long silence)

Are you still with us, Sheila?

Of course I am, Josie.

Well then, Sheila, why don't you speak up now and tell us what your problem is. Is it something to do with you self-esteem? Thousands of women throughout Ireland are just dying to hear what you have to say this fine spring morning. Spring is bursting out all over as the poet once said. It's on the cards, Sheila, that many of our listeners out there are suffering from the very same problem, whatever that is. No man, or woman if it comes to that, is an island, as it says in the Bible. Encouraging words, don't you think, Sheila! Was it Shakespeare or James Joyce first thought of them? But what do we care, and spring bursting out all over, as the poet said. So away you go, Sheila, let our listeners out there have the full Monty, if you don't mind. And we want all our listeners out there to listen carefully to what Sheila says as she describes her personal problem, whatever it turns out to be. And if you have some good advice to give her, well Josie's Morning Show always keeps the lines open for listeners to have their say.

Well, Josie, to tell you the God's honest truth, Josie, I'm sort of ashamed of meself to be letting the whole world know what my problem is. You know what I mean In all fairness, I mean to say, Josie, that it is a problem that only we women know about, you know what I mean. I have the fear of God on me that some of the people listening to me are going recognize my voice. If that happened, I'd die of shame, you know what I mean. Honest to God, Josie. They'd all be laughin' at me. And if my mother heard me, she'd kill me, so she would. You know what I mean, Josie! Because the problem has to do with my tits.

(Silence)

With your breasts. Did you listeners get that? The problem has to do with Sheila's breasts. Please don't think for a moment, Sheila, that this Josie, sitting here in this studio, this fine spring morning, is blind to the problems of the fair sex. Far from it! Our regular listeners, the thousands of you out there all over Ireland, will know that many is the time we have discussed openly the problems women can have in this changing Ireland of ours, emotional problems, health problems, the whole gamut of problems that are specific to the fair sex.

You know, or should all know, that this program welcomes free and open discussion of questions that were taboo up to now in Ireland. No hot potato is too hot for Josie Thornton to handle! We want our Morning Show to be the breath of fresh air that is needed to sweep out all that stale air that has stifled free debate for far too long in the dark and fetid corners of poor ould Mother Ireland's kitchen. You know what I mean. Fresh light on dark corners, as the fella says. For far too long, the women of Ireland have been smothering under a pile of meaningless superstitions that have no basis at all in fact. Out with the dark, I say, and in with the light!

And let all of you listeners out there, the women of Ireland, know that the Josie Thornton who Sheila is talking to is a married man. Yes sirree! Your sympathetic host for whom tits, breasts and other private parts not usually given an outing over the air waves, are far from being a mystery. Things that are as natural as... Are you still on the line, Sheila?

Why wouldn't I be, Josie? In all fairness, did you think I was going to run away or something?

Fair play to you, Sheila! The beauty queen of Glenawney is still with us. Put on a brave front, girl! Fortune favors the brave, as Shakespeare said. All of us, meself and the entire nation, are waiting to hear what you have to tell us. And we're here to support you, no matter what you have to say. This is your moment of fame, Sheila, and to hell with the begrudgers. You were talking about your breasts...

That's just it, Josie. The problem is their size. In all fairness, you know what I mean...

Not really, Sheila, love. Could you be a little more specific, love. Are they too big? Or too small?

There you have it Josie.

So, they are too big, those breasts you are telling us about, Sheila?

No, Josie! Too small! That is what the lad I am walking out with tells me, anyways. All the time! He never stops bitchin' about me tits! He is always making me cry, but tears don't stop him. No, not him! And now he is saying to me that I'll have to go and get something done about them...

Hold on there, Sheila. Let's get this straight. You think you have a problem because your boyfriend thinks your breasts are too small. I might mention here that not all men are attracted by enormous mammaries. In any case, what you are giving me to understand is that your boyfriend's behavior, his macho attitude, is lowering your self-esteem.

In all fairness, Josie, I wouldn't know anything about that. All I know is that my breasts are too small. Even though I am well into my twenties, they hardly fill the A cups of my bra. I have to stuff the bra cups with cotton wool or stockings to make my you-know-whats look presentable. So that I look as if I am well-stacked, as they say! You can only imagine how I would feel, if that secret got out at work. So, that's my problem, Josie. And I don't know what to do about it. But I'll have to do something or I'll go mad. Jason says—that's not his real name (and I'm not Sheila either)—that if I don't do something about it, I'll live to regret it.

Hmmm, I see! You've all heard that, listeners. Sheila's boyfriend doesn't like the small size of her breasts and she is becoming desperate. But Sheila (although you aren't really Sheila), how did this Jason (who isn't really Jason) discover your secret?

(Silence)

Sheila, are you still with us?

I am, Josie. But I'd be ashamed to give you the real answer to that question.

No need for shame now, Sheila—nobody knows who or where you are. And fortune favors the brave, as the great Sligo poet W.B. Yeats once said. Just take a deep breath and let the truth out and be done with it!

Righto, Josie! Well, he was, well, messing...You'd know what I mean, in all fairness, Josie, messing, when his fingers found the cotton wool. I nearly died from shame. And he got into a right bad temper. Saying that I had been fooling him all along and if I didn't do something about my "tiny tits", as he called them, our *engagement would be off. And that June wedding as well, he said. You can just as well forget about the confetti! And I wouldn't mind that, Josie, only that I am head over heels in love with Jason. It was love at first sight from the word go. And he says he's madly in love with me. But wild horses couldn't drag him into a marriage with a woman with small tits. That's just the way he is. I would be heartbroken if he left me, Josie. I just can't help it. And that's God's honest truth, you know what I mean!*

Ah, now I get you, love. In all fairness, it seems to me that your Jason has a breast fetish that has led him into making an unreasonable demand, for all intents and purposes, on your good self, Sheila. But tell me: what do you think he means by doing "something about it".

He's been talking about plastic surgery, Josie. And that puts the fear of God into me, you know what I mean. The thought of those sharp knives gives me the shivers. I read in a magazine about a woman whose life was ruined by a plastic surgeon's botch job; that's what the article called it. You should have seen the photographs that showed her face before and after the operation. They were awful! Scarred for life she was, the poor creature. What do you think I should do, Josie?

Before I'd ever venture an opinion, Sheila, I'd like to listen to the opinions of all those women who are listening to us out there, some of whom are bound to have undergone successful plastic surgery and proudly display their silicone enhanced breasts, modestly covered of course, to the world. I'm sure there are hundreds, if not thousands, like them throughout Ireland who are now pondering Sheila's story and thinking up words of advice for her and willing to share with her the benefits of their own experience. Among whom my own wife could be named. I'm on safe ground here for, to tell you the God's honest truth, Carmel never listens to our program. It's more than enough for her to hear me sound off around the house, she says. Can I really be all that bad... ah, we have a listener on the line, Adrienne who will be talking to us from...Portarlington!

But first of all, a little question for you all: is Stacey pregnant? And, if so, who is the guilty party? Has Howard anything to do with it, if we indeed find out that Stacey is expecting? Since Stacey ended her affair with Courtney, Howard appears to be coming more and more into the picture, rushing in where angels fear to tread, as James Joyce used to say. Be that as it may, Adrienne, let us know what you think of Sheila's breast problem! And, given that you have had silicone breast implant surgery, what advice have you got for the beautiful Sheila of beautiful Glenawney, whose tale of woe you have just heard?

+++++

THERE IS A SUDDEN TURN in their road just outside Glenveal. A road sign, almost fully concealed by overhanging foliage, warns approaching motorists of that impending danger.

Jaysus! As he tries to negotiate this unexpected stretch, The Citroën almost crashes into the wall on the far side of the road, having been forced to jerk the steering wheel suddenly in order to avoid hitting a red-haired woman cycling in the other direction. Lucky he didn't flatten her.

This near miss drives his heart into his mouth.

His attention to driving had been distracted by Josie's prattle, of course. And by the latter's obscure references to Stacey and her pals, Doug and Howard. Who, in the name of Jaysus, are these creeps, both the male and the female ones? The nose of the bonnet is scarcely one half inch from the stone wall on the other side of the road as his car screeches to a halt. The shrill voice of Adrienne of Portarlington explains that Howard has damn-all to do with Stacey and that, in any case, Stacey, being the careful woman that she is, is hardly likely to let herself get into the family way.

He opens the car door, descends, and hurries over to the other side of the road, *Josie Thornton's Morning Show* continuing on its merry way behind him. Hoping to Jaysus that this red-haired woman cyclist on the other side of the road is uninjured.

Are you okay there, he asks anxiously. She descends slowly from her bicycle and turns to The Citroën, her broad peasant face drained of color with the start her near brush with death had given her. Or with her anger at The Citroën's driving?

Am I fucking well all right? Well you may ask, you bastard. Who do you think you are, fuckin' Brad or what?

The Citroën does not understand this obscure, for him, reference. Who the hell is Brad? The shrew continues to bombard him with expletives: fuckin' this and fuckin' that!

They take to arguing. Each blaming the other. She, drawing on the riches of her seemingly endless repertoire of swear words, accuses him of being drunk.

Don't try to deny it! I can smell your shaggin' breath from here, she says. You're fuckin' fluthered!

The Citroën, speaking as softly as the circumstances permit, accuses his furious protagonist of cycling carelessly on the wrong side of the road. Just then, the context of their heated *tête-à-tête* changes suddenly. And definitely not for the better as far as he is concerned!

A large-framed thuggish looking character now appears on the scene, a sudden apparition of a demon of simian aspect from the lower reaches of hell. With a three-day beard and the bloodshot eyes of the habitual drunkard. He is the husband of the combative redhead, it transpires. Hands like shovels, curling into fists as soon as his spouse explains the cause of the altercation to him. "More gorilla than human being", summarizes The Citroën's assessment of this unwelcome new arrival. A surviving Neanderthal in this arsehole of nowhere!

This fuckin' bastard here nearly killed me, says the red-haired woman to her spouse. He was speedin' along like a fuckin' bat out of hell, just as if the bollix bleedin' owned the shaggin' road.

If that is what the fucker was at, Kate, you get right up

on your bike and get the fuck quickly down to Glenveal and bring the fuckin' Guards here. I'll stay here to keep an eye on this bollix, says The Gorilla, glowering at The Citroën, as he stands menacingly in front of the car door. The only escape route available to The Citroën is, thus, blocked.

If you come near that car, yeh fuckin' cunt, I'll fuckin' mangle yeh.

The Citroën, thinking quickly, realizes that he is stymied. He has absolutely no time to waste on this sort of tedious nonsense. He has a flight to catch later from Dublin airport along with Anna. He has lots of time to spare, bags of it. But a holdup of this nature could last for hours. Time to enter into negotiations!

He reckons rapidly that Glenveal should be three miles at least from this ill-fated twist in the road. Glenveal, from the Gaelic *Gleann na bhFaol* (Wolves Glen). Hardly a more appropriate toponym! Just as sweet-mouthed Kate is about to take off to call the Gardaí, The Citroën announces a proposition. He explains to this quarrelsome twosome that he is on his way to succor his terminally ill mother. And, furthermore, that he is willing to pay them a small compensatory sum in order to let bygones be bygones. A sort of goodwill gesture! The instant flash of greed from those four eyes tells him instantly, bingo! A deal is possible. The only problem now is the price.

How much the fuck for each of us?, asks The Gorilla brusquely.

For both of you?

That's what I said, you bollix. You said you were goin' to fuckin' pay. Don't try to fuckin' back out of it now!

Why in the hell should I pay him? The Citroën asks himself silently. But he understands that he is now well and truly cornered by this menacing harpy and her simian consort. And, as is clear from the self-satisfied look on both of their faces, they understand clearly that they are just about to snag this unexpected bonanza.

How about 5 euros each? asks The Citroën.

The red-haired woman laughs sarcastically.

Jesus Christ! Are you fuckin' mad or do you think we were born yesterday, me bucko? Did you hear that fuckin' joke, Mick. He is as stingy as that fuckin' Ben who didn't even buy a present for Stacey on her fuckin' birthday. Fuckin' 5 euros compensation after the bastard nearly killed me. 5 euros and look at that shiny new Citroen you've got to go cavortin' around the bleedin' country in. And, of course, a woman by herself out in the country could accuse a fucker like you of more things than speedin'. Dead fuckin' right she could! 'No problem at all! Fuckin' pawing, and worse: that'd get the TV and the papers to nail you! Not to mention the fuckin' Guards...

€50 each, you cunt, says The Gorilla, a gentleman not given, plainly, to flowery rhetoric.

€20 each, says The Citroën.

The red-haired woman and The Gorilla eye each other briefly. They do not speak. But the telepathy of greed works just as efficiently in their case as speech.

Shove €30 each into ours hands and we'll let you fuck off with yourself out of Glenveal, growls The Gorilla.

The Citroën doles out this sum into the eager waiting hands, sits into his car, backs it out from the wall and drives away, with an angry screeching of tires. Leaving his curse on that sharp bend in the road, on the foulmouthed red-haired woman, on her Gorilla/Neanderthal mate, on thrice-damned Glenveal before concerning his mind with questions that are of much greater import to a young middle-aged man hurrying to keep a tryst than an unpleasant, and un-necessary, squabble with a pair of quarrelsome troglodytes on an out of the way rural lane!

The Tourist Board (or was it Aer Lingus?) slogan that the Irish are "the friendliest people on earth" flit incongruously across The Citroën's mind. But where are all these gregarious Celtic bumpkins of the commercial myth hiding themselves?

Not in Glenveal. That's for sure!

+++++

ON HIS LONG JOURNEY towards the great Central Plain of Ireland that will shortly stretch out before him, The Citroën now understands, somewhat ruefully--but much too late now for regrets--that he should have commenced his trip a lot earlier and taken the new motorway, the so-called *Autobahn*, to Dublin. Instead he started late and took the winding byroad between Glenlongan, Stonecairn, Moykarka, and Mullaghmawm.

This is the price he is paying now for all those pints he drank last night back there in the cozy ambience of the Glenlongan Arms Hotel. For the after-hours football *craic* in the small resident's bar with some locals who had been driven there from the public bar by a noisy wedding party. Penance for those extra two hours he had spent dreaming between cool crisp bed sheets of Anna, when he should have hit the road earlier to keep his appointment with her! However, taking this shortcut, he reasoned, would make up for time lost in erotic reveries. However, he had not reckoned on this constant braking in twisting laneways or on that unpleasant incident, involving Kate the Valkyrie and the simian Mick, Glenveal's resident Gorilla.

Bad enough to be already behind schedule but, to add to his annoyance, the traffic is now beginning to slow down. Since that surly lout, with his Liverpool United jersey, filled his tank in a garage at the commencement of the motorway, at the edge of Clooneen Bog, the speed of the line of traffic in which he is now irremediably stuck is growing progressively slower. The long procession of cars in front of him stretches as far as his eye can see. A little later, and you would say that it is hardly moving at all. The Citroën has never seen traffic so dense on this stretch of road.

Must be all heading to some big game on in Dublin, he says to himself. Although he has heard of no such event scheduled for today or tomorrow. He would surely have heard about it last night in the Glenlongan Arms. They hardly speak of anything else out here in the West. Football from morning to bloody night and Rome burning to a cinder in the meantime! Or could it be that all of these motorists and their passengers are returning early from a few days out west, beside the Atlantic? Possible, though hardly likely in the month of May, in spite of this unseasonably early heat wave! But, for whatever bloody reason, we appear to be running into some sort of traffic jam...

We are now down to a crawl, God blast it!

And now we are stopped altogether! He turns off the engine. Starts it again! We move forward. Three shaggin' meters, if that! Stop again! Turn off the engine. Godammit to hell! We are stopped altogether again and there is no movement at all now up front. Two motionless lines of cars on this new motorway out here in the back of beyond! All heading eastwards; westward traffic in the right hand lane is nonexistent. Without a house or any other sign of civilization in sight! Nothing but black bogland stretching away hazily to the horizon!

Fuck this for a game of cowboys!

He opens the door of his car, gets out and stands on the road looking eastwards. There is absolutely nothing to be seen from where he is standing to an elevated section of the road about 5 km to the east of them but two lines of cars, interspersed with trucks, vans and lorries and a bus in the distance. Even the occasional tractor! Just two glittering metal lines snaking eastwards, parallel to each other, as far as the eye can see!

Small groups of motorists gather here and there along the grass verge of the westward bound section of the motorway. Mainly men! Blue-gray clouds of cigarette smoke float above them. Energetic movements of their arms expressing their sense of frustration, anger, their sheer powerlessness to alter this unwelcome turn of events. Their womenfolk remain in the cars. Mutinous howling youngsters are pacified by them by cheese 'n onion or vinegar-flavored crisps. And the ubiquitous Kong Kola, of course. As they all half-listen, without doubt, to the inanities of *Josie Thornton's Morning Show*. Opinions regarding Sheila, the Queen of Glenawney, and the cosmetic surgery she may (or may not) be facing, are being bandied about. Along with the predictable meaningless chatter about the state of Stacey's womb, whoever she may be.

The Citroën prefers to enjoy his own company. Always has. To pass the time, he makes a report in his journalist's notebook on the imagined conversations of men, standing and smoking there in groups by the side of the road. He cannot visualize much variation on a common theme:

Jaysus! What in the hell is the reason for this delay?

And not a house, village nor town within 50 km of this shit-hole!

Nor a bleedin' bar in sight where a fella could wet his whistle!

Whatever bollix of a Minister who is responsible for roads and traffic needs to get his fuckin' marching orders, because this is nothing less than a fuckin' disgrace!

That gang of chancers is more on for spending big money on junkets to Europe than on using it to solve problems here in Ireland.

The money we earn by the bleedin' sweat of our brow being used to grease palms and to be spent wastefully.

On luxury fuckin' hotels!

On booze!

On expensive hoors!

Hear, hear, my friend! But the money that that gang wastes on junkets is as nothing compared to what is being swallowed up by all the black holes in the banks.

Throw them all into some shit-hole of a prison and throw the fuckin' key away! That is what I would do with the whole fuckin' lot of them.

I'd put the bastards up against a wall and let a firing squad take care of them!

The promises this new crowd made. And broke as

soon as we voted them in!

Hollow fuckin' promises that will never be fulfilled!

And then you have this new Taoiseach and his useless overpaid advisers!

It is these *bowsies* that have got us where we fuckin'-well are, not that bumbler!

We should wake up, shake ourselves and realize that Germany runs the show now!

There you have it, boy!

To hell with the all them foreign bastards! Ireland for the Irish!

Up ManU!

The Citroën is well accustomed in these ailing times to plain balderdash, harebrained projects, the whine of eunuchs, the vaporings of alehouse patriots.

He keeps his own counsel.

+++++

THE DOOR OF THE FORD ESCORT directly to his right and just opposite to him opens. The driver, a young woman, neither plain nor pretty descends to the road.

She treats herself there to a long luxurious stretch.

Two well-developed breasts strain against her tight-fitting pink sweater. Apart from that, decides The Citroën, she hardly merits a second glance. This Ford Escort creature is far from being an Anna, that is as sure as that eggs are eggs. Not by a long shot. She walks across the road towards him, waving her right arm in his direction. He lowers his window and smiles at her.

She says, this Ford Escort, her earrings dancing to the rhythm of her voice, that she makes this journey at this time every week. And I've never seen the road so choked up with cars. Never ever! There must have been an accident somewhere up ahead? There's a really dangerous stretch of the road just beyond Derryshinnagh. I always say that it is nothing short of miraculous that nobody—as far as I know—has been killed there yet. You would think that they would have flattened out that bend when they were turning this road—it used to be just a plain bog road—into a motorway.

And why didn't they?

Seems there was some mad talk of a fairy bush they didn't want to uproot. The European inspectors who were monitoring the project could hardly believe their ears when they heard that one...

The Citroën nods his agreement with her. Smiles inscrutably! He says: remember, girl, this is Ireland! With all the money they waste here on inflated salaries for fools and winnings for gamblers who have lost their bet, there are inevitable capital expenditure shortfalls whose effect is to put public safety at risk.

As he says this, he continues to scrutinize The Ford Escort. Her face will never launch a thousand ships, he surmises, but her figure may have that classical much sought after S look. Unfortunately, the outline of her thighs and her calves are hidden by the loose-fitting trousers she is wearing. If only she was wearing a skirt, his judgment of her esthetic qualities would be more complete.

She is a teacher, he says to himself, basing that conclusion on the authoritative tone of her voice. Not to mention those thick-rimmed spectacles sitting on the bridge of her nose, giving a vaguely owlish look to her rounded face. Her midland accent struggles to be heard beneath a heavy overlay of Dublin Four. Like a small sharp stone in a shoe that one struggles to forget.

The Citroën opens the door of his car, gets out and stands beside The Ford Escort. He tells her that what she is saying makes sense. There has to be some rational reason for this appalling traffic jam. A traffic accident up front, without doubt, he says. This delay could be due to just that or, maybe, the Gardaí are looking for somebody traveling eastward. Wasn't there some talk in the media recently of agitators or terrorists being holed up somewhere out West!

I never thought of that, she says. But with the way things are going in this unfortunate country the days nothing like that would surprise me. In any case, all we can do is hope that we will not be delayed for too long.

She is almost as tall as he is. Would she be better-looking if she abandoned those awful spectacles, with their thick black frames? Probably!

A traffic snarl like gives a person to understand that half of the population moves about on wheels these days, he says. Which is hard to believe, now that the good old days of the Celtic Tiger are gone the way of the dinosaur and the price of petrol is no joke! And then you have the cost of insurance. Why are they all on the move today? Is there some sort of major game on in Dublin?

She glances at him, surprised.

So, you really don't know why there are so many cars on the road today?

Not the faintest idea! If you know the reason why, I'd be grateful if you'd tell me.

However, The Citroën is not destined to hear the answer to his question.

For, just as The Ford Escort is about to answer, they both realize, standing there together on that country road, that something is about to happen. The ancient silence of the bog that stretches away from them, almost to the horizon, on both sides of the road, is punctuated now by the sudden distant bleating of car horns emanating from the rise on the road to the east of them. They then note that cars there are now beginning to move slowly. The traffic jam is beginning to unsnarl.

Better now than never, she says.

Thanks be to Crom, he says.

They race to their respective cars.

+++++

THE CITROËN STABS HIS KEY into the ignition and turns it. The engine starts up immediately. It is hard to beat this make of car, he tells his friends, often to the point of satiety on their part. It never lets me down. Who would be without a good car, these days, as shopping malls move further and further from the domiciles of their customers? This one glides along like a dream. And it isn't too heavy on petrol. When looking for a car, one should be just as discriminating as when seeking a wife. That's right! Buying a car is just as serious a business as contracting matrimony...

The radio starts up as soon as he twists the key. *Josie Thornton's Morning Show* is still under full steam. Another phone-in guest is now being questioned by the King Blatherer himself. Some woman with a strong American accent. She explains to Josie that she was a prisoner of gluttony until she was saved by the Buddha:

Seven meals a day, Josie, and a supersize of French fries with every one of them and a serving of potato crisps on the side. Those Taystees that have a lovely taste of cheese and onion. Not counting the fistfuls of sweets I'd be eatin' between meals, Josie. You know what I mean. I swear to God! No kiddin', I was McDonalds' and Burger King's best customer. Not to mention haunting Kentucky Fried Chicken and the Chinese. And the Indians sometimes too, in all fairness! I can hardly believe these days that I was so greedy then, Josie. Shoveling in food throughout the day! And I really mean shoveling, Josie. Day after day! Night after night! I was your original food junkie, Josie: the original fat fiend, as the fella says. And, worst of all, I was in complete denial. My self-esteem was not worth a bloody button in those days. I couldn't even look at myself in the mirror. Honest to God! There was no way I could resist the temptation of the good oul' cholesterol carousel. The full Irish breakfast and all of that!

But you managed to break that habit, Shirley?

Well, but for that book I chanced upon in a bookstore window, Meditate Your Fat Away, and the Buddha of course, I wouldn't be alive today to tell you my story, Josie. I'd have been making clay in some graveyard or other, and that is God's honest truth, no kiddin'. But for Meditate Your Fat Away, A Buddhist Guide to Weight Reduction, I still wouldn't be able to look into the mirror, Josie. And that is a truth that is as true as true can be...

The Citroën half-listens to this spiel. Josie must have solved the problem of the prospective cosmetic surgery patient while he, The Citroën, was talking to The Ford Escort. Or, maybe, it happened when he was in fractious dispute with The Gorilla and his loving spouse! Will timid Sheila---it was Sheila, wasn't it?---Queen of Glenawney, face the cosmetic surgeon resolutely and with the courage of her heroic breed? Or will she shrink back, terrified, from the challenge of the knife? Who gives a continental damn! The cars start to edge slowly forward.

And now, both lines are moving at the same speed. For about a kilometer, or so, they crawl. And then, goddammit to hell, they begin to slow down to snail pace. Jesus! Let there not be another delay!

The Yank, she of the excess avoirdupois, isn't really a Yank. *Not at all, Josie, I was born and reared in Boolabrack, and proud of it. But I spent a week in New York and another week with my Auntie Mary in South Boston when I was a teenager. Gee, know what, Josie, I just loved it, no kiddin', along with Hollywood movies and especially* Cougars. *Stacey and Beth are role models for me, Josie. And maybe that has something to do with my accent that you mentioned a few second ago...*

Jesus H. Christ!

The traffic grinds now to a complete halt. More delay. The Citroën once again curses his heedlessness in not having started on his journey earlier to beat the traffic. But how could he have known that his progress towards Dublin on this old motorway would be reduced to a crawl. He imagined that most drivers would have opted for the recently inaugurated *Autobahn*. He sits back resignedly in his driver's seat, stretching to give relief to his shoulders. What a bloody day! Between sudden road bends that don't appear on the map, that misnamed "short cut" and the run-in with the sweet-mouthed blackmailers who are now, without doubt, scoffing back €60 euros of his hard-earned *spondoolacks* in the form of big creamy pints at some sleazy hostelry in distant Glenveal.

Glancing into his rear mirror, The Citroën notes the ashen face of The Opel behind him. The scowl on the latter's face, gives him, The Citroën, to understand that this present delay is far from the liking of his fellow motorist. Could it really be that The Opel is wearing on his lapel the big golden *An Fáinne*, the superannuated symbol of the Irish Language movement? The symbol that indicates to all and sundry that he is a fluent Irish speaker, always able and willing to converse in the native tongue!

It is a long time since The Citroën has seen such a symbol. A smaller, more discrete lapel pin had taken the place of *An Fáinne*. And since, with the complete abandonment of the traditional national goals, total discretion then took the place of both of those symbols.

Is The Opel one of the old school of civil servants, then? Every possibility that he is! Or a teacher, maybe? A pensioned-off member of that professorial tribe? Or a university lecturer?

Well, the latter is the least likely option, decides The Citroën.

The holders of such sinecures prefer the murmur of social approval in their ears rather than pot-pourri of language revivalist slogans. Or, still less, having to rub shoulders with language cranks! But here behind me, at least, is one old Fáinne, ready and willing to discommode the comfy-holes of academia.

And ould Ireland shall be free!

+++++

THE CITROËN is not a gregarious sort of hail fellow well met. He is forever loth to be taken as such. If you were to canvass his acquaintances with a view to ascertaining his personality, they would probably tell you that he is a "private" sort of individual. Depending on whom you ask, of course. His enemies (he has some) would describe him as "anti-social" or "dark". Yet, he drinks his pint and is never shy about standing his round. Your average citizen? An Everyman, all things to all men? Can he be trusted not to add a discordant note to the lowing of the herd?

Could be! Unless you listen to him very carefully! Unless you happen to notice that he has the look of a person who listens to a music that seldom reaches the ears of the same herd.

However, most would agree that The Citroën is an obliging sort of fellow, one that you could depend on in times of woe. And now, bearing the ashen face of his fellow motorist in mind, he decides upon a work of corporal mercy. That is to say, he will find out if The Opel behind him is lacking water to alleviate his thirst, perhaps?

With this intention in mind, he grabs a plastic bottle that is full to the brim with water from the holy well near Letterfree, given to him by his wife's people before setting out for Dublin. He opens the door of his car, glancing to his right and noting that the nose of The Ford Escort across the way is buried in a newspaper spread out on the steering wheel in front of her. As he walks towards The Opel, he fills his lungs with that clean air of the countryside about them. But for his marginal anxiety about missing his flight later in the day, the perfume of new growth in his nostrils would inspire him to Spring giddiness, like the young lambs he saw earlier, kicking up their heels with excess of energy.

The veteran than sitting in his Opel observes his approach and, closing his eyes, with pretends to be dozing. The Citroën taps on the driver's window to draw his attention. The Opel "wakes up" with a "start". He grimaces as he lowers his window.

Well?

The Citroën greets him Irish. I don't want to disturb you, he says, but seeing that you are wearing the Irish Language

Fainne, I thought to come over to see how you were doing. Have you ever seen the likes of this traffic jam on an Irish road? If you would like some water…

I don't need your water. And if you want to speak the language, please learn to speak it in its pure form and not according to the pronunciation of some corrupt dialect. Indeed, the kind of Irish you speak is so littered with barbarisms, bad grammar and lazy expressions that it isn't worth speaking at all.

You are joking, surely, says The Citroën.

There you go again, says The Opel, mangling the pronunciation of our ancient tongue. A language that has come down the centuries in its purest form, only to wind up as an uncouth gibberish in the mouths of those who would claim to be its speakers! I am afraid you spend too much time listening to the Gaeltacht radio station, which I prefer to call "The Radio of Rotten Gaelic". In any case, I've have not the slightest interest in listening to the murder of our ancestral speech. I'll speak as much Irish as you want as long as you speak the language as it should be spoken. Otherwise, we'll stick to English!

Having delivered this parting salvo, The Opel raises his window abruptly. Conversation over! He shuts his eyes again.

The linguistic sermon of this pallid old veteran gives The Citroën a start. What a comic opera requiem for a dying tongue this encounter is! To argue the toss with him? A pure waste of time! But at least I didn't have to waste any of my precious water on the old crank.

With the way this jam is shaping up, you'd never know but that you may need it!

+++++

WITH HIS CAR SEAT again under his backside, The Citroën decides to to open all the doors of his car. To let the pure air of spring waft through the vehicle to purge it of all of its accumulated stale air! He twists the screwtop off his water bottle and, unthinkingly, drinks about one third of its contents. Better me than that ould bastard, he says to himself.

The couple in the Cortina in front of him are eating sandwiches. A small somewhat obese child observes The Citroën from the rear window of his car. He laughs and sticks his tongue out at the driver of the car behind him.

The Citroën, seeing nothing else to do, switches on the car radio.

Obese, like 56% of the population of European Union, Josie Ireland's Agony Uncle Thornton is now reminding the far-flung band of his listeners. *And isn't it an awful thing, he asks, that more than half of us are suffering from some form of obesity while millions are starving from hunger?*

It is obvious that the parents of that living dumpling in the Cortina there in front of me have not been in touch with the Buddha, thinks The Citroën, regarding their child's obesity. Nor have they read *Meditate Your Fat Away*. With a grunt of annoyance The Citroën extinguishes the jabbering voices of Josie and that other dumpling: faux Yankee dame from Boolabrack.

The thought-triturating thump-thump-thump of trance music emanating from an old renovated DAF van, covered with multicolored painted flowers, that is stationed behind The Opel, further depresses the spirits of The Citroën.

He curses himself for not having brought a book on this trip. Or at least a newspaper! Boredom impels him to switch on the car radio again.

Josie is now promising us that we will soon hear a terrifying story from the mouth of a woman who has spent years working in a part of the world where famine is the norm. But, before that, we'll have an advertising break.

The nutritional virtues of a fantabulous Three-in-One deal that everyone is talking about: the biggest burger yet, the Maxiburger, that comes with a triple helping of French fries and a king-sized Kong Kola are being touted hysterically by some media clown affecting an ostentatiously mid-Atlantic twang. *The Ge-nu-wine Taste of Manhattan. Your Super-Dooper-*

Sized Burrrrger For a Price that All can Afforrrrd...

And now, folks, let's get back to that, em...famine we were talking about!

+++++

THE CITROËN REMINDS HIMSELF AGAIN that he must reach the airport before half past seven this very evening. But, in spite of this temporary (he hopes) traffic holdup, he figures that he should be well able to meet that deadline, with (he calculates) three and a half hours to spare.

Which will give him lots of time to while away in the bar of the airport Duty Free before boarding time for his Ryanair flight to Girona. This is where Anna has arranged to meet him. They will have two unforgettable days together in that luxurious apartment in Estartit, on Spain's Costa Brava. Sipping *daiquirís, caiparinhas* or *mojitos* in the warm evening under the palm trees on the patio...

The Mediterranean stretches away eastwards from that flower bedecked balcony, a panorama of living glitter, as far as the eye can see. A sun-bronzed (or spray-tanned) Anna, lolls naked on the broad bed. He presses on the nipple of her left breast with his lips. Then nipple of her right breast is being massaged simultaneously between his thumb and forefinger. He hears her sensuous moan as his fingers delicately explore the warm damp valleys of pleasure…

This reverie is suddenly interrupted. The insistence beeping of The Opel behind him indicates that it is time to move again. He turns the key in the ignition.

The engine starts and the car lurches forward. The two long metal lines crawl forwards at snail pace towards the eastern horizon. They manage to cover about 50m this time before the stationary cars in front of him proclaim another halt.

This Citroen gives vent to his anger with a loud shout. To hell with all this fucking messing about! After spending about five minutes there, as stationary as the Rock of Cashel, he switches the engine off again. How long more do we have to endure this damned creeping from halt to halt?

A sudden sensation of acidity in the gullet just behind his throat remind The Citroën of the cholesterol carousel he enjoyed last night, prepared for him by Maura's folk, before he hit the road early last night.

Eat up, *a mhac*, because you have a long journey in front of you tomorrow. Good God almighty! The mother of all fry-ups! Eggs, sausages, black pudding, white pudding, mushrooms, tomatoes, fried bread. But Maura's people, to hand it to them, were always like that: generous to a fault, hosts of the old school.

Not to mention the rake of pints he threw down on that feast later on in the Glenlongan Arms on his way from Letterfree. Pints that cost nary a red cent! A thank you prize from the management of that faux-Victorian hostelry, with those god-awful foxhunting reproductions on its walls everywhere one looked, for a tourism (whorism?) color piece he wrote ten years ago at the editor's behest. A comfortable enough rural hotel that certainly never merited the gushing praise he heaped on its "French" cuisine and "friendly" staff.

All that you can drink, sir! The manager's invitation! Never look a gift-horse in the mouth, as the fella said!

Another cholesterol carousel downed, with all the trimmings, free of charge again, before easing his Citroen out of the mock-palatial driveway of the Glenlongan Arms earlier on.

And that entire unholy food 'n drink cocktail churning about in his stomach is now aided and abetted by the growing anxiety that all of this stopping and starting is cultivating in my innards. My kingdom for a Rennies!

And, thinking of Maura's folk, I wonder did they notice the cold formality and silence that now stretches between us?

Or that our marriage is now as dead as stone?

+++++

IT ALL SEEMS SO MUCH SIMPLER when you are young, muses The Citroën. Sitting there in his stationary car, his imagination unbound, he relives his first stay in the Gaeltacht. He almost senses the clean sting of ocean air in his nostrils, punctuated by the occasional oddly comforting whiff of turf smoke. Currach crews, rowing their frail craft across the Letterfree Bay, bouncing them across the waves, plying their fisherman's trade, just as their fathers, and their fathers before them! The backdrop of those towering cliffs to the east is a romantic real-life Paul Henry landscape painting...

How a raw urban youth could be so entranced then by all of this furniture of another age! By those tough frieze-clad coastal dwellers! By the ancient tales of Stiofán Pháraic Neil, the greatest storyteller of the parish! By the witty cut and thrust of Gaelic talk! By the first pint of stout he ever drank, there in the company of his future father-in-law! By a life that may have been basic but that appealed to the romantic cast of his thought in those distant days! The unceasing rhythm of Atlantic waves crashing on the beach below the house was the metronome that dictates the rhythm of the daily round. Just as it has been here for thousands of years! Permanent? Unchanging?

Not really! What if I had had a vision then of the coming times? muses The Citroën. If I had known then that another universe was to supplant the frozen "permanency" of this Gaeltacht life by a new reality that all but ignored the time-old metronome of the waves. A new universe in which frieze britches, *bawneen* and colorful Gaelic were becoming hazy memories in the minds of the aged. Images and sounds of another life, another age! What had the impetuous romanticism of youth gained him?

Had he married a woman's voice, the ghost of an ancient heritage, rather than a flesh and blood woman? Ah, the haunting voice of Maura, as she sang *An Droighnean Donn* (The Fairy Bush). That song from the sweet mouth of his future wife surpassed anything he had ever heard on the radio or on a record. It seemed to him then that he was listening to the very essence of his birthright rather than the voice of a mere human being. And still less, to the dying echoes of a vanishing, if not almost vanished, civilization.

But now, in the cold light of hindsight, he asks himself what or who did he marry. And what if he had understood then that the seemingly sound foundations of his dream were already fatally eroded?

For, even then, the Gaeltacht tide was already turning. But now the ebb-tide strand is all too plainly visible. And the tide is on the rise. A thrusting Spring tide, carrying with it the star-spangled universe of the Maxiburger and Supercoke, floods in, unstoppable, across the deserted strand it is destined to fill.

Just as the emptiness that Maura left in his heart is now being filled by Anna?

+++++

THE CITROËN AWAKENS FROM HIS MUSINGS with a start. From a dreamland of whose geography he was still uncertain! He glances at his watch. Dammit to hell!

It is already two o'clock.

He must have spent the last half hour dozing. In the meantime, these long lines of cars haven't budged even a measly centimeter. Still parked bumper to bumper! Why, he asks himself once again, have all the motorists of the country, it seems, chosen this narrow old motorway instead of the spanking new *Autobahn* that was opened by the Minister last week? Are they objecting to the fact that he spoke only in German at the opening ceremony? And that he has chosen to exercise his ministerial function from Berlin rather than from Dublin?

Or could it be that my fellow citizens are so fleeced by taxes and sundry other charges these days that they are unwilling to pay that controversial toll that privileges them to enter the *Autobahn?*

However, as we are stopped here, and there is damn all I can do about it, I may as well get out of the car and stretch my legs. If only to find out who my fellow unfortunates are and what they think of this mess. Who knows, maybe the editor would be interested in carrying the story: 'Citizen Rage at Traffic Holdup!' Or, even, 'Angry Motorists Boycott *Autobahn*!'

But let me not stray too far from the car! For one never knows when the moment when the cars will begin to move again will arrive unexpectedly. One never knows. So as to avoid being the object of the threats, curses, and the angry beeping of car-horns behind him, he had better be ready to jump into his car as soon as this traffic jam begins to unsnarl.

He ambles slowly past The Skoda that is parked just in front of the Cortina. It is occupied by two priests. One elderly reverend gentleman and the other somewhat younger! Their heads are close to each other, as if they are in deep conversation. Some obscure theological point? Angels dance on the head of the pins again? Or, much more likely, the prospects of some fancied steed in the 3.15 steeplechase at whatever racecourse in England? Or, maybe, the scandalous price of golf clubs?

He reaches the silver BMW, the "Beamer", that is parked just ahead of the Fiat 1100, in the opposite line of cars. A middle-aged balding type, pushing 60, sits ensconced in this vehicle. Spectacles sit above the bulbous end of his nose as he scans the newspaper spread out on the steering wheel in front of him. Noting out of the corner of his eye a presence of on the road outside, Mr. Beamer lowers his car window and beckons imperiously towards The Citroën. He scrutinizes the latter keenly from head to toe, over the horn-rimmed upper edge of his spectacles as he speaks:

Have you any idea at all what in blazes is going on here? he asks. Another D4 accent, with muted undefined rural undertones. A current of suppressed anger underlies his words.

It almost seems as if he were blaming The Citroën for having caused this holdup! The Citroën notes the small mustache on The Beamer's upper lip. Which reminds him of Adolf Hitler's toothbrush effort? Or of Charlie Chaplin's! Or of Chaplin's imitating Hitler! He also notes the whiff of expensive aftershave lotion wafting in his direction from the person of this irascible Beamer.

No more than yourself, I haven't the slightest bloody idea what is going on, answers The Citroën. Some others were telling me that there may have been an accident as there is supposed to be a dangerous stretch of road up ahead. Others are floating the idea that the Gardaí may be rummaging in cars up front, looking for agitators or terrorists. Or so they say. The only thing we can do, I suppose, is to stay patient.

Humph, says The Beamer. You, no more than myself, have not even the faintest clue as to what in the hell is happening to the traffic. But patience bedamned! Leave that to Job and to the nuns! Assuming that there was ever such an *eejit* as Job! Which is, as sure as eggs are eggs, is just another bloody cock and bull story, like the rest of them!

Having purged himself of that venom, The Beamer suddenly raises his window. And returns again to his study of the pink pages of his Financial Times! Paying no further attention to The Citroën on the road outside, indisputably a nobody, if ever there was one!

The latter then detects a light footstep behind him

Do you know that if the traffic was flowing normally, we'd nearly be at Angelbank by now? He recognizes that accent, that curious—but not unmusical—amalgam of Westmeath and D4.

He turns around. Well spotted, sir! It is The Ford Escort teacher, indeed. The Citroën imagines—not for the first time—how this young lady's face might appear without those awful spectacles. Whatever about that possibility, his inventive mind has no trouble imagining the possibilities of that curvaceous slimto-full figure in front of him. Whose attractiveness is emphasized by the clinging white dress she is now wearing instead of the loose trousers and blouse she sported earlier. She must have changed clothes in her car since he saw her last.

Talking of traffic jams, I'd say we've seen nothing yet, opines this renovated Ford Escort. Cheerfully! Wait until you see the chaos once we get beyond Clooneen Bog, she says. Especially when the flow of traffic coming from the north merges with this mess at Angelbank! It is then we'll get to see a real mess, unless I be greatly mistaken—real honest-to-God bumper to bumper confusion.

Have you noticed that not a single car has come in the opposite direction up the other lane since this traffic jam began? The Citroën asks her.

The word is going around that there was a really bad accident up front, another voice chimes in. Another motorist from down the line has sidled up to them.

The driver of The SUV that is lying behind The Ford Escort now does the talking. A thin lanky youth, wearing a yellow designer Lacoste t-shirt, with its mandatory embroidered alligator. Screaming out: *look upon my shirt, ye losers, and despair!* The back of a light jacket The SUV is wearing informs us that golf under the Bermudan sun is for winners. The back to front peaked baseball cap he is wearing informs us that its owner is in love with New York.

Maybe checkpoints for cars are being operated by the Gardaí, ventures The Citroën. Rumor has it, if we are to believe the half of what the newspapers say, and I don't, that we could be in for a new spate of bombing attacks.

Ignoring The Citroën, this SUV faces The Ford Escort and his words are aimed directly at her. A worn old package this, says The Citroën to himself. Emptiness in its armored suit of arrogance!

Whatever obstacle is holding up traffic should have been cleaned up long ago by the Guards, says the bean pole from the SUV. Isn't that why bucketfuls of taxpayer's money is supposed to be being spent on reinforcing public security? He continues to ignore The Citroën.

But, to be honest, I have not the remotest idea, continues The SUV, how all the money we pay though the nose in taxes is spent… But that's the way it has always been in this shit-hole of a country. If there is a cock-up to be made, leave it to the Irish! What other nation under the sun would spend billions on idle civil servants and not a bloody Guard in sight, just when Guards are desperately needed.

They are probably all up in the capital, busy battering demonstrators, says The Ford Escort. She looks directly at The Citroën as she says these words.

I would hope that you are not complaining about the behavior of our security forces, young lady, says a polished voice behind the threesome.

The Citroën, The Ford Escort and The SUV turn around. The Beamer has lowered his window again. The small pale blue eyes behind his spectacles sweep the body of The Ford Escort from head to heel.

I think you have misread my intention, sir, she says.

But The Beamer continues as if he had not heard her.

For nothing stands between us and absolute chaos in this country but the forces of law and order. It is the plain responsibility of every citizen to support their defenders in every way. Irresponsible criticism of the Gardaí does nothing but help those ruffians and madmen who would destroy the country if they were given a free hand.

And how in the hell could the country be in a worse state than it is at the present moment, The Citroën mutters under his breath. What with flooding and infrastructural damage caused by the constant succession of winter storms and no money in the State kitty to repair the damage. He himself just read how the harbor in Letterfree was reduced to rubble by the most recent storm and the fish storage facility flattened.

He says nothing out loud, however. No point in starting

the usual useless Irish argument that never goes anywhere! That loses itself in all sorts of irrelevant byroads. The Beamers of the world live, immured within the cast-iron cocoon of their own certainties, enchanted by the circular surfaces of their self-serving arguments. The Citroën senses that more than words would be needed to shatter that cocoon.

But, in all fairness, given the mess that the country is in, as we speak—what with poverty, unemployment, emigration and so forth—you can hardly deny that people these days have all the reason in the world to take to the streets, says The Ford Escort.

Look here, young lady! Of course the country has grave problems these days, says The Beamer, the tone of his voice giving witness to his annoyance. Any fool with half a head can see that. Nevertheless, we do have the capacity to overcome our difficulties. But only on condition that we remain a united people! The problem with these agitators and their crazy ideas is that they are destroying the very unity that can restore us to prosperity.

But why do the riot squads attack ordinary people so brutally when all they are trying to do is to express their democratic right to express their opinions, asks The Ford Escort.

And, tell me this, young lady, should communist ruffians be given a free hand to stir up the people, asks The Beamer. To divide the people when a united people is what we most need. As far as I am concerned, I believe that the Gardaí are too soft on agitators and on the people who are influenced by them. If I were responsible for our national security, do you know the first thing I would do?

Not a clue, say The Citroën, The Ford Escort and The SUV, all at once.

Well, the first thing I would do, says The Beamer, is to reopen the Curragh internment camp. Immediately! That camp should never have been shut. And what I would do is lock up in there those disruptive evil elements that you foolishly call "demonstrators".

A stony silence follows this statement.

Which is quickly broken!

For just right then, as if on cue, a chorus of car horns to the east is heard. And the voice on some unknown individual, with a strong Belfast accent, shouts that the traffic jam is over. Everybody get ready to fuckin' move!

Those who have taken the liberty of stretching their legs run back to their cars as fast as their legs can carry them. Leather and rubber soles pound the road. Shouts are heard! Doors open and slam shut. Engines cough into life. As he runs past The Skoda, The Citroën is greeted with a hand wave by its gray-haired priest driver. But such is his hurry that he has no time to respond to this greeting.

The deteriorating situation does not allow of such niceties.

+++++

NO SOONER HAD THE CITROËN sat into his own car than the red Cortina in front of him starts to edge forward. Master Cortina appears again in its rear window, grinning and pulling faces. Sticking out his tongue! Thumbing his nose at the driver behind him! The Citroën pays little attention to this live puppet show as he keeps his eye on the speedometer.

Things are looking much better this time, he says to himself. 10, 20, 30, 40 km an hour, indicates the needle. And every centimeter traveled is that one centimeter nearer to Estartit.

He can hear Anna's sensuous whisper in his ear already. I love the missionary position, she says laughingly. As long as I am always on top!

He glances over at the other moving line of traffic. Just as The Ford Escort is glancing in his direction! They smile briefly at each other!

Then he presses the radio button. That infernal creep,

Josie Thornton, is still blathering away like the superannuated cokehead he is reputed to be. Ah, if only there were such a thing in the universe as a just God!

You know, or should know, that this program welcomes free and open discussion of questions that were taboo up to now in Ireland. No hot potato is too hot for Josie Thornton. We want our Morning Show to be the breath of fresh air that is needed to sweep out all that stale air that has stifled free debate for far too long in the dark and fetid corners of Mother Ireland's kitchen. Fresh light on dark corners, as the fella says. For far too long, the women of Ireland have been smothering under a pile of meaningless superstitions that have no basis in fact.

And let you all of you listeners out there who are listening to me, the women of Ireland, realize that the Josie Thornton that Sheila is talking to is a married man. Yes sirree! Your sympathetic host for whom tits, breasts and other private parts not usually given an outing over the air waves, are far from being a mystery. Things that are as natural as... Are you still on the line, Sheila?

Why wouldn't I be, Josie! In all fairness.

Jaysus H. Christ and His Blessed Mother! Am I fucking-well dreaming? The Citroën asks himself. It must be that I'm going bloody-well bonkers. Didn't I hear that pure-as-the-driven-snow bullshit earlier today? Or didn't I? Ah, they must be doing a rebroadcast of that useless rubbish. Or has time itself stopped? Could it be that I am dead?

Take it easy, man! That sort of speculation will land you in cloud-cuckoo land.

Damn! The Citroën steps on the brake pedal suddenly to avoid crashing into the red Cortina that has stopped dead just in front of him. And making mush of that brat who continues to mock him through the Cortina's rear window!

Will there ever be an end to all of this stopping and starting? Will I ever make it to the airport before boarding time?

That doubt, once entertained, burgeons...

+++++

WHATEVER ENJOYMENT The Citroën might have obtained from the flowers of May, which offer their modest feast of perfume and color from the edges of the motorway, is negated by the stink of the exhaust gases from the vehicles in front of him. And by the blinding sunlight that flashes towards him, amplified by its reflection from the windows and metal bodies of the cars.

He thinks: I should have brought those snazzy designer sunglasses, genuine Gucci, a present from Anna in Biarritz. And, to top it all off, the mind deadening trance-beat pulsing without respite from that damn flower-plastered DAF sitting behind The Opel. Like a hammer thumping down on the top of his head, so it is, disintegrating all his attempts to make rational sense of the situation in which he now finds himself.

He glances at his watch, a Rolex, yet another gift from the munificent and elegantly manicured hands of Anna. It is already almost 2 o'clock. He senses the first pangs of anxiety, their acid fingers probing the lining of his duodenum. Yet, if traffic began to move again, he could still make it to the airport with a half hour to spare.

But, what if that movement fails to materialize?

Maybe the *News at One* will provide some information about this traffic jam. He turns the radio knob until he finds the Gaeltacht radio station:

The Gardaí are continuing to search for some rogue bankers who may have already left the country. Interpol has been alerted. The price of a barrel of oil is set to rise. €3.5 million slated for welfare payments has vanished without trace. Riots rage in various countries of the Middle East. Another huge car bomb in Bagdad. Huge floods in India and bush fires rage somewhere or other. Military reinforcements are being sent from some obscure place to quell unrest in yet another obscure place. The Arctic is melting faster than we originally thought it would, sea-levels are rising continually and low-lying coastal regions are already being inundated. Experts warn that over- and inappropriate use of antibiotics is causing the development of antibiotic-resistant strains of bacteria that cause many dangerous infectious diseases that are now spinning out of control…

And now for some local news. A call for taxes to be further lowered to offset falling living standards caused by the crisis. Two killed in a traffic accident in Carlow. A gun-battle in Dublin West, apparently drugs-related, leaves one man dead and two injured, one of them seriously. A priest appears before the court on sexual molestation and pedophilic charges…

Every damn thing except the news The Citroën wants most to hear: the reason for this accursed traffic delay in the middle of this accursed bog outside of thrice accursed Clooneen,

Suddenly, it occurs to him that he has heard this very newscast somewhere before. Yes, he certainly did! It came through that ancient crackling radio out west, in the house of Maura's parents in Letterfree. And doesn't he remember Maura's father, Dan Mór, remarking that stories of that ilk are a sure sign the Doomsday is fast approaching. This realization gives him a sudden start. *Josie Thornton's Morning Show* can be—and is—re-cycled, of course. But never the news, that ever-shifting kaleidoscope of opinions and events. The realization that he can no longer access fresh news sends a shiver down his spine.

That is when The Citroën begins to suspect that this hiatus in his life is no normal traffic jam. But, if not, what could be happening, then? He tries to quell a sudden irrational spasm of fear that now grips his innards. He thrusts the vague irrational presentiment that surfaced down into his subconscious. Where it festers like some sort of poisonous stomach parasite.

+++++

MANY WEIRD THOUGHTS CROWD a person's mind in a car that has come to a full stop in a monster traffic jam like this one. In order to lessen the mounting anxiety that his tryst with the exuberant Anna is in jeopardy, The Citroën now concentrates on the delights that the coming weekend with her holds in store for them both.

He would like to tell her now that, thanks to this delay, it is hardly likely that they will have time for their traditional parting cup, the "stirrup cup" she calls it, before boarding their flight to Girona.

He had wanted to travel on an Aer Lingus flight to Barcelona and spend a night there in the Catalan capital before moving on up to the Costa Brava. But the forever pragmatic Anna bought Ryanair tickets for Girona for the simple reason that Girona Airport is much closer to their journey's end. He could hardly complain. She who pays the piper calls the tune.

It was she who had chosen Estartit, a resort town on the Mediterranean. An incident in the Glendalough Hotel had caused them to decide that the island of Ireland no longer afforded them a safe place in which to conduct their affair.

They had spent a crisp sunny autumn day before they reached this decision strolling on the tree-shaded paths around the placid lakes of Glendalough. Examining the stones and ruined churches, all that remains of Kevin's spiritual empire in that wooded valley among the Wicklow Hills. In his mind's eye, the foliage on the trees on the heights above the monastery have already turned yellow and brown, waiting to be torn from their branches by the teeth of an easterly wind. *Sic transit gloria mundi.*

Now he imagines a table fully set for dinner laid out tastefully in front of them. A bottle of red wine, an Argentine Cabernet Sauvignon, is already uncorked, sampled and accepted. Courteous and discrete Polish waiters hover about, ready to rush to serve. All indicating that the pleasantest of pleasant weekends is in store for The Citroën and Anna! An exquisite meal, Anna's astringent wit (at the expense of her husband, by the way) a bout of ardent and imaginative lovemaking, a deep sleep and a slow drive the following morning, taking in the scenery, after the full Irish breakfast, through the Sally Gap, stopping and descending from the car to view Lough Nahanagan, Lake of the Otters, holding hands, and then over the Feather Beds to Rathfarnham and finally down into Dublin!

This idyll is suddenly shattered.

For who the hell should walk into the hotel restaurant just as he is about to bury his fangs in that prime sirloin steak from the grill, done rare to his taste? None other than Martin and Betty O'Donnell, next door neighbors of Maura's people, a couple who have been long and well acquainted with both me and Maura.

The Citroën' heart jumps into his mouth. Jesus Christ and his Blessed Mother! If this pair see me here with—as far as they are concerned—a painted unknown floozy and the word gets back to Maura, my goose will be well and truly cooked!

Who could ever have imagined the homey O'Donnells travelling so far from their home base in Letterfree to potter around ancient ruins in such a remote mountain valley! Did a special devotion to Saint Kevin bring that pious couple here to completely *banjax* his meticulously planned evening?

Anna and himself just about manage to slip out of the restaurant, unperceived by the O'Donnells, (she giggling and he with a handkerchief held to cover his lower face), leaving the best part of an expensive meal, that succulent steak included, behind them. And most of that expensive bottle of red wine.

Lesson learned!

In bed afterwards, Anna says: no more Ireland for us, darling. This damn country is far too bloody small.

No matter where a girl goes on this damn island, she can never be at her ease. No matter where you find yourself, there's no telling who or what is about to pop out of the blue. With God knows what ridiculous consequences…

+++++

ANNA'S HUSBAND, BRENDAN, DOESN'T GIVE A FIDDLER'S about us. *Catholic Ireland is dead and gone/It's with Mick Cleary in the grave* he said laughingly when Anna told him about our adulterous little arrangement.

Our marriage is one of the most modern kind, my dearest, says Anna to me. As far as Brendan is concerned, my little "adventures" on the side are strictly my own business. He knows damn well that they work wonders for my self-esteem. It is this perpetual openness to new experiences that keeps a modern marriage like ours alive and vibrant. And, then, we do have this no-jealousy pact. He does his thing and I do mine and ne'er the twain shall meet So, after that debacle in Glendalough, I'll go right ahead and compensate with a memorable weekend for us both together in Estartit. It will be pure magic—that much I can guarantee you. Like nothing you have ever before experienced. On one strict condition, lover boy: you must never allow yourself to fall in love with me. Because, in my book, falling in love is definitively one of the most uncool things you can do. Love is always a messy business and leads to all sorts of complicated problems. Look at the condition in which it has left poor Stacey in *Cougars!*

The great thing about this exotic tryst is that it won't cost me an arm and a leg.

Brendan, your prototypic Celtic Tiger, owns that luxury apartment facing the harbor in Estartit. He also owns a brace of apartments in Dublin and one pretty opulently furnished one in picturesque Carcassonne, just over the French border, as well as a couple of housing estates in Ireland. A brash shaker and mover type, and never one to hide his light modestly under a bushel, he announces candidly to all who will listen sundry that he has never paid even a penny to Inland

Revenue, in Ireland or elsewhere. His business, whose real nature The Citroën has never been able to ascertain, is based in Amsterdam, while various fiscal paradises figure in his scheme of things. And my legal eagles have it all sewn up, he says; the revenue sleuths would want to be up before daybreak to catch the bold Brendan!

The hubby will be over in the United States while we go on the rampage in his Estartit flat, says Anna in her cold matter of fact voice. That new secretary of his, Miss Miniskirt Number IV as I call her, will be going with him. Brendan tells me that he is involved in some property deal in Manhattan. Along with some other deal he is trying to organize to buy some small Caribbean island or other.

The Citroën figures he must find some way to warn Anna about this damn traffic jam. For, If these lines of motor vehicles don't start moving soon, her carefully drafted plan will have to be scuttled. He removes his mobile phone—a present from Anna—and from his briefcase and rapidly taps out her number.

With this phone do you marry me, she intoned with mocking solemnity, that afternoon they met for coffee in Bewley's Café in Grafton Street. On the one condition: that you never fall in love with me, dear. Anna's constant refrain! And that you leave all of that juvenile mush to antediluvian Hollywood movies…

You have turned that old marriage ceremony cliché back to front and upside down, Anna!

So you get it, dear! For we, the modern womanhood of Ireland, have learned how to use our beauty and our brains to entrap men. While those ridiculous old feminists were haranguing us with their "Dictatorship of the Patriarchy" we just wiggled our hips and went calmly ahead to wrap those patriarchal bullies around our little fingers.

Anna's mobile number is a secret between us two, or so she says. And whoever betrays that secret, the other, be it me or you; and as long as this capable and well-practiced young cougar is able to entrap some virile young male, it will be the end of our somewhat unholy—but fun—humping pact.

The tinny tinkle from The Citroën's mobile signals that Anna's mobile is disconnected. That's altogether weird! Didn't he speak by phone to her this very morning, before he left Glenlongan to assure her that he was on his way to the airport!

You and I in Estartit, she was said then, without mobile, without internet, without fax, without clothes! And our consciences left a long way behind us, in the dour old rainy Land of Saints and Scholars! He almost feels the breath of her sensual laugh on his cheek...

The Citroën taps out Anna's number again. With the same fruitless result, the same mocking tinkling in his ear.

He then calls the numbers of his acquaintances—without any result other than that now familiar tinkling.

That damn mobile is out of order, he mutters savagely to himself. Along with the bloody car radio!

All of which rightly screws up my contact with the outside world!

+++++

TO ALLEVIATE HIS FRUSTRATION, The Citroën decides to stretch his legs.

Leaving the car, he makes for a small group of his fellow motorists who are assembled in a huddle on the side of the road beside the blue Peugeot. Who knows, maybe somebody there has some news about what is up. All the drivers of the surrounding cars seem to be gathered here. Even that tattooed hippy from the DAF is part of that glum conclave. All except that cranky old Gaeilgeoir, The Opel driver.

Having discussed the situation soberly, and in detail, the general consensus appears to be that the idea of reaching Killmorna soon should be abandoned. Extensive road works ahead are the problem, asserts The Beamer, the Hitler/Chaplin of the silver BMW. But there is a fine broad stretch of road—whose construction was generously funded by Europe—from Killmorna on. So that when we reach that place the going should be much faster and we'll easily be able to make up lost time. In the meantime, the main attention of the Gardaí should be directed to getting the traffic flowing between here and Killmorna, opines The Beamer.

I expect that we'll see the police helicopter before long, he says. He talks confidently and with the confident air of one who is privy to the inner workings of the Jam. And as he talks, he peers keenly over the top of his spectacles at the assembled motorists and at their passengers, as if gauging the reaction of each and every such soul to his words.

The Citroën is wondering if it occurs to anybody but himself to question the source of the new-found information that is being so authoritatively divulged by The Beamer. The same Beamer who, a short time ago, indicated that the cause of this traffic jam was a mystery to him! Is he a chancer talking through his arse or has he managed in such a short space of time to connect with a reliable source of information? And, if so, how did he manage to achieve that?

Could it be that there was an accident on the road between here and Killmorna? ventured the grey-haired priest from The Skoda. Speaking quietly and with a faint Northern accent! The Citroën notes the broad purple belt that encircles the capacious paunch of the cleric. No mere common or garden priest this! But a buck bishop, *begod*!

The Beamer calmly disputes The Skoda Bishop's suggestion. I know for a fact that road works a short distance ahead are the cause of the delay, he asserts, but without disclosing the basis for his opinion. But he says this again with such a secure sense of certainty that most are convinced that he has managed to access some recondite source of information that he is, as yet, unwilling to disclose.

A brief silence falls on the group.

This is broken by a spurt of inconsequential car-talk. The BMW is compared to the Mercedes Benz, the Renault to the Ford Escort, the Volkswagen to the Fiat 1100, the Skoda to the Saab, the Citroën to the...

The conversation switches to the prospects of Manchester United in the game tonight. The general opinion is that they will win. 2-0! But it all depends on the form of some player or other with a Spanish-sounding name who has only recently recovered from a knee injury

It is agreed, with no dissenting voice, that the temperature is unusually hot for this time of year. Which is hardly surprising given the Winter that has just mauled us. It is unlikely that Stacey is pregnant, as some of the women think (but we should all have a definite answer to that question tonight).

That the tax burden is already too heavy, without having to bear the brunt of this proposed new tax, is carried without a dissenting voice.

Likewise: that super Viagra could be a danger to the health of the old.

That politicians only look after themselves.

That Golf Club fees are scandalous.

That a miraculous monkey in America learned human sign language as good, if not better, than most human beings.

That the increasingly frequent and ferocious Atlantic storms are the result of sun spots.

That snails know how to count.

That a Chinese woman had twins at ninety years of age!

That this is Kerry's year!

That this isn't Kerry's year!

Friendly disputes and conversational bric-a-brac, long sentences, short sentences, clumsy sentences. Great oaths, tiny oaths. Old jokes and new jokes. Any bloody sound to hold the boredom of this Vale of Tears, now located definitively on Clooneen Bog, safely at bay. Until this damn traffic starts to move again…

The Skoda Bishop would like to be in the capital before four o'clock, he says. His younger clerical companion has just give a mission to an order of nuns in some convent in the West. To thank him for imparting his spiritual edification, nothing would satisfy the good sisters but to give him a big parcel of prime beef. The brother in charge of cooking in the monastery has been apprised of this windfall and will waiting to prepare it to the taste of seventeen hungry monks.

Apart from that detail, he himself, the Bishop, will have an important function to fulfill in the Pro-Cathedral at four o clock. At that time, if all goes well, he will be at the baptismal font, pouring holy water over the head of the latest addition to the family of An Taoiseach and his good wife. Irmgard is the name they have chosen for the little girl.

A beautiful name, don't you think? And practical?

Especially given the times we are living in?

+++++

RETURNING FROM THE "MEETING" beside The Peugeot, the young couple in the Cortina greet The Citroën. They are in their mid-thirties, give or take a few years. Both wear light blue and white track suits emblazoned with symbols of the Dubs football team. Both are shod in trendy sports shoes. The Cortina himself is tall, dark and lean, his partner complements he first two of these attributes, being much shorter and fair-haired, but also exhibiting the same trim fit build. Both are epitomes of the sort of health enthusiasts one can sometimes see on the early mornings of the capital's fashionable suburbs, loping grimly along grassy verges, their bodies responding to mysterious instructions relayed to them through their earphones, as they jog their way to perfect health.

The male component of this sporty twosome is holding

the hand of the pudgy brat who enjoys making faces at The Citroën from the safety of the rear seat of his parent's car. Seeing the latter, this young Master Cortina opens his mouth and sticks out his tongue.

Now, now, don't be so bold, darling! Where have all your manners gone? says The Cortina's female party. The brat pays not the slightest attention to his mother's command, assuming that he even recognizes it as such.

I hate to be always telling him: don't do this or don't do that, says Ms. Cortina apologetically. It says in *Raising Junior for Tomorrow* that too much emphasis on obedience can do great damage to a youngsters self-esteem. And it stifles their creativity. Or so say the psychologists, and if they don't know, well, who the hell does?

Have you ever seen a traffic fuck-up as bad as this one? says The Cortina himself. (Rhetorically). But now that it seems we are going to be stuck here for a while, I may as well grab the opportunity to let Junior here stretch his legs. He hasn't been out in the fresh air all day.

And, without further ado, away with the pair of them, holding hands, walking westwards along the narrow strip of road that lies between the two lines of cars. As they pass the Gaeilgeoir's Opel, Ms. Cortina addresses The Citroën:

Well, what do you think: is Stacey pregnant, or not?

This question leaves The Citroën at a complete loss. He had heard it mentioned before on *Josie Thornton's Morning Show*, but assuming that it was just another of Josie's frivolous inanities, had paid not the slightest attention to it.

What Stacey do you mean? he asks, somewhat falteringly. But Ms. Cortina seems not to hear him, appears as she seems to be to be trying to give voice to some convoluted inner vision.

Well, as far as I am concerned, she says, I think that it is a dead certainty that she is up the pole, if you'll excuse the vulgarity. But in any case, we'll know for sure tonight; I can hardly wait for her to confirm what I think she'll confirm. In all fairness, as far as I am concerned, there can only be one question, which is: who is the father? That is, if she is really pregnant, of course! But if we do find out that she is in the family way, who do you think is the guilty party?

Well, to be honest with you…

Ah, there you have it. I agree fully with you, says Ms. Cortina. One hundred percent! But people seem to be in two minds about it. Some of the people I talk to say that she isn't pregnant at all. That she is only letting on! That she's only looking for attention! So that some of the others won't be so bitchy with her. Especially, that hard-hearted whore, Beth! Not a bleedin' chance, say I. Why? Because that schemin' get is trying to grab Ben from her. Anyone who can't see what she's up to would need to be blind as a bloody bat. I know that Beth is good looking—more than the average, even—and you'd have to give her that. And she is a past mistress at twisting men around her little finger. And, maybe she'll get away with it this time, with seducing Ben, I mean. I wouldn't put anything past her after what she did to poor Doug. And the mess she landed poor Susan in as a result. But I know Stacey better than that. She is like a sister to me, honest to God. A modern woman with a heart of gold, even if she is a little bit too fond of the cocktails when she gets half a chance. But, in all fairness, you'd do it yourself. And as honest as the day is long; remember that heart-to-heart she had with Susan, that nice black-haired lassie! That showed, if nothing else, that she has bucketfuls of self-esteem, fair play to her. The only question is—and, to be dead honest with you, it's really killing me—who put her up the pole. That is, if she really is preggers, of course! Do you think that Doug, might have, well?…

To tell you the honest truth, I don't…

I fully agree with you. That's what I always say to myself. Doug is a decent sort of a fellow. Too decent for his own good, I say to myself sometimes. But, above all, he is a doctor. And, of course, he'd well know how to put an end to, well you know what I mean. But you could never say that that sly boyo, Howard, could ever compete with him when it comes to decency. I cannot, for the life of me, understand what possessed her to go out on a date with that smooth-talking creep. Especially as she already knew that it was because of him that Brad left Barbara. Let me tell you, between ourselves, what I really think. I think that Howard did the job on her, you know what I mean, in the back of the taxi when they both were leaving that night club, The Golden Peacock, they called it, I think. Do you remember that incident?

Lookit, I…

Yeah that's it! I'm not certain either that it wasn't called the Moulin Rouge. Something Frenchy like that! But that doesn't matter. What matters is that I am as sure as I am standing here that that's what happened. She was a little merry at the time, you'll remember… Cocktails and more cocktails, and before you know where you are….you know yourself how it goes…

And you saw the way Howard slipped some sort of white powder into her drink. We didn't get to see what happened in the back of the taxi, of course; it was away too dark there. But the fadeout on that scene didn't leave much to the imagination. You can never be fully sure, of course. But why did she let him, if indeed she did, when you remember that the whole of Ireland knows that the same Stacey was never really in love with Howard? To get her own back on Courtney, what else! Did that ever occur to you?

Lookit, I never…

I knew that you never imagined that. Not too many people would think that Stacey is the kind of woman who goes around looking for revenge. Her pound of flesh, as the fella says. Yet, neither of them knew yet what Courtney had in store for them. There's a bloody dangerous bitch for you, if you don't mind me saying so. And a tricky one too! Imagine!

She spikes her husband's drink with poison, though they were never able to prove that in court. So there she went, as free as a bloody bird, although she had already been condemned by all the newspapers. She hired a good lawyer, though: Jeb Sleimberg, one of the best in the business, even though he's a complete slime ball! That's what you'd always need in a jam like that: a good lawyer. So, when she arrives, that bastard, Howard, had better be on the lookout. What do you yourself think is going to happen?

Lookit, to tell you the God's honest truth, I haven't the remotest clue who any of these people you are talking about are, says The Citroën. Not an iota...

C'mon, You are just having me on, says Ms. Cortina. Are you tryin' to tell me that you are retarded or somethin'? Or that you have no ears? Sure the whole country these days is talking about nothing else but *Cougars*. Men, women and children! On the buses, the trains, in the shops, everywhere! The newspapers are full of it. And Josie Thornton, fair play to him, he's always on the ball, he always keeps us up to date about *Cougars*. My own other half, even; he'd never miss an episode. It's just about as important for him as the Sports Channel or *The Contraltos*.

I wouldn't have thought that shadows flitting across a screen could generate such interest, passion, even...

Shadows? Aha! I knew you were having me on. Let me tell you that *Cougars*' night is always a special night in our house. We get in a bottle, or two, of wine, Pringles and pizza and we look all together, even Junior, at Cougars. Jesus, it would be no word of a lie to say that Stacey, Beth, Barbara, Ben, Courtney and even that, may God forgive me, that lousy creep, Howard, are now part of the family. And Courtney, the fashion model, of course, even though she still has a lot of questions to answered about the death of Jeb, her husband. But, sure, wasn't he a crook, anyway, and even the Mafia wanted to stiff him? To be honest with you, I know the girls of *Cougars* better than I know some of my own flesh and blood. They're no shadows as far as I am concerned. And that's the God's honest truth.

I see. You are talking about some sort of television soap, then, says The Citroën.

Are you still having me on? By far and away the best TV entertainment ever—that's what the newspapers and Josie say—is nothing but "some sort of television soap"; is that what you are trying to tell me? You're a real "odd man out", so you are, and millions all around the planet hooked on *Cougars*, as Josie Thornton tells us, day in day out. But, in all fairness, I just know from the twinkle in your eye that you're having me on...

If you want me to tell you my God's honest truth, honest injun, I have no time to waste looking at television, says The Citroën. Except for certain news programs, which I have to watch regularly, being the news reporter that I am. And current affairs programs, of course, especially when some subject I am working on is being discussed. But, to be frank with you, I'll always choose the solidity of the written word over shadows on a screen.

So, you only go for the boring programs, then, comments Ms. Cortina. Which means: you're about the only person in the whole of Ireland who hasn't a clue about *Cougars!* Which means that if you're not up to the minute with the shenanigans of the Cougar girls, you have sweet damn-all to say to anybody! Doesn't that make you feel, well, sort of out of it?

The Cortina returns from his stroll, pucker-faced Junior in tow. When the latter observes The Citroën in front of him he, predictably, pulls a face and sticks out his tongue. Not wishing to inhibit her son's urge to self-express, Ms. Cortina ignores his facial expression and greets her partner:

Wait till you hear this one, love. Our friend here from the car behind us (indicating The Citroën) says he has never seen *Cougars*.

The eyes of The Cortina sweep The Citroën from head to toe and back again. As if inspecting the bizarre phenotype of some alien life form, previously unknown to man. But then, looking at The Citroën, he winks his left eye:

And now pull the other foot, he says.

+++++

By the time the following extracts were recorded, it seems that the motorists and their passengers had adopted the custom of calling the informal assemblies that were wont to gather beside a blue Peugeot (a make of automobile) every time the lines of cars, stretching eastwards as far as the eye could see, ground to a halt: the Dáil. And, once again, it is obvious that the term "The Parish" refers to a group of cars in the immediate vicinity of The Citroën, whose drivers and passengers got to know each other and organize during those interminable halts in order to allay whatever hardship might arise from the protracted Clooneen Jam, and to defend themselves.

Levi and Levi (2447) draw attention to the similarity of the structure of this, seemingly, spontaneous organization and that of the faux-democratic structures that organized society administratively until The Great Collapse ended the hegemony of all such primitive modes of social organization. It is clear that the word "parishioner" pertains to denizens of "The Parish" as so defined, whether drivers or passengers.

(The Editors.)

+++++

WEIRD WEATHER ALTOGETHER, as someone said a short while ago, that interminable subject being bandied about once again. 'Climate change' says Bishop Skoda.

True for you, says The Fiat 1100 Dub. I heard a report on the tele some times ago that said that both the poles are in advanced meltdown and that the weather systems of the planet are *banjaxed*.

Global warming, they say, chips in Ms. Toyota Starlet.

No wonder the polar ice is melting! But, in all fairness, we've only ourselves to blame with all of the greenhouse gases we're pumping into the atmosphere.

The SUV Yuppie, wearing his Ralph Lauren shirt with its polo-player badge, gives a contemptuous snort.

That's the sort of alarmist codswallop you always hear ecofreaks bleating about, he says. The climate is always changing, nothing weird about that. Only scientific lefties out to get a bit of publicity for themselves say the opposite.

The Citroën was about to enter the fray, saying that the Bishop's opinion had, indeed, a scientific basis and that the idea of man-induced climate change accords with the current scientific consensus. But why waste my breath in these PoMo days, where magical thinking, if not bland indifference, almost invariably trumps scientifically proven facts in the public arena.

The sun is still high in the sky. Blazing down, its unseasonal heat beats down mercilessly on the two metal columns that stretch between this desolate place and Killmorna. And even further to the east, for all we know. How far does this Jam extend? Only God himself, in the unlikely event of His having survived the rationalist onslaught, could answer that one.

The Citroën is reminded by this temperature of the dead heat of Jemaa El-Fna, the great square in the center of Marakesh. Their honeymoon, Maura and himself. Descending from the Agadir tourist bus, into the square, they are faced by snakes swaying gently to thin whistle notes, stalls laden with sheep heads with their staring glazed eyes, and a wall of heat, 47 C, that all but immobilizes them. They take refuge in the cool shadowed narrow streets of the Medina, the traditional Arab (or Berber) quarter. And that was the time and the place, under the curious gaze of local urchins, where Maura first confided in him that she wanted a family of ten children.

At the time that he thought that this preposterous proposition was the innocent fruit of pure infatuation. A whim that would evaporate like a puff of nothingness on exposure to economic reality. Really, nothing to be concerned about.

The Renault 4 Ponytail is an artist (self-defined), his long grey ponytail appearing to confirm his profession. He has news for us. Reliable sources have informed him that the heat is making people nauseous further up the line. That children are vomiting. And that an old lady in the yellow Anglia in front of the blue Peugeot has lost consciousness.

Heat prostration, is it? asks a refurbished green Volkswagen, who joins the group assembled beside the blue Peugeot.

I suppose so. The heat has the poor old creature totally banjaxed. She revived a little bit when I gave her some of my water. With the result that I have scarcely a drop left for myself.

The Beamer advises everybody to drink a lot of water. Dehydration can kill you, he says. The problem is that there is so little water left in the surrounding cars that their inhabitants prefer to conserve it as best they can.

Just in case.

+++++

THE CITROËN IS THE FIRST TO NOTE that the hands of his watch are no longer moving.

When he suddenly recalls his appointment with Anna at the airport, he glances at his watch. To observe that—although this bunch has been blabbing for the last half-hour, at least—the hands of his watch appear to be frozen at two o clock.

He explains this to The Fiat 1100 Dub and asks him for the correct time.

Jesus H. Christ, exclaims the latter out loud, my own shaggin' watch is stuck at 2.00 pm. Just like yours.

Each and every person in the group hurriedly scrutinizes

his, or her, own watch. With the same disquietingly sinister result: the hands of every watch in the Parish are frozen at 2.00 pm. The changing position of the sun in the sky above, which has slid perceptibly from the zenith towards the western horizon, however, demonstrates conclusively that 2.00 pm is long past and that time itself has not come to a full stop.

Some time later, The Renault Ponytail, had concluded a survey of all timepieces within a reasonable radius of the Parish. He reports that every single watch in this Parish, and in the surrounding parishes as well, is fucked, to parrot his artistic eminence's elegant turn of phrase. Yes, they are all stuck at 2.00 pm. And not only watches. Each and every radio and mobile phone is incapable of moving beyond that time. Press on the button and all you will ever hear is a re-broadcast of some shit program that you have already heard ad fuckin' nauseam.

Josie fuckin' Thornton?
Yup! Josie fuckin' Thornton, there you have it!
That same cokehead blatherskite!
Josie Every Irish Woman's Darlin' Fuckin' Thornton!

+++++

A SUDDEN PANIC GRIPS THE CITROËN. More than that relaxed pre-flight cocktail in the airport lounge is now at stake. The future of the whole bloody Estartit adventure now hangs in the balance. He must find the correct time somewhere: Ponytail was probably talking through his arse. Try the damn radio gain! He runs to his car, pulls open the door hurriedly, and presses on the radio button. Just in time to hear the beginning of *The News at One*:

The price of petrol is shaky again, a car bomb in Bagdad, the Taliban on the offensive in Afghanistan, soldiers to be sent from some unknown zone to some another unknown zone... two killed in a road accident in Carlow, an Orange Hall set on fire in Fermanagh... a youth drowned in Donegal, a gun battle in Dublin West leaves wounded, one seriously...

But, isn't that the same goddam news, exactly as he had heard it before—word for word—some days ago in his in-laws' place in Letterfree. And that he had heard again earlier today?

He now sees people emerging from the other cars, shrugging their shoulders, the same question mark emblazoned on all foreheads. The Citroën makes another attempt to contact Anna on the mobile she herself had given him. A forlorn hope, destined to be dashed. The same maddening jangle in his ear! Even the texting function is totally banjaxed.

She would be setting out for the airport by now, very likely. If she isn't already there. There is no way that a person as prissy and as punctilious as Anna is ever going to forgive a let down like this. Even if his excuse is based on true and verifiable facts! For Anna, being a Gorgon to the manner born, facts that fail to conform to her beliefs and desires belong to some alien universe that she prefers never to know.

But how can he help it if he appears to be now enveloped in such a universe? Who could ever imagine such a monstrous traffic jam involving almost every car in Ireland, it seems, on such a normally quiet stretch of road? Anna would never believe such an improbable yarn, anyhow. Of that he is in no doubt.

Bad enough that the traffic hasn't budged an inch over the past hour, at least! But this observation pales into insignificance beside the big question—that as yet unanswered question he poses to himself again—why has time itself, or time as it is defined and measured by man, at least, ground to a full stop here on the Bog of Clooneen?

While the earth's movement relative to the sun is the reason why the latter is sinking now towards the western horizon!

As it always has!

+++++

HE IMAGINES ANNA'S SARCASM as he tries to explain his current fix. Time itself ground to a halt, you say. For God's sake! What do you take me for? Do you think I'm some fucking birdbrain, like that Maura of yours, or what? Every idiot knows that time stops, space too, when the lights go out at the end of the journey. And only then! Are you trying to tell me that you were dead for a while as you drove towards the airport? What in God's name do you take me for!

I'm not trying to say that I hadn't some sort of afterlife experience, or something I cannot rationally explain, on my way here. But there it was, believe it or not! There I was, stuck in the middle of the traffic, and not a budge out of it. And all watches—mine and those of the other drivers—stopped, and stayed stopped, at 2.00 pm

The chances of my meeting Anna in the airport are rapidly disappearing, muses The Citroën, as he gulps a few mouthfuls of lukewarm water from the plastic bottle he keeps within reach of his left hand. Unless some miracle happens soon!

Glancing out of the window, he observes that the usual suspects are assembling on the side of the road beside the blue Peugeot. The Peugeot himself, Renault, Beamer, Volkswagen, Skoda, Cortina, Fiat 1100, Saab, the yellow Anglia and Mercedes-Benz! Another Parish Dáil session is about to commence, it seems. The only notable absentee, apart from himself, is the gold Fáinne Opel, who has yet to attend even one such meeting. The Citroën glances into his rear mirror. The Opel looks as ashen-faced as ever. Neither is The Ford Escort present and her car is empty. She had said told him earlier that she had friends further ahead that she wanted to contact. The Citroën takes in the gathering to his left and a short distance up the road.

The Cortina, standing on a low mound at the side of the road, is now addressing the assembled parishioners. His energetic air-punching lends forceful emphasis, undoubtedly, to whatever points he is making. Ms. Cortina isn't there to applaud him; she must be feeding their undisciplined offspring in their car.

The Beamer is there, his eyes hidden behind dark spectacles, as he listens impassively to The Cortina, his arms folded on top of the capacious corporation that thrives there under a multicolored Hawaiian shirt.

Should he join his fellow motorists beside The Peugeot to combat this boredom that continues to mount as this delay is drawn out? Damn! If only he had foreseen this and brought a novel with him or a newspaper or a magazine with which to while away these tedious hours. However, as he lacks such wherewithal, whatever screenplay his imagination can rustle up will have to take up the slack.

He is sure, from the position of the sun, that Anna must be in the airport by now, if not already airborne. Wearing that tight-fitting black dress, and high heels, an ensemble that she knows pleases him mightily. A dissatisfied scowl puckers her elegantly made-up face as she sticks metaphorical pins in a lifelike wax image of himself, The Citroën.

His reverie is interrupted by the furious blaring of the siren of an ambulance coming at breakneck speed in the opposite direction down the right-hand lane of the motorway on which westbound traffic is driven. This is the first vehicle that has come from that direction since this Jam began. It must be doing at least 100cm/hour, surmises The Citroën, though he is not the most reliable of witnesses concerning such matters.

Those who are not attending the Dáil session emerge from their grid-locked cars to gaze after the ambulance. Concerning this new development in the traffic jam story speculation is rife. Handclapping and a cynical cheer is the contribution of the DAF riff-raff to the ambulance debate. The Citroën wonders, idly, if these ragamuffins might not be some kind of alternative music group. The words THE MUSHROOM DRUIDS, emblazoned over their windshield, appear to accord with such an idea.

Ms. Cortina, the ill-mannered brat tugging at her skirt and sticking out his tongue at The Citroën, opines that the passing of the ambulance augurs the impending end of the traffic jam. She moves up and down the lines of stationary cars spreading this good news among all who are evidently relieved, judging from their smiles, to hear such a heartening prediction.

Never a one to give much credence to non-evidence based auguries, The Citroën holds his peace.

As the infernal racket created by the ambulance siren gradually fades into the distance, the primeval silence of the surrounding bogs reestablishes itself in the Parish. Punctuated only by murmurings from the Dáil, still very much in session after that brief interruption!

As the temperature of the interior of his car is now verging on the insufferable, The Citroën decides to take a stroll along the road. He walks back past the DAF, source of the incessant loud thumping of heavy metal that so annoys the rest of the parish, and past the Saab parked behind it, that seems to mark the western boundary of the Parish. As he crosses this boundary, he is greeted cheerily by a Nissan.

We'll be on the move again shortly, says the Nissan cheerily. Which is just as well because my wife will commit suicide if she doesn't get to see *Cougars* tonight…

That's great news. But how do you know we'll be moving soon, asks The Citroën, fearing that he already knows the answer to that question.

A woman from your neck of the woods put us in the know a short time ago. She told us that the ambulance was carrying all the people who had been injured in the accident up front and that the road will soon be open again to traffic.

The Citroën decides to hold his silence. Let people cling to whatever illusory hope promises to relieve their distress, no matter what grim reality lies behind such illusion!

The lines of traffic fail to budge, of course… Half an

hour later—time being measured subjectively in the complete absence of timing devices—the Parish is still at a complete standstill, witnessed by the sole flowering chestnut tree growing in a small fertile island of land just inside the bog and outside the left margin of the motorway. The ambulance has, by now, become incorporated into Parish folklore, though probably not quite as centrally as the shadowy Stacey and her shadow universe.

Strangers from other parts of the jam arrive, now and then, in the parish. Walking on the sides of the motorway or between the two lines of stationary vehicles! Many of them have stories to relate. The reasons for this traffic holdup, for example. These stories are eagerly rebroadcast, with emendations, among the parishioners, avid—as always—for whatever light might illuminate the true nature of the jam they in which they find themselves.

And who am I to blight that hope that forever springs eternal in the human breast? asks The Citroën of himself. Yet, the propensity of his fellow motorists to put their faith in mere rumor, not backed by even a shred of hard evidence, disturbs him. He wonders if profession of this unsubstantiated faith is a characteristic of humankind, in general…

This traffic jam is 30km long, according to one rumor recycled by The Ford Escort, after she had gathered stories for some considerable distance up front. It would be interesting to compare that assessment with some of the other fanciful yarns we've been listening to over the last few hours. I don't think they would form a coherent narrative! she says.

Teach your grandmother to suck eggs, thinks The Citroën.

But where is the truth of the matter, then? asks Ms. Anglia (yellow), a grey haired veteran, still flushed looking but obviously recovered from her earlier heat prostration.

Ah there you have it, Madame, says The Citroën to himself. That very answerless question that still exercises the human intelligence, as it did that of those ancient Greeks.

+++++

NO ANSWER APPEARS NOW to dissolve this fundamental mystery of things, as the engine of cars away to the front of us cough and roar into action.

The Dáil session beside the blue Peugeot terminates abruptly. Each driver and passenger seeks to find his or her allotted seat as quickly as possible. Does this sudden movement verify the prophecy of the sagacious Ms. Cortina? By happenstance, yes! That merit can hardly be taken from her.

Except, cruel fate, the cars crawl forward about 10 meters before halting again. After a couple of minutes, shouts of disappointment and rage are heard from the motorists, goaded beyond endurance by such an insignificant improvement of their situation. The same chestnut tree is still in plain view, resplendent under its bright cargo of flowering candles. A living witness, as it were, mocking by its very unchanging presence, the harrowing plight of motorists ensnared here by this traffic jam in the midst of the fabled bogs of Clooneen.

As the Dáil reassembles on the edge of the motorway beside The Peugeot, The Ford Escort announces that she is the bearer of important new information. Facts culled, she indicates, from information possessed by some DKW or other some hundreds of meters to the east of the Parish.

This fresh news throws a totally credible light on the episode of the ambulance, she says. According to her, a double accident occurred at 2.00pm just outside Angelbank. In the first one, a Rover that was coming full speed from the Dublin direction crashed head-on into a Seat Malaga. Two were killed and another pair gravely wounded, including a young child. And then, to add to the horror, a bus, full to the gills with tourists from Italy or Japan, somewhere like that, while trying to skirt to skirt the Rover and the Seat Malaga, which were interlocked, crashed into a Renault van. And, if that were not enough, a Jaguar sports car, doing 100km an hour, at least ploughed into that tangled mass of metal and blood.

The appearance at that moment of a second ambulance, speeding westwards with horn blaring, lends credence to this horror story. As soon as it disappears from sight and hearing, The Beamer announces that he does not believe The Ford Escort's story, "as well intentioned as it, undoubtedly, is." He would never question her, The Ford Escort's, *bona fides*, of course. That would always go without saying. But he would question, seriously question, the reliability of DKW's informant.

And then, surveying the assembled parishioners (a name coined by a lone Trabant in the next parish) over the rims of his spectacles, he inform them that he is in receipt of "certain knowledge" that a grave accident occurred—and this he can affirm with absolute certainty—to the east of Angelbank and closer to Dublin. This is proven by the fact that this traffic jam extends far to the east of Angelbank.

The Fiat 1100 Dub asks The Beamer how he managed to acquire such information given that the radio appears to be permanently hijacked by Josie, the unspeakable turd, and his Glenawney bimbo, not to mention Lardina *Meditate Your Fat Away*. Not to mention that repetitive *News at One* dose, adds The Renault 4 Ponytail.

I can confirm the accuracy of those observations, says Bishop Skoda, with appropriate episcopal solemnity. And, on top of that, all our mobile phones have ceased to function.

And don't forget that all our watches are stopped, adds Ms. Peugeot (blue), an aged, but still vital, wrinkly.

The Beamer informs them, surveying his audience over the rim of his spectacles, a slight sardonic smile (some would say sneer) on his lips, that he has his own methods for accessing information. Infallible methods that have never let him down! Whose proven success are more than worth a vote of complete confidence. People of the highest standing, he says, have revealed to him the true state of play. Sources of the highest possible probity and reliability!

It surprises The Citroën that nobody thought to comment that the story that The Beamer's supposedly totally reliable sources have sold to him totally contradicts his earlier explanation of this traffic jam, presumably emanating from the same sources. Can it really be that the parishioners have such short memories? Or is pathological docility encoded for in their genomes?

Tiring of such a fruitless wrangle, The Citroën leaves the vicinity of the Dáil and proceeds eastwards in the direction of Angelbank/*Baile an Dá Ghadaí*, surveying as he does so the long lines of stationary cars on either side of him. This jam could almost be a second-hand car showroom, he says to himself. For, almost every make of vehicle is here: Peugeots and Toyotas, Datsuns and Fiats, Ladas and…

It is clear that many of the drivers in this part of the jam are immigrants. Pale-skinned Slavs, the darker skins of arrivals from the South and the lightly tanned features of those from the Orient!

From where he is standing now, The Citroën sees an elevated stretch of the road, seven kilometers, at least, away and covered with vehicles, their roofs glittering in this unexpectedly warm sunshine. Straining his eyes, he can detect no movement whatsoever in this metallic mass. Farewell to the luscious Anna! Farewell to the warm blue seas of Estartit!

A driver from this neighboring parish hails him. A gentleman whose accent clearly indicates that he was born not a thousand miles from the Falls Road, Belfast! He cannot recognize the blue car from which the Belfast man addresses him, unless it is a mutant Lada, totally unfamiliar to him. The latter is obviously keen to impart a piece of information he has heard from some Daimler or other further east along the line. And a grim story it is, without doubt. That car accident rumor is just a fuckin' cock and bull story, he says vehemently.

The real story, which I'm goin' tae tell ye nigh, is much more horrifyin'. Aye!

A small aircraft—a Piper Cub, which seats two people only—crashed on the motorway between Angelbank/*Baile an Dá Ghadaí* and the Capital. It seems that it hit a petrol tanker which immediately exploded in a burst of flame. Five dead, at least, says the Lada (if that is what he is driving), his hoarse Belfast accent lending urgency and dramatic impact to this piece of sensational news. And then: they couldn't recognize the corpses. Burnt to a bloody cinder they were. Nawthin' left but cinders thar.

Cinders, he adds, for further dramatic impact.

And that wasn't the end of it. Not by a long shot, bejasus! Scores were wounded, so they were, many seriously, when the cars behind the tanker rammed into each others arses. It's goin' to take two hours, at the very least, to sort out that tangle, not to mention gettin' the bloody traffic movin' again.

A refurbished Morris Minor , who happened to be passing by, remarked that he had heard that a lot of these amateur pilots are given the run of aircraft that they hardly know how to fly. And that this meant that an accident of the type described by the Lada was only waiting to happen. It's hardly a fortnight since I said those very words to the other half. As sure as I'm standing here!

But a Honda motor bike, who joined our small group, said that he had heard rumors up front to the effect that a suicide Al Caida pilot may have been behind the disaster. And that's something that had to happen sooner than later, he opines. When you think of the way Shannon Airport is being used by the US army to transit prisoners to Guantanamo and troops to the Empire's many battle zones. In a country that claims to be neutral, if you don't mind! That Al Caida crowd are the boyos who know very well, so they do, the uses to which that airport is being put by the US army.

The sudden bleating of car horns to the east reminds The Citroën that the lines of traffic are about to move again. And that he is at some remove from his own car. He runs back past the Fiats, the Datsuns, the Toyotas and The Peugeots. Breathing heavily, he reaches the familiar boundaries of his own parish. The engines of the automobiles of his neighbors are already ticking over.

The Cortina, his arm extended through his lowered door window, greets him with a handshake. The Opel surveys him sourly as he opens the door of his car. If looks could kill! Whence this hostility?

Another of these mysteries whose roots lie buried deep in the long tragedy of Irish history?

+++++

THE CITROËN TURNS THE KEY in the ignition. The engine purrs into action immediately. When The Cortina in front of him starts to move—the brat making faces at him, predictably, from its rear window—he moves into first gear. And then, as they gather speed, into second gear. The two columns move ahead slowly, side by side, the left column moving slightly faster than its companion to the right. So that The Citroën is now almost directly opposite The Fiat 1100, just ahead of The Ford Escort.

But, as if these minor discrepancies between the lines were being monitored and annulled by some imaginary Garda, the right column accelerates just ever so slightly, so that The Ford Escort catches up and is now directly opposite him.

Glancing over to his right he sees that she, The Ford Escort, is looking in his direction. The two glances meet and both of them smile involuntarily. He notes, for the first time, just how dazzlingly white are her teeth. Could be that she is wearing cosmetic caps or can it be that they are exhibiting their natural color? If the story of the aircraft crash has yet to percolate through to the Parish, he would welcome the opportunity to be the first to acquaint her, The Ford Escort, with his latest gleaning from the impressive output of that rumor factory up the road. Almost as if he has already consigned his tryst with Anna to the realm of the impossible.

Was there any point, really, allowing Anna to intrude on his consciousness while he, The Citroën, was very far indeed from being within an ass's roar of crossing the Shannon. She, being the punctiliously organized lady that she is, would already be in the airport. She would have the tickets safely stored in her handbag. Would her anxiety mirror his, at this stage? Hardly! She knows that The Citroën can always be relied upon to show up on time, a characteristic that endears him to her. Or so she says, probably hypocritically. A slight delay caused by slow-moving traffic, but he'll show up in due course. And if not? Her elegantly made-up brow darkens.

As The Citroën, now in fourth gear, glides effortlessly eastwards, he imagines Anna surveying the offerings of the shops in the airport's general lounge. Wishing that he were there so as to be able to pass the inspection barrier and eye the more extensive range of products available in the passenger lounge. And assessing the "performance capability", as she calls it, of every young male (and even some not so young) within eyeshot!

Remember, she said to him once, that I'm a little bit like Stacey, if you know what I mean. On that nudist beach near Cadaques one blazing summer day last year, the Mediterranean glittering to the eastern horizon. I haven't a clue what you mean, love, never having met this Stacey. Anna just laughed. That's what I love about you, dearest, she said, the amazing naiveté of eggheads!

Haven't you noticed that I'm a man-eating tiger. Just look at the equipment of that brute over there! He's like a bull! Doesn't that make you feel somewhat…insufficient? And a little jealous? Maybe I'll go over and introduce myself to him. What would you say to a threesome tonight?

Jeez, Anna, if I didn't know you better, I'd say you were a thorough nymphomaniac!

Ha, dearest, if you really knew your Anna, you would know that she's the mother of all nymphomaniacs.

Anna, is probably in the plane by now. An empty seat—his own—beside her. The craft taxies slowly to the beginning of the runway. They pause, waiting for the go-ahead from the control tower. Then, the roar of the engines announces a sudden surge of power, and the plane races down the runway, gathering speed. Lines of blue lights on the edge of the runway flash past and then, suddenly, they are airborne...

Vehicles crawl like ants along the roads beneath them. Lambay and Ireland's Eye are partially obscured by wisps of white cloud... Dammit it to hell, I've been carried away by a daydream sparked by that memory...

For want of anything else to do, he selects another DVD. His imagination paints a picture, this time, of that plane crash up the road, announced to him earlier by that Lada (or was it?). A merry band travels towards the Capital. Animatedly discussing Arsenal's prospects, this weird weather ("more like fuckin' Africa"), the heavy traffic, ManU, Liverpool (the team), the Heineken Cup. The women while away the time discussing Stacey and the $64.000 question: is Stacey pregnant? And, if she is in the family way, who is the guilty party? Could it be Doug? Or that creep Howard? Or, maybe she isn't pregnant, after all...

And then, a lightning fast forward: cinders in the place where living flesh was thinking, imagining, holding forth! Ah, the transience of human existence! That frail curtain that separates life from death is suddenly rent; nothingness replaces the material universe. All of which could be a gigantic illusion, anyway, the supreme trick of the Great Magician!

The sun hangs like a great red ball over the far horizon beyond the tedious flat expanse of bogland to his right. Not a tree nor decent-sized bush in sight, to distract his mind from that latest sinister thought. He concentrates now on his driving. The traffic is slowing down and he has already slipped down into second gear. A little later, he notes that the speedometer needle is now hovering, shakily, near zero.

Soon, the setting sun will make contact with the horizon; dusk will soon be upon us!

Anna's flight should be crossing the Pyrenees just about now. Snow lies here and there in the shadowed valleys between those towering peaks. Now the plane descends over Girona. The illuminated bulk of the great cathedral, in the heart of the city's medieval district rises up behind that phalanx of tall buildings that line the banks of the River Onyar.

+++++

THE CATHEDERAL ON THE RETINA OF HIS IMAGINATION is suddenly displaced by an unusually large white butterfly as it descends on to the windscreen of The Ford Escort, that/who is still to his left.

The Citroën and The Ford Escort both see at the same time, out of the corners of their eyes, the descent of this butterfly. They then look at each other. The butterfly uniting them in a split second in a look of seeming mutual understanding!

Is it a look that presages the commencement of another complicated chapter in the life of The Citroën? Could this butterfly be other than accidental, he asks himself, though predestination doesn't figure normally among his confused retinue of assumptions.

In fact, The Citroën prides himself on being totally free of such superstitions and the blind Fates, together with their enchanted looms, have been consigned by him to a point outside the known, and knowable, universe. But can absolute certainty in anything, including Descartes' "I think, therefore I am", ever be vouchsafed to man? So can any happening, no matter how ephemeral, really be accidental? The Citroën reminds himself that contemplation of such profundities is as bad for the mental hygiene of motorists as estimating the number of angels that can dance on the heads of pins.

The butterfly takes off again from The Ford Escort's windshield. The Citroën's eyes follow its erratic flight over the Bishop's Skoda, as far as the Volkswagen. And then it veers in the direction of the Renault before fluttering across the divide between the two lines of vehicles, high above the blue Peugeot before finally coming to rest on the rear window of the Cortina in front of him. Little pucker-face puts out a (probably) jammy paw to grab it.

So, the butterfly takes off again, its fluttering and directionless flight a symbol of freedom and arbitrariness, in The Citroën's *weltanschauung*, as it carries the insect over lines of vehicles groaning their way in first gear on the road across the never-ending bogs of Clooneen. He loses sight of it altogether as it disappears behind the grey Opel of Mr. Gold Fáinne that appears to be glued to his rear bumper.

+++++

THIS UNINTERRUPTED SPELL OF DRIVING could never last for long, of course. With scarcely a few kilometers of this bog road traversed, all vehicular movement comes to a full stop. Effing, blinding and blasphemous swearing is heard once again all along the length of the road.

As a consolation, The Citroën reminds himself that, at least, that they are no longer under the malignant shadow of that chestnut tree. Certain progress has been made, albeit minimal. But one must be grateful for small mercies. Furthermore, The Parish has remained intact, situated as it is now between two rises in this ill-fated road. And neither bush nor tree can be sighted on this monotonously flat bog that surrounds them now on all sides, stretching to the very horizon.

In a now monotonous reflex action, The Citroën turns

on the car radio. But continuous programming from the one station he can locate, having traversed the entire dial, appears to be kaput. For all he can hear is the irritating faux-Yankee twang of that bimbo explaining once again to Josie, the *Morning Show* windbag, how "Buddhism" cured her of obesity. And this narcissistic rant to be followed, undoubtedly, by the *News at One*, with its all too familiar repertoire of stories whose stale outlines are almost palpable.

With a snort of annoyance, The Citroën, extinguishes the Thornton windbag's flow of unsought banal familiarities. The seeds of doubt, even fear, are beginning to germinate in his mind. The sun is now sinking beneath the horizon; suppose we have to spend the night, or part of it, in this isolated place before normal traffic resumes? Is this purgatory a real prospect?

He surveys the vicinity of his car. The out-of-control brat in the Cortina, not being at his usual station by the rear window of his parent's car, must be asleep.

He can just make out The Ford Escort damsel as she applies her makeup in the semi-darkness. She squints into her rear mirror as she defines the shape of her lips and eyebrows with, presumably, cosmetic pencils. Eye shadow will undoubtedly follow; he knows the routine from having observed Maura's ritualistic self-beautification procedure prior to sallying forth with him to one of those tiresome events that configure their social life. But for what purpose is The Ford Escort now applying mascara to her eyelashes in such a god-forsaken place as this?

He imagines a decade of the rosary being intoned in The Skoda. Hopefully, with the intention of getting the Almighty to intervene in this crisis, as the efforts of the temporal powers are remarkably conspicuous by their absence. His rear mirror presents him with a view of The SUV Yuppie, baseball cap and all, and the Mercedes Benz accountant, in his shirt sleeves, sitting together on the grassy verge of the right-hand side of the road, quaffing beer from cans and eating sandwiches.

This sight reminds him that he himself has eaten nothing since early morning. Anxiety appears to have displaced hunger in the constitution of his sensorium for the time being. However, when it reasserts itself, he will investigate the packed lunch bestowed on him by Maura's people, generous to a fault, as he set out on his journey from Letterfree yesterday.

Not worth wasting time thinking of Anna! She'd have reached Estartit by now in the white limousine and driver that Brendan keeps there "for comfort and convenience". And he has no way to inform her of the unbelievable predicament in which he finds himself this ill-fated evening. Will she ever believe the fix I am in, unless this monumental traffic cock-up is reported in one of the national papers? And by some neutral correspondent, not by him, The Citroën?

He opens the door of the car, descends to the roadway and, standing there, looks towards the west. Just in time to see the upper part of the sun's red disc being swallowed by the dark edge of the bog.

At least, he says to himself, the cool night air will soon dispel the dead heat of the day, traces of which are conserved by the interior of his car.

A small comfort!

Well, better than no relief at all! he mutters, the banality of the shibboleth being scarcely noticeable in the reduced universe he now inhabits.

+++++

THE SUN SANK beneath the horizon. Ragged red clouds hovered above the point of its disappearance in bright pale blue sky whose color will soon drain away to be replaced by the darkness of night.

The Citroën directs his footsteps towards the Dáil, which is being convened, as is its wont, on the roadside beside the blue Peugeot. Ordinarily, such assemblies hold little personal interest for him. But, who knows, maybe he will hear something there this time that may throw light on his and the common predicament of all his fellow parishioners. And, failing that, he himself will always have that story of the Piper Club crash to contribute to the conversation. Thus he will be able to feed that insatiable rumor mill whose sensational products serve to divert the gaze of us parishioners from a too critical contemplation of our common Clooneen Jam reality.

    He is startled momentarily when some animal or bird out on the bog, whose loud scream he does not recognize, awakens the residues of certain childhood fears. The arrival of the banshee, for example, whose wail announces death, as his rural aunt related to her young and impressionable nephew, her voice adopting an appropriate sepulchral tone. The Fiat 1100 Dub says he recognizes the screech of an owl; he had seen some nature film on the television recently featuring the life of owls. Mr. Anglia (yellow) adds that that very bird is common in these parts, according to something he had read somewhere lately…

    Impossible, says The Beamer authoritatively: Everybody knows that owls feed on small woodland mammals like mice and voles. How could their likes survive in a desolate hole like this where there isn't even a single tree in sight?

    An interloper from another parish passes along the way. Carrying a new take on our predicament! A story, to boot, that contradicts all the stories that have been circulating up to now. And that gives us to understand—to compound our woes—that an early release from the distress to which we are all now subject—the result of this long drawn-out traffic jam—is far from being in the offing. A megadisaster is the cause of our predicament, claims this Johnny-come-lately.

    There's a story going around in some of the parishes to the east of here is that small aircraft crashed into a petrol tanker up the way, and that the mess that that caused is the reason for this bloody hold-up that is driving us all mad. I don't know if that story has reached you here so far. Well, that is all so much bullshit as far as our parish is concerned. The real story is a thousand times worse than that, according to this latest harbinger of disaster:

Yes sir! A plane crashed up front, all right, but it was no two-seater aircraft. No sirree! It was a big passenger plane en route from Sweden to Shannon. It's too early yet to say if the Taoiseach and a couple of other ministers were on board. They might well have been returning from that summit meeting in Stockholm. That is what some of them up front are saying. And, furthermore, instead of hitting a tanker, as some early reports indicated, it seems that it hit a minibus in which a hurling team was returning from Dublin to the West.

The place where this disaster happened is like a slaughterhouse, with dead bodies and pools of blood all over the place.

Another messenger arrives to corroborate the story we have just heard, but to dispute certain of its minor details. The minibus was not travelling to the West, as alleged by the first "reporter", nor was it carrying a hurling team. Rather, it was travelling eastwards, full of drunken passengers returning from some fishing competition, or other, over in the West. Or, maybe, from some Bingo convention; that part of the story has still to be verified. Furthermore, this accident happened closer to Dublin than was indicated by the initial, understandably confused, reports of the disaster. So, yez can all see, this bleedin' traffic jam is much longer than most of us thought at first. This fuckin' line of misery may bloody-well extend as far as Dublin itself, remarks this second messenger jocosely, before the same misanthrope takes to the road again to deliver, with sadistic glee, his tale of death and destruction to those who still desperately want to believe that this traffic jam is just a local hiccup, soon to be resolved.

That is more or less what I was saying, says The

Beamer to the assembled members of the Dáil, although I didn't know the details of that horrific accident. But somebody has to say the unsayable. It strikes me that we could very well be in this mess for the long haul. And, if that's the case, we'd better take certain measures sooner than later. Unless we pull together, I dread to think of our future.

The Fiat 1100 nudges The Citroën with his elbow. Do you think Arsenal made it in today's match, he asks. Somebody up front told me that they had won, but that only one goal was scored, and that in an extra time shoot out. Pilsudski scored the clincher he said, but you'd wonder about some of these stories when our radios are no longer functioning.

And did you yourself hear anything about what might be happening to Stacey in *Cougars*? intervenes Ms. Cortina.

Not a word, says The Fiat 1100 Dub. But, in all fairness, you'll have all of that story if we manage to make it to Dublin in time for *Cougars*. Half the country has been driven fuckin'-well mad by that story, if you'll pardon my posh talk…

These latest rumors catapult the members of the Dáil into a frenzy of speculation. Some are disposed to call these rumors "stories", and true stories at that. The opposition balks at accepting their veracity, and describe them as, simply, "unfounded rumors". They point to the fact that most sports reporters, the ones who really know, have put their money on Manchester United. The opposition point out that, as Pilsudski had recovered from his ankle injury, an Arsenal victory was generally forecast. Their manager usually gets it right, says The Cortina, togged out, as usual, in his Dubs track suit. And as far as Chelsea is concerned…

Yet another bearer of tales arrives on the scene. From one of the parishes that lie to the west of the Saab, it seems. He seems determined to scotch the rumors that have been entertaining the Dáil for the last half-hour, or more. Night has already fallen as he explains that the story of the airplane crash is nothing but an egregious fabrication, although he doesn't express this thought in precisely those words.

That story is noting but a bleedin' load of horse shit from a fuckin' crowd of liars, he says. A pile of steaming fuckin' ould cobblers cooked up by a crowd of fuckin' chancers with fuck-all better to do than to go about looking for attention.

His far less sensational story is that a portion of the motorway to the east of Angelbank collapsed beneath the weight of traffic. Five motor cars, a van and a long lorry with some foreign registration are trapped in the crater caused by that collapse. Luckiliy, given the nature and scale of the accident, only two people were killed.

The Dáil considers this new rumor briefly.

Ms. Ford Escort opines that building a motorway across a stretch of bogland might not have been the best solution of the west-bound traffic problem.

The Beamer says, however, that this latest story has the semblance of truth. And much more so than any of the other stories that they had heard up to now.

But you said before that all the other stories we have heard up to now had a "semblance of truth" as you call it, notes Ms. Toyota Starlet.

Exactly, says The Beamer smoothly. But the word "semblance" is just that, the appearance of truth is not, *per se*, necessarily the truth itself. A truth may have many semblances, only one of which corresponds to its true essence.

I've no idea what in the name of Jaysus you're talking about, replies Ms. Toyota Starlet.

The Renault 4 Ponytail says that, although he is now an artist, he does have an engineering degree and practiced that profession for many years. That was before he discovered that he had been harboring this unsuspected artistic talent, although he had never gone near an arts school. Nor ever felt any need to do so. However, thanks to his specialized engineering background, he is in a position to say, definitively, that this latest "crater in the road" hypothesis has no foundation. No, sir! None whatsoever! Furthermore, and coincidentally, he happens to know, personally, some of the engineers who had planned this very stretch of this new motorway. Indeed, it is many the creamy pint he downed with them before he gave rein to his artistic calling. So that he, Renault 4, is in a privileged position to say, without the slightest fear of contradiction, and has the letters after his name to prove it that yes, by God, his erstwhile drinking comrades are past masters in the art and science of road construction and for any bloody bowsie to assert anything to the contrary, anything so ill-informed, if not downright malicious, only underlines the dark and cavernous depths of his own ignorance.

Mr. Toyota Starlet, presumable aggrieved by the cavalier dismissal of his wife's allegation of inconsistency on the part of The Beamer, says he wouldn't give a "two fucks" for all the so-called "expert knowledge" in Ireland, full stop. And that, anyhow, the airplane crash story is the one he prefers. Full stop! And that it is more the pity that the whole bloody Government wasn't travelling in that shaggin' plane from Stockholm.

Fuckin' far play to you, shouts a fashionably ragged Mushroom Druid, who sports a mullet hairdo (thereafter named The Mullet by most parishioners).

Sides are taken. The debate is fast and furious. If you don't take back what you've just said, says The SUV Yuppie to Mr. Toyota Starlet, I'll twist your bloody neck. I'll break your head. (The male Toyota Starlet has, unwittingly, introduced a personal note into the proceedings. As The SUV was to explain, *ad nauseam*, in other such assemblies, a cousin of his is among the newly appointed ministers.)

With the help of the Terminator himself, a scrawny fucker like you wouldn't even be able to twist a chicken's neck, says The Toyota Starlet.

As these heartfelt exchanges become increasingly heated, exacerbated by the creative expletives of the Mushroom Druid, The Citroën figures that it is time for him to pour oil on such turbulent waters. He point out calmly that none of the stories that have been presented to the Dáil up to now can be proven or disproven, since all contact with the outside world has been definitively broken.

Unless you have your own reliable sources, says The Beamer, mysteriously. Everybody looks towards him. And then towards each other. As if further elucidation of that point could somehow make a terrible new beauty—or at least a name or two—emerge.

An elucidation that was not destined to be forthcoming at that juncture, however.

For, just then, the blaring of car horns to the east rent the night air...

+++++

IT IS GOING TO BE A MOONLIT STARRY NIGHT. The moon, a great red balloon whose string has been released suddenly from the grip of some youngster, impelled by curiosity, bounds up into the sky from the distant edge of the bog.

The frightening screech of that animal, or bird, punctuates the silence of the bog at irregular intervals.

The sudden bitter cold reminds The Citroën that Summer could still be a long way off. Didn't that snowstorm in the North only last week spawn a clatter of road accidents. He returns to the car to retrieve his gansey. Although the interior of the vehicle still conserves something of the unnatural heat of the afternoon, The Citroën figures that the possibility of frost later on can hardly be discounted.

Surveying his surroundings through his windshield, he sees parishioners with electric torches scurrying back and forth. Looking for companionship, news and, maybe, food, he reckons. Ah, the draw of bodily warmth, whose mysterious attraction sometimes puzzles The Citroën. Heavy metal sounds thunder out from the DAF. Two women stroll slowly past to his vehicle. The raised tones of their voices indicates that are arguing, but in a friendly way. One of them, he cannot see which, asserts that she doesn't believe that Stacey could be pregnant.

That lady is far too intelligent, and as sly as a hungry fox, to allow herself to be put in the family way by anybody. I'm not saying that she couldn't pretend to be pregnant, if that suited her ends. I mean, if she saw some sort of advantage for herself in telling people that she was pregnant. I wouldn't be surprised if that is what she is up to. And that the gaffing of Doctor Ben could well be the object of her machinations. Don't forget that I was the one who told you first.

I don't agree with you, says her companion, but the people of Ireland will be viewing *Cougars* shortly and they'll be the ones who'll be able to answer that question. Not like us who have this bloody cross to bear. They say we'll be stuck out here among these shaggin' bog holes until the bloody traffic begins to move again.

Anna, if I read her script rightly, is comfortably ensconced by now in that cane armchair under the palm tree on the apartment patio. Probably still sticking pins in a waxen image of The Citroën! Or, much more likely, preening outside one of those open beach bars, *chiringuitos*, sipping a *mojito*, her posture announcing to all and sundry her easy availability!

For, The Citroën knows all too damn well, that if he is not on tap to cater to her needs: well, my dear, there are so many other fish in the sea. And, now that I have come all the way to Estartit, do you seriously think that a man-killer like me is going to spend the night all alone? You must be joking! And he, The Citroën? Should he be thinking of The Ford Escort? Was that butterfly earlier a favorable portent?

Maybe this whole traffic jam episode is nothing but a nightmare and I'll wake up beside Maura in Letterfree.

He glances obsessively at his watch from time to time. The luminous hands and numbers inform him, mockingly, that it is still 2.00. The moon is already riding high in the sky, its strong light is a silvery patina on the metal roofs of the cars in front of him. Away over to the right, captured by the moonlight, he sees the dark outline of a person out on the bog is squatting on his, or her, hunkers. On his way back to his car, The Citroën drums lightly with his fingers on the metallic body of The Ford Escort.

No answer!

Looking into the car, he sees it to be empty. Where could its occupant, the elusive Ford Escort, be hiding herself at this hour of night? And she made up like a bride on the morning of her wedding! He returns to his own car, without being able to summon up a realistic answer to that question...

Some time afterwards, a light tap on the window, awakens him from a fitful semi-slumber. It is The Skoda Bishop, and he effusively apologetic about waking up The Citroën at such an unearthly hour. But he comes bearing a welcome gift, a fine big sandwich, which the latter accepts eagerly. The Bishop says that the nuns in a convent over in the West, where the younger priest—his travelling companion—was giving a mission over the last few days, had lumbered them with a load of sandwiches that the pair of them alone could never consume. So, he was going around the Parish in the dark to feed the hungry. And, if you would like one...Bloody right, he would like one...

Even if he had his own "larder" as a back-up supply in case the going gets rough. Wrapped up neatly in a copy of *The Sunday Star!* Presented to him a seeming infinity ago by Maura's people, just in case he became afflicted by "the hungry grass", as rural folk describe insatiable hunger, on his long journey from Letterfree to Dublin. He had planned to throw it later into the rubbish bin in the airport. Better to keep it in reserve for just now, though. There has not been the slightest indication up to now that this traffic jam is on the point of breaking up soon.

Would you prefer ham or cheese?

Ah, the luxury of choice! He selects ham, but go ahead says His Eminence, you may as well take the pair of them, since we have lots. So he takes a pair of them, ham and cheese. And fine substantial sandwiches they are. Leave it to the nuns to know how to make real sandwiches!

Later on in the night, The Ford Escort pays him an unexpected visit. Where has she been all night ? Visiting some old friends who are further ahead in the line. Or so she says.

Is she hungry? Would she eat a sandwich?

Would a duck swim?

She offers to share a tablet of chocolate with him. A gift from her friends, she says. Thanks, he says, but keep it all for yourself he says. The thirst is the divil that's really killing me, he says. For, parched he truly is, with a throat as dry as the floor of the Gobi desert.

It is a long time now since he pissed the last of those Glenlongan pints into this damned unending bog. People are astir now. Having been aroused from their slumbers by the ministrations of the Episcopal sandwich dispenser, they can be seen walking about in the moonlight, swinging their arms and stamping their feet on the road in order to warm themselves up. There is a sharp icy nip in the air, and it is certain that there will be frost on this road before morning.

But how is he going to solve his thirst problem? The Ford Escort says that she has finished the last of her water.

The perfume that she is wearing is beginning to remind him of The Beamer's shaving lotion. Jesus! This is how this excruciating thirst, and this accursed traffic jam that looks like as if it is never going to end, are both affecting my perception of reality, he mutters to himself.

When they descend from the car to stretch their legs, they quickly find out that they are not alone in their plight. The contents of water, milk, lemonade, Kong Kola, Pepsi, Fanta, Sprite etc., between cans and bottles, have all been drained to the last drop, even the occasional can of beer. The Cortina's brat is the first to start howling with the thirst. His piercing screeches freeze the very marrow of The Citroën's bones. His father and The Skoda Bishop go in search of water...

+++++

SUDDENLY, WITHOUT ANY WARNING whatsoever, the Mushroom Druids raise a ruction designed to awake the dead from their sepulchral slumbers.

It seems that, in some mysterious fashion, these "alternative" people have managed to locate a fresh water spring out there somewhere on that desolate bog that surrounds us. They flaunt the bottles and plastic containers that they have filled with this precious liquid before the longing gaze of the parched parishioners.

Are they disposed to share this bonanza with their parched parishioners? Or even reveal the source of the spring that keeps their thirst at bay?

Are you having me on? In this "Greed is Good" epoch? In a celebration—as it were—of our currently fashionable hip selfishness, The Mullet mockingly "offers" a glass of water to the surrounding parched parishioners, and then mockingly withdraws the glass before anyone else can even touch it.

Later, having returned to his car, The Citroën has just about started to slumber and gently snore (probably), when the familiar cacophony of car horns to the east of the Parish indicates that the traffic is about to move again. With the help of the unseen powers, this could very well be the final chapter of this unexpected, unsought and unloved odyssey.

O great God almighty, vouchsafe to look down on us, Thy suffering children of the Clooneen Jam, on this dark night of our souls! Vouchsafe that dear old dirty Dublin be designated as the next and only stop on this final leg of our journey!

Shouts, imprecation, entreaties once again break the primeval silence of the surrounding bog. Car doors slam, engines splutter, cough and roar into action…

But, horror now heaps upon horror. Instead of being Dublin-bound, the two lines of cars are now moving westwards, under the gaze of the cold and indifferent stars, in reverse gear. The night pulsates with the whine and groan of thousands of vehicles, as they go about reversing the minuscule gain made during the penultimate leg of their journey.

As he participates in this retreat, The Citroën realizes that his goal, Dublin, is retreating once again away from him. He now senses, more clearly than ever before, that he and his fellow parishioners are in the grip of huge and complex forces whose powers are unchallengeable. Not to mention unchangeable!

This nocturnal cavalcade suddenly grinds to a halt. Peering through the windshield, The Citroën sees by car headlights that they have returned to the very spot where the Parish was located before its last migration. That accursed chestnut tree stands mocking the disconsolate denizens of the Parish, as it were, its erect flowering candles picked out by the bright moonlight. Car lights are extinguished. Each vehicle retreats back into the dark of its own silence. Except the DAF, whose musical repertoire has now extended to an eclectic sampling of techno-rock, loudly and freely and generously available to all parishioners, whether they want to hear it or not.

The Citroën is unable to get back to sleep. He cannot think of anything to do, or anything worth doing, in these dead hours of the night. The hours are melting into one another, symbolized by this perpetual 2.00, which seems to him to have become a metaphor for some primal time that can never be manipulated by human thought. But, whose human co-relative is this perpetual boredom which so wearies his spirit. To facilitate his re-insertion in a more human dimension, he gives the radio another try:

Righto, Josie! Well, he was, well, messing...You'd know what I mean, in all fairness, Josie, messing, when his fingers found the cotton wool. I nearly died from shame. And he got into a right bad temper. Saying that I had been fooling him all along and if I didn't do something about my "tiny tits", as he called them, our engagement would be off. And that June wedding as well, he said. You can just as well forget about the confetti. And I wouldn't mind that, Josie, only that I am head over heels in love with Jason. It was love at first sight from the word go. And he says he's madly in love with me. But wild horses couldn't drag me into a marriage with a woman with small tits. That's just the way I am. I would be heartbroken if he left me, Josie. I just can't help it. And that's God's honest truth, you know what I mean!

If that spiel illustrates some essential aspect of the human condition, he mutters silently to himself, the sooner I renounce my membership of the human herd the better. He twists the radio knob. Both the local and national radio transmitters emit a crackling silence only. Is the whole damn nation caught up in this traffic jam? Or have all their staffs fucked off home or been abducted by aliens? Or been silenced by some mysterious natural disaster?

In that drowsy half-awake, half-asleep state, the screen of his imagination is now featuring the amazing amatory adventure of Anna the Man-Eater. With whatever German, Swede, Catalan, Russian, Greek or Turk she has managed to hook in Estartit standing bollix-naked in front of her, as her eyes, made sultry with generous applications of mascara, assess the worth of his offering.

He now pulls his overcoat about him to keep out the cold. Thus protected, he now makes another unsuccessful attempt to get to sleep. Trying to imagine himself as an embryo, lying there in the warm womb of his automobile.

But the same imagination sips the leash and persists in leading him back along memory's convoluted highways and byways...

+++++

WHAT WAS LEFT after his experience of real life weakened and finally eliminated youth's romantic impulse? Consigned its youthful idealisms to the attic where childhood baubles are stored. While the tamed spirit, chafing occasionally at the bit, is tightly reined by the dictates of duty all the way to journey's end.

Nor was this the limitless spiritual and physical communion he had imagined true love to be. At every level! The standard missionary position is all that is allowed in The Citroën's marriage bed. Night after night! In the beginning, that was! After that, it was once a week.

And leave those weird antics you are looking for to ladies of the night!

Forgetting, or ignoring, those distant early warning signs in the Marrakesh medina, he failed to understand Maura's early enthusiasm for those nightly lovemaking sessions. A genuine zest for the sensual aspect of love? Or, was she merely answering to the dictates of the Irish herd as ordained by Holy Mother Church? That would be credible, given her ban on contraceptives. Never, she said, would she consent to the use of such "filthy things". Nor would she ever consent to the use of such a medicament as "the pill", which is both "unnatural and, anyhow, sinful". And how about the Billing's method which is based, after all, on a woman's fertility cycle? And which is permitted by the Church!

Priests who do not understand their own religion gave that permission, she said. Shame on them! They will have to answer to Almighty God. For they, above all, should know that the fundamental aim of marriage is the procreation of children. Full stop! If you don't believe even that much, you should never have married me.

However, religious faith does not seem to be the real reason for Maura's rejection of all contraceptive methods. She returned, unexpectedly, to her Medina theme of five years ago while they vacationed with her family out west.

I won't be satisfied with anything less than eight children, she announced.

There were a dozen children in her own family. My

mother always says that happiness and love are to be found wherever there is a large family, she said. Yes, it'll be eight children, at least.

Why not make it eighteen, says The Citroën jocosely.

You don't appear to be seriously listening to me at all. I said that I want eight children. I'm really serious about this and I'm going to hold you to it!

That demand effectively neutralized his taste for lovemaking that night.

Eight children would bankrupt him, for God's sake. Freelance journalists these days live a precarious enough existence, and the three offspring we have already stretches my resources to the limits. Isn't that threesome enough for us?

Neil says he will be a footballer with Manchester United when he grows up. Little Sarah aims to be a television actress or a pop singer (she isn't yet sure which), whichever will make her "famous" fastest. And then Seán, whose bad behavior—bullying, even—are constantly getting him into hot water with the school authorities. An unexpected—and unwelcome—strain on the family purse is the exorbitant fee that has to be paid to that shrink who has been charged with "normalizing" the behavior of the recalcitrant Seán. In whom 'there is not a stim of harm, basically just energy and high spirits', according to Maura. An aficionado of self-help books, of which she has a veritable library by now, is the same Maura. She claims that Seán's Attention Deficit Disorder is basically one of low self-esteem. Together with a clutch of old-fashioned teachers who just refuse to understand the mind of the modern child.

When the costs of these family difficulties are added to the huge mortgage they have to pay for that new house they bought recently in D4, the ability of The Citroën to make ends meet is sorely tried. Mortgage rates are set to rise shortly; the increased property tax will clip the family's wings; rises in the price of petrol and water are forecast by pundits whose infallibility regarding these affairs is a matter of record. Along with the many other blows to the family's economy that are in the pipeline as citizens struggle to pay their banks' crippling debts! He, The Citroën, would not be surprised if direct and indirect taxes will have to be further increased in the near future. If only to pay for the losses incurred by that clatter of international steeplechase gamblers who placed their bets on Ireland before that ill-fated horse broke its back at that dangerous mid-course jump. Try to forget that such payments mortgage the futures of Neil, Sarah and Seán!

And that is the somewhat bleak landscape that stretches out in front of the five of us. And, if that weren't enough, these crushing burdens will be augmented by preposterous educational fees when the youngsters come of university age. Making ends meet with three adolescents is purgatory enough. But with eight? What sort of Never-Never Land does Maura inhabit?

For God's sake!

Not that he didn't try to discuss the economics of their plight with her! She, for her part, always imputed selfishness and snob values to him.

Your own comfort is all you ever think about, she said. Your membership of that damn golf club, for example. Sometimes, I think you'd rather live there in your hideout than here with us.

Dead right, I would, he had breathed silently to himself. If only she had understood the truth of that statement. But he can hardly divulge the real reason for his frequent visits to that establishment, of which the glamorous Anna is a member. Even this secret compartmentalization of his private life involves an extra expense.

So, tongue-in-cheek, he explains his frequent visits to the golf club as being a necessary part of a journalist's work. It is where the nation's shakers and movers meet to do deals. Politicians, bankers, developers, bishops, the lot! There's no accounting for the number of exclusive stories that escaped between the 17th and 18th holes. Or, most especially, at the 19th hole, once the details had been worked out between putts out earlier...

And then, continues Maura with her harangue, this fancy mansion in this yuppie suburb when something much less ostentatious would have done us just as well! And two cars in the garage when we could have done just as well with one! Why do we need that Citroen, for example? Or is it that you are afraid I'd have to give up my job if we had a large family? That we wouldn't be flush enough then to keep this insane show on the road?

He had to restrain himself that evening from saying to Maura that poverty is generally the bosom companion of the "love" and "affection" that binds the members of poverty-stricken families together. He could have related then episodes from the history of her own family that are at complete odds with the absurdly romanticized *Little House on the Prairie* type of domestic arrangement that has monopolized her perspective on such matters up till now.

What would she have to say about Colm and Máirtín, who high-tailed it to the U.S.A. when the arse fell out of the fishing in Letterfree? And nary a word from the pair of them since! There is a rumor (admittedly unconfirmed) circulating these days in the village that Máirtín has been seen wearing an American army uniform in Afghanistan. Or was it in Colombia?

And isn't it true, Maura, that your other brothers have spent the best part of their lives navvying on the "lump" on England's motorways? And spending their weekends in an alcoholic haze in some sleazy Irish ghetto over yonder?

Not to mention your sisters, Maura, those "civil servants", God help us! I like your fanciful naming of skivvies as "Sanitation Officers". What about Bridget and Sarah and their West Indian husbands. Why is it that your family warmth is so overpowering that they never return home? You yourself related to me that Bridget told you in London that she could never go home with her husband and family for fear of shocking your parents. Do you think that this fear might have to do with your family's possible distaste for black people and mixed-race children?

These were some of the things he wanted to tell Maura that evening, just about four years ago, to this very month. But he kept his silence. He had little choice at the time, being on a holiday visit with Maura and the kids to his Letterfree in-laws.

A university scholarship enabled Maura to escape the fate of her sisters. Then, a good B.A. degree gained her a good pensionable position in the Civil Service and a one way ticket away from the poverty that condemned her siblings to downward mobility, at best.

But it is now clear to The Citroën that all of that education and the superficial layer of urban culture Maura affects had never managed to create an impermeable barrier between her and the culture of poverty in which she had been raised. "Eight, at least", for Chrissake!

She may as well have bought a return ticket to Letterfree!

Stuff happens!

Donald Rumsfeld, *referring to the torture of war prisoners in Abu Ghraib Prison, Iraq.*

BOOK TWO

BECAUSE OF USURY

THIS UNCEASING TWISTING AND TURNING OF HIS BODY in his frenzied quest for a comfort that is unobtainable in the back seat of this car lasts right through the night. Or through the entire length of eternity, it sometimes feels to The Citroën. Dawn seems as if it will never materialize.

    He finally sits up, throws off his overcoat and rubs the sleep out of his eyes. He notes a sour taste in his mouth and the fact that he is still wearing his day clothes. He feels sweaty and dirty. He would walk ten kilometers, or more, to have a decent shower, if such were available. He permits himself a long luxurious stretch to try and ease the stiffness in his cramped limbs. For a fleeting interval, he isn't quite sure where he is. In Foxrock, Letterfree or Estartit?

    You are in your own Citroen, you eejit! On a dark road between two God-forsaken rural villages, sandwiched between the two halves of Clooneen bog! The silence of the night is rent at all too frequent intervals by the piercing wail of the brat in the Cortina in front of him and the monotonous thump-thump-thump of Mushroom Druid trance.

    He glances at the luminous hands and numbers of his watch. Still frozen at their eternal 2.00! A bitter laugh escapes him inadvertently. This frozen number reminding him once again that the nightmare in which he is embroiled is no creature of a fevered imagination. And that both he and thousands of his kind are trapped in a monstrous and unprecedented traffic jam that never ever shows signs of breaking up. And that Dublin is as far from him right now, and just as unreachable, as it was yesterday evening as the setting sun slid below the western rim of the bog that surrounds them on all sides.

The morning star is visible through the windshield, its frosty brightness suspended, as it were, from the rafters of the heavens. That, and the faint paleness of the sky to the east, confirms for The Citroën that the dawn cannot be far distant.

His attention is deflected from the star to the shadowy figures scurrying about the cars in the thin pre-dawn light. They seem to be making for clumps of low bushes in the bog, just a short distance in from the edge of the motorway. The insistent signal sent to his brain by his own lower innards reminds him of the reason for this unexpected flurry of activity. Informing him that he himself must descend from the comfort his car to satisfy his own body's most basic demands!

As he opens the car door, he is surprised by the cold outside. This, in spite of the fact that Summer has arrived officially! But it is clear from the crunching under his feet, as he seeks a suitably secluded spot to perform his morning evacuation, that the surface of this ill-starred Bog of Clooneen is covered by a thin film of ice. However, he keeps on walking through the pre-dawn chill. Nothing lies to the north of him but the formless dark of this vast bog, weakly illuminated now by the silent starry sky above. Eventually he reaches a slight hollow that seems to be out of the sight of his fellow parishioners.

However, occasional grunts from unseen neighbors nearby remind him that his exertions are not unique to him alone.

Returning shortly to his car, The Citroën almost bumps into The Toyota Starlet. He is almost certain, at least, that it is in fact The Toyota Starlet, although the latter, fails to respond to The Citroën's greeting. Indeed, he moves furtively away from the latter, as if he were seeking to avoid being recognized. The Citroën cannot help wondering if the exercise of this bodily function was a matter for such shame on the part of our distant ancestors, some of whose remains lie, undoubtedly, far beneath this blanket of peat. Most unlikely he concludes! Probably just another part of that Jansenist heritage that has so scarred our people!

Safely ensconced in his car again, The Citroën twiddles his thumbs. Fully awake now, there is nothing for it but to wait patiently for the dawn to fully break. Why not kill boredom by trying the radio again. Maybe whatever glitch that was causing it to repeat incessantly those boring old programs has been eliminated. And, with a bit of luck, we will be back to regular programming. Maybe, there'll be some news about this traffic jam, even. He presses the radio button:

... Saying that I had been fooling him all along and if I didn't do something about my "tiny tits", as he called them, our engagement would be off. And that June wedding as well, he said. You can just as well forget about the confetti. And I wouldn't mind that, Josie, only that I am head over heels in love with Jason. It was love at first sight from the word go. And he says he's madly in love with me. But wild horses couldn't drag me into a marriage with a woman with small tits. That's just the way I am. I would be heartbroken if he left me, Josie. I just can't help it. And that's God's honest truth, you know what I mean!

Ah, now I get you, love. It seems to me that your Jason has a breast fetish that has led him into making an unreasonable demand, for all intents and purposes, on your good self, Sheila. But tell me: what do you think he means by doing "something about it".

The Citroën already knows the answer to this puerile question. Fucking cosmetic surgery, Josie, you unspeakable gobshite, he shouts With a groan that signals boredom, impotence and muffled rage, he presses a button to cut the "unspeakable" *Josie Thornton's Morning Show* short.

Good Christ Almighty, please send your unfaithful servant a sign that this nightmare traffic jam will end with this coming dawn!

+++++

A GREY HALF-LIGHT SIGNALS the surrender of night to day. Glancing over to his right, he notes that The Ford Escort has returned in her own car. She now seems to be asleep in the driver's seat, a gansey heaped on the steering wheel serving as a pillow for her head. She faces in his direction, a rebellious lock of jet-black hair falling across her forehead that must have escaped during the night from a mass of hair she normally keeps well combed back, culminating in a bun, traditional schoolmarm style.

He entertains himself briefly with a short erotic drama he projects on to the flickering screen of his imagination. Just two actors figure in this spectacle: himself and The Ford Escort. This idyll is interrupted, however, by a sudden burst of loud heavy metal music designed, it seems, to awaken the very dead. It emanates once again from The Mullet's refuge, the flowery DAF van of The Mushroom Druids, that is parked just behind The Opel…

Traffic movement is minimal throughout the morning. Just a couple of meters back and forth at random intervals! But sufficient to maintain the hope of the parishioners, albeit increasingly forlorn, that this traffic jam will unsnarl itself shortly and that traffic towards Dublin will flow freely. According to rumors that percolate through from parishes to the west of the Parish, this mass of all but stationary vehicles now extends back as far as Glenlongan. And even further west, if some of the more exaggerated stories are to be believed.

Having nothing else to do, except indulge in meaningless chit-chat with his companions in distress, The Citroën switches on the car radio. Hoping against hope, that some semblance of normality has returned to air waves had that seemed up to now to be parasitized by Josie Thornton and his gormless guests. Maybe a news flash will throw some light on the predicament of all us who are trapped here by this fucking appalling inconvenience, to put it as politely as the facts warrant.

A forlorn hope not to be realized, alas! The faux-Yankee eulogist of *Meditate Your Fat Away* is explaining once again to Josie Thornton that boredom, the product of a sense of spiritual emptiness, was what set her at first on the road to gluttony. And there is damn-all else to do in the capitol, she asserts, except to: *go drinking. And to go looking for the "craic", wherever and however that entertainment is to be found. And with the price they charge these days for drink and fags, you know what I mean, it was cheaper for me to fight the boredom with hamburger and pizza-feed-your-face feasts, Josie, rather than with piss-ups. Binge drinking would bankrupt you, you know yourself, Josie. And, in all fairness, French fries don't leave you with a morning-after hangover, you know what I mean?...*

And so it goes...

+++++

A FEW MINUTES AFTER MIDDAY, a messenger from some outlying part of the Clooneen Jam (as just about everybody here now calls it) arrives in our Parish, bearing the one tale that all of us have been longing to hear.

At long last!

The crater in the road that has been holding us up has just been filled in, he says. And traffic will be moving again shortly, in about twenty minutes or so. Both drivers and passengers, all assembled on the edge of the motorway to give ear to the latest tidings, greet this news with a sustained and full-throated roar of approval that is lost in the primitive vastness of Clooneen Bog. They are as a cohort of concentration camp inmates who have just been told that their guards have fled and that their release is imminent. Mullet and his Mushroom Druid comrades celebrate this imminence by amplifying their heavy metal repertoire up a number of decibels.

As The Citroën complains to Ms. Ford Escort about this assault on his ear drums, she explains to him that what he is listening to, or being assaulted by, is a fusion of "trance" and "house", legitimate heirs of the "rave" music that preceded them. As he ponders this subtle, for him, distinction, two of the Druids—The Mullet and a stocky gap-toothed shaven-headed youth wearing badly torn jeans—climb up on to the roof of their van. The latter is stripped to the waist and a prominent tattoo of a naked woman is seen by all to adorn his back. Their shouts and bodily contortions answer to the rhythm of the music, pouring out from the guts of their van.

The Citroën sees little reason for this ebullient celebration. Yesterday's false alarms have immunized him, effectively, against a euphoric reception of stories that arrive, not backed up by hard evidence. His doubts concerning the tidings of great joy of this latest messiah are confirmed when he sees the latter, taking advantage of the parishioners' euphoria, go begging for food and drink from them. He manages to wheedle a banana from The Toyota Starlet and a half-bag of Taystees from The Renault 4.

Water, the little of it that is available, is being jealously conserved by the parishioners, for obvious reasons. The bringer of good news then disappears from view, still parched, seeking refuge, presumably, from more generous water providers elsewhere or in the familiar environs of his own parish.

At least an hour later, and without the slightest budge in the meantime, another bearer of good news arrives on the scene. Bringing with him more or less the same spiel as his predecessor! Nobody listens to him.

He then knocks on the rear door of the DAF, begging

for "a bit of bread and something to drink". The Mullet appears, still stripped to the waist, a can of beer in his hand, roaring that he'll "cut the fuckin' balls" off this unfortunate indigent with a "big fuckin' rusty knife" unless "you get the fuck outta here as fast as your fuckin' legs can carry you". False Messiah No. 2 immediately takes this unsubtle hint; his future presence hereabouts can be safely discounted.

As the temperature of the day gradually mounts, so does its humidity. Nevertheless, the majority of parishioners remain in their cars. Not that they really believe the optimistic forecasts of the vendors of false hopes who visit the parish in quest of food and drink. Yet, one never knows! Hope springs eternal in the human breast, as that old hoary cliché has it. And what parishioner would want to be caught unawares on this abnormally oppressive sultry day by a sudden movement of the traffic while socializing at some distant remove from his, or her, vehicle?

All of the windows of The Citroën's car are rolled down; nevertheless its interior is a veritable oven. And although he himself has divested himself of his shirt, he senses a constant stream of sweat dripping from his chin on to his chest. The merest breath of wind wafting through the car would feel like a drop of ice-cold spring water on a parched tongue...

In spite of all the discomfort that this almost tropical heat has visited on the Parish, The Citroën cannot but admit that it has also brought certain advantages. The Ford Escort has removed her blouse, leaving a black brassiere as the sole garment clothing her upper body. This disrobing also reveals a multicolored tattoo, that seems to him to be based on some Celtic design from the Book of Kells, on her upper arm just beneath her left shoulder.

As he gazes now at those graceful shoulders and that delicately carved back supporting her black tresses, on that intricate Celtic design beneath her shoulder, on the black brassiere that emphasizes the ivory smoothness of her skin, how in the name of all that is holy did he ever imagine that the driver of The Ford Escort was anything less than surpassingly beautiful? Anything less than a Goddess?...

The Cortina brat starts his shrill screeching again, hunger gnawing at his vitals, without doubt. As if on cue, The Ford Escort wriggles into her blouse, buttons it up and, then, descends from her car. She walks over to the Cortina, her left hand clutching a paper bag, doubtlessly containing—as before—morsels to pacify the source of the piercing screams emanating from within the vehicle. The Citroën can hardly avoid taking in the shapeliness of her figure. How did he ever designate this apparition as "dumpy"? Her shapely calves and derriere! The narrowness of her waist! The gentle way her breasts bounce with her gently swaying walk!

What a pity that this unexpected beauty of The Ford Escort's body is not congruent with the set of her features. Her face is just that little bit too rounded for The Citroën's taste, her cheekbones too broad, evidencing her peasant origins. He prefers a more classically molded countenance, such as represented by Sir John Lavery in his portrait of his wife, Hazel, Lady Lavery, on the old green Irish pound note. Ah, but that was in those distant times before television brought Stacey to the masses and Ireland had begun to shed her sovereignty. But whatever lack he detects in The Ford Escort's features is more than compensated for by the dazzling smile she directs in his direction as she walks towards the Cortina.

He knows that she knows—with that ancient and unerring instinct of woman—that he is carefully observing her. That smile in the context of the sultriness of the day, and the other feminine attributes has observed and appreciated, has served to awaken desires that now compete with the hunger pangs that rack his lower innards. Now, if only she removed those spectacles that give her face that slightly owlish look! But, as one of his drinking companions in the Glenlongan Arms had remarked the other night: "Who'd give a tuppenny damn about the mantelpiece when you are poking the fire!"

As his mind travels again in this well-worn circuit, a vision of Anna swimming in the warm waters of the Mediterranean pops into his mind. Along with her new acquaintance—some vigorous young bull, undoubtedly—doing a "show-off" butterfly stroke just ahead of her. Later, in the evening, they'll wind up in El Bulli, Ferran Adrià's gourmet restaurant near Roses. One of the world's most famous restaurants, thanks to the quality of its *Nouvelle Cuisine*, much touted by the Michelin Guide. For, such a sybaritic indulgence figured on the schedule devised by Anna for what was to be their mini-holiday together.

Brendan will foot the bill, of course. Afterwards, commencing with a *hors d'ouevre* of a different kind in the marble Jacuzzi of the apartment, the Goddess will so exercise the young bull that he will be left as weak as a kitten...

+++++

THE DÁIL IS IN SESSION on the edge of the road facing the blue Peugeot. Among the faithful, The Citroën notes the presence of The Renault 4 Ponytail, The Skoda Bishop, the middle-aged Ms. Toyota Starlet, she who is parked just behind the yellow Anglia that forms the eastern boundary of the Parish.

The Citroën ambles as far as this meeting. Who knows, but perhaps some suggestion will emerge as to how the hunger and thirst of the parishioners—their and his greatest growing concern—is to be assuaged. He notes the burning heat of the day as he approaches what seems, if loudness of voice is any indicator, to be a vigorous discussion group.

Ms. Toyota Starlet is shouting—her shrill voice has a strong north midlands twang—that this traffic jam is a "bloody disgrace", so it is, and a resigning matter for whatever "bloody minister" is responsible for the upkeep of roads. She regards this jam as not only a blot on the good reputation of Ireland "among the nations"—"as sure as eggs are eggs" there must be tourists among those of us who are trapped by this "disgraceful and unacceptable exhibition of the worst side of our national character"—but as a "massive personal insult."

The soothing voice of The Skoda Bishop advises her to be patient. He suggests that she, and her listeners, offer up their suffering to Almighty God, in the hope that he will give us all the grace to use this, admittedly most unpleasant, experience to grow in our love of God and our neighbors.

Ms. Toyota Starlet was visibly unimpressed by this pious intervention and gave a snort of disgust. This insufferable heat does not breed moderation, thinks The Citroën. Consider the excitable Southern races compared to the phlegmatic Northerners! Are we or are we not living in the 21st century, asks a combative Ms. Toyota Starlet, a little more truculently than this debate demands, thus interrupting The Citroën's train of thought. Or does anybody here seriously believe that we are still ruled by medieval superstition, she asks?

The Bishop, in reply, advises Ms.Toyota Starlet, who is clearly somewhat less enamored of Holy Mother Church than his Eminence would like, and all other parishioners to pray for the intercession of Saint Fiachra, the patron saint of all drivers.

And what the hell good will that do?

So that he will intercede for you up above to win the grace that will enable you, and all of us, to suffer this torment resignedly!

Up above? Up in the sky, is it? Hiding behind the clouds? Is that where your Saint Fiachra hangs out? Yourself and your likes have kept the Irish people bamboozled with that kind of codswallop for generations now. But, mark my words, that day is long past...

Having delivered herself of that thought, Ms. Toyota Starlet turns her capacious posterior to the assembled Dáil deputies and heads back to her car.

Heat and hunger, says The Citroën to the somewhat crestfallen Bishop, make a dangerous cocktail. Shake them up together and frayed tempers are the result.

This jam may a sort of purgatory here on earth, answers the Bishop, interpreting The Citroën's words as support for his stance. But it won't last, with the help of God. Could it be that this suffering has been visited by the Almighty on his errant people? To remind them that an even greater suffering lies in wait for those who would challenge His divine authority!

Oh, I heard that last remark, shouts Ms. Toyota Starlet from the door of her car, though obviously she was not yet out of earshot. If there was such a thing as hell, yourself and the rest of your crew would be burning there throughout all eternity. That is, if there was such a thing as justice to be had in the universe. And if the devil is what you people crack him up to be, he'll be waiting there at the gates of hell, with a white hot poker in his fist, ready for your arrival...

You know very well what I am talking about, you unctuous *ould* scumbag!

+++++

SHARP HUNGER PANGS continuously rack The Citroën's guts.

Especially since he discovered that the unwholesome smell of the contents of his own secret larder, brought all the way from Letterfree, points to the inadvisability, if not foolhardiness, of using the said vittles to relieve that hunger. The heat of the interior of the car must have kick-started the putrefying bacteria into speeding up decomposition of these comestibles. This is the unexpected and unwelcome result of the rigorous fast he had undergone in order to conserve this food for the time it might be needed, if this traffic jam fails to dissolve very soon. So, he deposited the stinking remains of his lunch behind a low bush on the edge of the bog. Now he was left with not even a solitary crust of bread...

Pondering possible solutions of his dilemma, he considers

the possibility that The Toyota Starlet may harbor food and drink. Hadn't he seen The Toyota Starlet promenading earlier eating what appeared to be a big cheese sandwich? However, he had heard it said that midland peasants, and their offspring, have the reputation of being excessively closed in on themselves, of being unwelcoming to strangers. Even that they lack articulate speech and imagination, though the lucid anticlerical spiel of Ms. Toyota starlet seems to give the lie to that prejudice!

In any case, necessity knows no laws. And to hell now with dignity! He will make himself known to these midlanders, prefacing his plea for food with spoken evidence of his urbane normality.

Ms. Toyota Starlet is in the driving seat, her right elbow resting on her door's window frame, as The Citroën reaches the target vehicle. He opts for a conventional opening gambit:

This traffic jam is a national scandal, don't you think?

Dead right, it is. Not only that, but we're all going to miss the latest episode of *Cougars* tonight!

A television soap is far from being central to the concerns of a famished Citroen just then. However:

Wasn't that shown last night? he says.

Of course it was! On the BBC! But sunspots destroyed the reception, they say. They'll be showing the same episode on RTE tonight. Most people opt for seeing the two showings. In fact, I know one woman who records it. So that she and her family can see it every night to give them something to talk about.

Um, I see. So, we won't know whether Stacey is pregnant or not, unless the traffic starts to flow again, says The Citroën. His eagerness to demonstrate that he is at one with the plain man and abreast of the latest doings in the never-never land of those *Cougar* phantoms that have parasitized the popular imagination knows no bounds. He has learned, as his forefathers before him, that hunger is the most effective spur to humility.

That's the great question that the whole country is talking about: is Stacey pregnant? What do you yourself think?

In all fairness, I'd say that she is pregnant!

Not too many would agree with you there. Why do you think that?

Unless she wants to get her own back on Susan!

I never thought of that. But, bydad, it does makes sense, when I come to think about it. Pure common sense! I never took Susan into my reckoning. But, now that you mention her, I seem to remember that odd thing she said to Doug. I couldn't make head nor tail of what she was saying at the time...

+++++

THE WELCOMING MIEN of the Toyota Starlet parishioners—two men and three women, including their fiery orator—belies the image of plodding stolidity and just plain dullness often assigned to the denizens of the country's great central plain. Like most such stereotypes, it seldom corresponds to the facts. For these midlanders cheerily invite this stranger, The Citroën, his human credentials established, to sit along with them in their car.

They are all returning to County Westmeath from a wedding reception in Glenlongan Arms Hotel: a son of Ms. Toyota Starlet had married a young woman from that storied glen of fighting men and ancient myth and that was why they were on this road, embroiled in this damn traffic jam. With generosity of spirit, they do not spare The Citroën the administrative details of the nuptials. After the reception, at which there were over one hundred guests, the newly-wedded couple took off for Orlando, Florida, where Disneyworld and its ubiquitous mouse will provide suitable contemporary background to the more intimate details of their newly-wedded bliss.

The Citroën attaches no ultramontane significance to

such coincidences. Or much else, if it comes to that! Thence, he doesn't see the point in divulging to his new companions the astonishing coincidence that the distant sound of their revelry in the public bar of the Glenlongan Arms had penetrated as far as the resident's lounge. Or that he himself had breakfasted in that same hostelry before setting out on this ill-fated trip.

It's a far cry from the old days, says her husband. Herself and meself spent the honeymoon—four days was all we could afford in them bad ould days—down in a B&B in Ballybunion. And it rained solid all the time we were there. Never let up...

Leaving another bout of conversation concerning Stacey out of the reckoning, (Doug is the guilty party is the unanimous decision of the crew of the Toyota Starlet, if indeed, that dastardly deed had been done at all, which is by no means certain), this damn traffic jam, not surprisingly, monopolizes the conversation in the car. The serious emergency now looming in the event of this traffic jam being prolonged figures large in the speculations that are entertained by the group!

Ms. Toyota Starlet puts it squarely on the line. If we don't budge almost immediately from this damn spot, she says, we had better organize ourselves appropriately.

What do you mean by "organize", The Citroën asks her quietly.

It's as obvious as cowshit in a meadow, says Ms. Toyota Starlet, turning towards him to answer his question. Take food and drink, for example! Can a human being survive without them? You know she cannot. Well, there are cars in this parish without a crumb of solid food in them, not to mention a drop of milk or water. I hear infants wailing from the hunger already.

And then there are health and sanitation problems. The bog on either side of us is becoming an open sewer.

Wild horses wouldn't drag names from me. All I will say is that there are certain cars in this parish whose occupants don't give a continental damn about the plight of their neighbors. And who are quite happy to gorge themselves sick on the food surplus they hide from the rest of us. They have it all: bread, meat, water, wine, you name it. But tell me when the glutton ever gave a damn about his starving neighbor.

I'm afraid you've hit the nail on the head, says The Citroën. Hadn't he himself seen The Beamer, with his own eyes, feeding himself yesterday. Sipping on a glass of red wine, held in his left hand, as he did so! His right hand holding a fine big baguette from which he bit chunks at regular intervals. However he managed to get hold of it! The Citroën imagined the filling of that huge sandwich: camembert, gorgonzola, parmesan ham, *pate de foie gras*….

The very thought of those words fills his mouth with saliva.

+++++

THE CITROËN FEELS THE HUNGER more keenly than ever. He images it now as a gigantic hungry worm wriggling around in the hollow of his stomach.

That is all very fine, Mam, says a lean looking youngish man sitting in the back seat of the car. His black hair is combed meticulously to cover a small bald patch on the top of his cranium- Thinks The Citroën: that youth is destined to wind up one day just as bald as his father, who is sitting directly behind me.

But what can we do?

Ms. Toyota Starlet appeared to have been waiting for that question.

The first thing we have to do, she says, is to estimate the quantity and quality of the food and drink we have in this parish. The second step is to gather and store all that we have in some agreed place. The third step is to distribute it equitably to all of us in need. Giving priority, of course, to the young and the weak…

But to do that, what we need is organization, energy and—above all else—honesty.

But, where the hell are you going to find those in this rotten little country, Mam? Remember that it ideas like that that got the buckeens to expel you from the party!

The husband of Ms. Toyota Starlet explains to The Citroën that his wife was once a Fianna Gael councilor, until she was drummed out of that party. And then that she wore the Fine Fáil label. Until the arse fell out of that pathetic pantomime as soon as the German roared...

You know right well that I had no time for any of those bastards, rejoined his wife. Nor would I have the time of day for any of their drinking butties in the Galway tent, if it comes to that.

And then, turning to The Citroën:

What do you think of my plan, anyway?

He opines that the plan is nothing but plain common sense. And that he would support it, one hundred per cent. He would be willing, indeed, to volunteer his own car for use as a food storage facility, if the plan could be got off the ground. But how is this going to happen?

Ms. Toyota Starlet says that the first step is to call an emergency meeting of the Dáil to discuss her proposition. In the event of its being accepted, it would be a question of assigning specific tasks to specific parishioners.

The Citroën agrees. I will support you, he reiterates. To the hilt! But, in the meantime, I was wondering if you might have something to eat.

I am starving...

+++++

The inhabitants of the Parish referred to their meetings on the grassy verge of the motorway, directly opposite the blue Peugeot as "Dáil sessions". As far as we can ascertain, these meetings attempted to mimic the structures that were founded on an ancient ideology referred to as "democracy".

The final Dáil Éireann session is believed to have been convened about 2028, at a rough estimate, and democracy is believed to have been commemorated annually in the area of its former jurisdiction up till approximately 300 years ago.

(The Editors.)

+++++

BEFORE THE CREW OF THE TOYOTA STARLET can respond to The Citroën's plea, the even tenor of the discussion within that vehicle is disturbed by shouting outside and the familiar blare of car horns to the east. The traffic is about to move again.

Apologizing to companions of the last half-hour, he quickly descends from the Toyota Starlet and runs back to his own car. Keys are being twisted in ignitions and car engines roar into action. The blue-grey effluent belching from exhaust pipes at least has the advantage of diluting, somewhat, the nauseating stink from unburied human waste lying on the bog that now permeates the air that is being breathed in by parishioners.

The lines of cars begin to move, all right. But The Citroën can scarcely believe the evidence of his own eyes. Another movement in reverse gear! If this goes on, it won't be long before we wind up at Mawmeen, that petrol station, with a small shop attached, that stands at the mouth of the accursed black bog of Clooneen.

In short, the place he had left some days ago. And all he was thinking about then was Estartit and the seductive charms of Anna. He passes that chestnut tree, with its erect white blossoms, as he drives in reverse gear westwards. The tree is soon out of sight. He is conscious of his parched tongue, lying like a wooden clapper in his mouth, and a hunger nausea in his guts.

The silence of the bog is now invaded by the groaning of the engines of hundreds, maybe thousands, of vehicles, trapped, like The Citroën, in this unending incomprehensible imbroglio...

This lugubrious rearwards procession eventually grinds to a halt. The composition of the parish, and the order of cars within it, do not appear to have been affected by this latest migration westwards. Almost making the parish into some sort of permanent entity, a source of small comfort, but a comfort nevertheless, for The Citroën: some stable point of reference in a world of whirl! That Cortina, with its leering brat, is still in front of him, of course. As well as The Opel Gold Fáinne behind him! A glance across the divide that separates the two lines of cars confirms that the nubile Ford Escort maiden is still directly to his right.

He opens the car door and descends to the road, intent on taking advantage of this interval to stretch his legs. The stench of sewage is, if that were possible, stronger here than in the bog of Clooneen up the road. The Citroën links this fact to unseasonable sultriness, for Ireland, of the afternoon and the swarms of flies, millions of them, that buzz about the Parish.

The surrounding countryside has an air of familiarity about it. He knows that behind that bend in the road, somewhere among that cluster of trees to the west of him, is a petrol station in which his tank was filled an aeon ago. Or so it seems to him now. And, unless his memory is playing tricks on him, a water and mineral water dispenser are to be found in the small shop there. Damn-all chance that there is a single drop left there to be dispensed! Still, no harm in giving it a try!

He walks westwards past the DAF, now as mercifully silent as a graveyard. It must be that its nighthawk inhabitants sleep by day. Even the devils of hell must take their forty winks sometime!

As he approaches the bend of the road, he is startled by the sight of dense clouds of black smoke, billowing upwards from behind the trees. Silent groups of people stand in the roadway, seemingly transfixed by this unexpected sight. At least it provides a little distraction from the all-pervading anxiety that has gripped the prisoners of the Jam.

A complete stranger, standing beside his grey-green Seat Ibiza 2000 addresses The Citroën:

When they had robbed every fuckin' thing from the petrol station, nothing would satisfy the bastards but to set the damn place on fire. In broad daylight, imagine! In broad fuckin' daylight! Without fear nor shame! And not a bleedin' Garda in sight, in spite of the fact that security expenditures were the only ones increased in the recent budget! The whole country, the whole shaggin' shebang, is going to the dogs, so it is. While the Gardaí are on the hunt for terrorists, robbers have a field day. And the honest citizen payin' for the whole show is nothing but fuckin' eejit!

The Citroën is about to comment that the booty of the small fry the robber's profession is as nothing compared to the billions being looted by the more polished and influential exponents of white-collar banditry. But he holds his peace.

They robbed the petrol, I suppose? he asks.

They robbed every fuckin' thing in the place, I'm telling you: petrol, food, minerals, everything they could lay their fuckin' paws on!

And the Gardaí?

Are you having me on? How, in the name of Jaysus, with this bloody traffic jam could a single Garda, not to mention a fire engine, get within an asses' roar of this place. So, of course, the bandits have a fuckin' field day!

But what did the folk of this parish do—there must be hundreds of you gawking at that inferno—to stop them!

Are you jokin'? They did nothin', citizen! Not a bloody thing! These days, the wise ould dog stays in his fuckin' kennel lookin' after his own bone. If you don't cross them, they say, why would the buggers interfere with you?

They remain there, silent, for a while, listening to the crackling of the blaze. Gazing at the thick black clouds that billow upwards from the leaping red flames beneath them. The sound of exploding windows is reminiscent of gunshot reports.

+++++

THE CITROËN IS GLAD to return to the familiar embrace of his own parish. The familiar knot of people is gathered across the road from the blue Peugeot signaling that the Dáil is again in session, even if its venue of this sitting has been displaced to Mawmeen!

Things have been developments during his absence.

We'll be electing a Taoiseach in a few minutes time, whispers The Renault 4 Ponytail in his ear, as he joins the assembly. If we don't have some sort of ring-master, this goddam circus will spin completely out of control. Did you see what happened to the petrol station back there?

A stranger, allegedly (from information volunteered by Mr. Toyota Starlet) another Beamer from the next parish, has already been elected Chairperson. They wanted somebody who didn't belong to this parish, says The Cortina, a neutral monitor to ensure that the election would be a clean and a fair one.

This Beamer II, a small obese man wearing an ill-fitting ginger wig, ascends a small rock that juts out of the motorway's grass verge and faces the assembly.

Only two names have been put forward as candidates, up to now, he says in a reedy pompous voice. A lady from the Toyota Starlet, proposed by her husband, and The Beamer, who has been proposed by a gentleman from the Saab! Are any other candidates putting themselves forward?

What about yourself? whispers The Renault 4 Ponytail, nudging The Citroën with his shoulder. I'll propose you, if you want.

Do no such thing, for God's sake, says The Citroën. I was never cut out to be a politician. And then, *soto voce*: bad enough having to report on mankind's irrational foibles without having to plunge personally in the politics of this lunatic asylum!

Well, if there are no further candidates for the post of Taoiseach, shouts Beamer II shrilly, and adhering to the agreed Order of Business, I will next call on each of the candidates to briefly explain briefly to you, the electorate, why they are worthy of your votes and of the exalted position to which they aspire. I stress the word "briefly". For, for all we know, we may be called upon at any moment to desert this place and return to our cars to drive to our destinations. Furthermore, given this intense sunlight, we want to avoid the risk of anybody here present contracting sunstroke. So, I first call upon Ms. Toyota Starlet to explain to us why she is the best qualified candidate in front of you to take over the leadership of this Parish!

Beamer II than leaps down off the stone, stumbling and almost falling, before being supported by The Saab and our Beamer.

Ms. Toyota Starlet is a short stout woman. The Citroën notices that, even when she stands to her full height on that protruding rock, she just about comes to eye-level with most of her listeners.

Some of you here probably think that it is, well, a wee bit presumptuous for a woman, a mere woman like me, to be running for this high office, she says. Especially considering the major challenges that face us! But, let me tell you all, the world is changing. Women are no longer second-class citizens. We demonstrate, day after day, that we are every bit as capable as the men, and maybe more so, when it comes to dealing with the problems that face holders of public office. Let me remind you of the grace and dignity that Mary Robinson brought to the public offices she occupied, whether in Ireland or abroad, of Mary McAleese in Ireland, of Cristina Fernandez in Argentina, of Michelle Bachelet in Chile, of Delma Rousseff in Brazil, of Angela Merkel in Germany.

These are just random examples, plucked from the pages of modern history, that show us clearly what determined and well-qualified women can do to advance the public good.

What about Maggie Thatcher, milk snatcher, then? some Dublin voice asks from somewhere in the crowd, that has now been swollen by curious onlookers from neighboring parishes. The jeers, mocking laughter and ribald remarks that greet this intervention encourage further such contributions. Tell us how the "good qualifications" Catherine the Great, Lizzie the First of England or Angela Merkel, ever advanced the "public good"(a Cork accent this time). Or Sarah Palin of the USA (a Belfast accent).

Beamer II loudly calls for order and threatens to suspend this meeting until said order has been restored.

Who could this heckler, who clearly has a mastery of the major Irish accents, possibly be? So The Citroën asks himself. He would almost be ready to swear that the completely unsuspected ventriloquist skills of The Saab, an innocuous personality he had scarcely noted before, succeeded in making a complete bollix of Ms. Toyota Starlet's speech. Although one would hardly suspect that the self-effacing Saab harbored such a talent, except for his half-open mouth and the faint movements of his lips.

The Chairperson shouts that it is incumbent upon him to exercise his democratic authority. And who invested Beamer II with this "democratic authority"? whispers The Citroën to The Renault 4 Ponytail. Our Beamer proposed him! And The Saab seconded! There was only the pair of them and Beamer II present when the meeting began, responds The Renault 4.

Ah, I see...

Furthermore, continues the Chairperson, it is incumbent on me to remind you all that this is no time for levity. All of the candidates who have had the courage to put their names in front of you have earned the right to a respectful and dignified hearing. But, I would also remind the present speaker that we are not here to discuss the problems of Argentina or

Chile et cetera, all of which have their own importance, undoubtedly so, in their appropriate contexts. We are here to hear strategies—if there are such—that will enable us to overcome the difficulties posed by the Jam in which we find ourselves, as long as the need for such a strategy exists. So, please continue, Ms. Toyota Starlet and, if you please, be as brief as you possibly can.

Thank you Mr. Chairperson! Before some macho bucko interrupted what I was going to say, I was about to give you a detailed breakdown of the policy I intend to enact when you elect me as your Taoiseach. I will be brief and to the point, as our Chairperson has requested of me. The big question that is staring us all between the two eyes is... sustenance. Food and drink, in other words...

+++++

THE CITROËN HAS ALREADY HEARD this spiel. His mind wanders now, opening and closing various doors in memory's convoluted labyrinth.

One opens, painfully, on the night of the showdown between himself and Maura. He tries hurriedly to close the door on that painful memory. But, alas, that particular door refuses to be shut. The film replay has already started.

We have been making love regularly for three years now, says Maura. For all the good that does either of us. Leaving the selfish pleasure that you get out of coupling out of the reckoning!

The Citroën knows all too well where this particular complaint is going.

For God's sake, Maura, aren't you satisfied with the three that we have already got? he asks.

At first, I thought that the fault lay with me, she says, ignoring his rhetorical question. Something down there that wasn't quite right, if you know what I mean. And that's why I spent a whole day in a gynecological clinic a couple of weeks ago undergoing a comprehensive examination of my reproductive parts. And comprehensive is the word... the whole thing makes me ashamed to think of it, though the nurses were very understanding. They told me then that their preliminary tests showed that there was nothing at all the matter with me. Well, the full results came in the post this morning. And they show, without the slightest shadow of doubt, that my fertility index is A1. That I am as fertile as my mother at my age! Are you listening to me? There is nothing, absolutely nothing, wrong with my reproductive parts...

And?

Well, doesn't that raise a big question about you?

What do you mean? You've never said that my performance ever gave you cause for complaint, he says, somewhat lamely.

You know very well that it is not that I am getting at, retorts Maura. You know damn well that it is not. So, in all fairness, you too must undergo a comprehensive fertility examination. There is no opting out of this one. So, I have booked an appointment for you in a clinic in the same hospital for next Tuesday. They'll examine you comprehensively, just as they examined me. To assess your fertility level! You could call in sick on that day. Or simply take a day of your holidays. The appointment is too important to be missed.

The blood freezes in his veins. There is no way that he is going to take a day off to have some clodhopper of a doctor poking around his private parts. What did she think he was: some sort of stud animal?

They both lose the block at that juncture; bitter feelings find their appropriate vehicles in the poisoned recriminations that now fly back and forth.

Why hadn't he found the courage to reveal earlier to Maura the dark secret he harbored in his mind's depths? The simple way he had found, in the very clinic she had just named, to frustrate God's plan, as she would calls her vocation for multiple motherhood. Yes! Courage to clear the air and put their relationship on a new basis, if such were possible and she could bear this new reality.

But, of course, the path of life is all too often the way of subterfuge and lies, *bealach na bréige*, as our language tells us. Secrets fester in the dark recesses of the mind that cannot be bought with gold or silver—or even with love itself. And this was one of them, in spite of Maura's entreaties, tears, threats and maledictions that tested his resolve—or his cowardice—to its very limits.

Threats?

If you refuse to accede to a simple request to undergo a fertility test at the clinic, I am going to have to organize my life in a very different way. He thought then that she meant that they would separate, go their own ways.

The more fool he!

+++++

THE DISCRETE HANDCLAP that marks the end of Ms. Toyota Starlet's discourse brings The Citroën's painful reverie to an end.

The Chairperson is standing again on the stone. And now, he says—blithely ignoring all his previous non-partisan pretensions—let us give the heartiest of welcomes to a man whose managerial talents have the respect of us all. Come up here, my fellow Beamer! And tell us what you are going to do when your parishioners elect you as their Taoiseach!

With respect, Chairperson, please allow me to address my fellow parishioners as I stand here in their midst! And then without waiting for an answer from the gentleman standing on the stone, he says:

Form a circle around me, friends, so I can describe to you, face to face, the policies that this united Parish must enact if we are to surmount the many difficulties and dangers that face us right now. And the many more dangers that will face us if this mother of all traffic jams does not soon end.

My adversary here, Ms. Toyota Starlet, spoke eloquently and persuasively about some of these problems. She explained how she thinks that the food and liquid sustenance we still have should be distributed. Fine! Personally, I have never supported the kind of communism she is advocating, but that is neither here nor there. I am a practical man. And the problem is, as I see it, and she doesn't address it at all, is what we are going to do tomorrow when all of our meager stock of food and drink runs out?

As these words fall calmly from the lips of The Beamer, the circle of parishioners draws in closer to him. His message, whose authority is now accentuated in the minds of his listeners by the faint mid-Atlantic oratorical twang, he has alloyed with his habitual D4 accent.

First of all, he says, I would very much like to praise my adversary's contribution to this crucial debate. The strategy that she is advocating comes from a heart that is pulsing with love for her neighbors. From a charitable disposition that derives from the noblest ideals that have been generated by the human race! This is all very fine! Admirable, even, in its own way! Except that the strategy she advocates ignores completely the grim reality of the problems that face us. Which I'll come to in a moment! In the meantime, let me stress the two words that are inscribed on my banner: one is "Realism"; the other is "Practicality".

I hope you don't think, my friends, that all of this is windy rhetoric! I don't mind telling you out straight: I am not a person without importance and considerable influence in the business life of this country. I am centrally involved in the affairs of a transnational hi-tech corporation whose business was estimated at €70bn last year. We have upwards of 30,000 employees, both in Ireland and around the globe.

Apart from that I have properties in Prague, in Bulgaria and in a few other places, as well. All of which I manage personally. I even own some luxury apartments in Lower Manhattan.

As I said before, this isn't all just hot air. It is just that I take seriously my democratic duty to demonstrate my mettle to you, fairly and honestly. For, after all, it is necessary that you know the quality of the candidates in front of you before you cast your vote. For, when the time comes to make a choice, who wants to buy a pig in a poke?

Who wants to cast a vote for a good-hearted lady, yes, I freely admit that, whom I imagine to be a fine housewife, as every good woman should be. I am sure she can put a fine tasty meal on the table, but what experience has she, I ask, in the fields of commerce and administration?

Character assassination! You've said more than enough, you bollix, a male voice shouts. I ask the Chairperson to get The Beamer to withdraw the insulting sexist comments he has just made about a lady who is a former county councilor.

Mr. Toyota Starlet is the source of this request. And then the ruction begins. Shouts attract the attention of idlers in the neighboring parishes who, bored and with nothing to do, drift over to share in the excitement. Some voices—most of them women's—concur that The Beamer has delivered a nasty sexist insult to Ms. Toyota Starlet. And to womankind in general, let's not mince words. The macho bastard! A brute who would chain a woman to the kitchen sink! Other voices call for silence: let the man have his say for God's sake!

The Chairperson—the other Beamer—climbs back up on to his stone and makes an attempt to call the Dáil to order. Silence, he shouts repeatedly. Let The Beamer speak! Not unless he apologizes, is the answer. But the parishioners and other hangers on, gradually tire of the ruction, worn out as they are by hunger and the brutal unseasonable heat. When The Beamer is satisfied that the hub bub occasioned by his remark dies down and that he has the attention again of every ear, he continues his electoral harangue:

As I was saying, before some of the heirs of Joe Stalin

in our midst interrupted what I was saying, (*You're a Hitlerite bastard yourself,* a voice interjects), interrupted my democratic right to explain to you my background and my policy and to let you know that I am a practical man, a man who can always find a solution, no matter how complex the problem. And I am at the furthest remove possible from the venders of superannuated ideologies that create insuperable problems wherever they are adopted and applied to the solution of economic and social difficulties.

(*Is democracy the ideology you are slagging?* a lone voice shouts.) The Citroën imagines he detects there the unique timbre of the voice of The Fiat 1100 Dub. Or, maybe, that of The Renault 4 Ponytail. The Beamer doesn't deign to respond to the question; such childish provocations are beneath his Patrician dignity:

My adversary here for whom I have the greatest respect (*Liar! Liar!* cry the hecklers) spoke of food and drink. About a central storage and distribution point from which our fast dwindling resources could be distributed equitably! Fine! But what food is she referring to? All she is offering to us, in reality is the remainders of the ideological rubbish of the 20th century.

Now that we are well-established in the 21st century, it is no longer acceptable—nor should it be accepted—that any responsible citizen who makes his, or her, own provision for the proverbial rainy day, should ever be penalized. On top of which, given our increasing food shortage—which is set to become even more exacerbated if this Jam continues—the policy advocated by Ms. Toyota Starlet is irresponsibly short-sighted.

What will she propose to do when the last bite if food has been consumed, all stomachs in the Parish are empty and we are still sitting in the middle of this mess? And this is no mere oratorical flourish, fellow parishioners, no abstract question. The grim reality is that we have scarcely food enough to go another day. So we are talking about a huge problem that will face us tomorrow.

I have given a lot of thought to this problem. And when you elect me to be your Taoiseach (*Never! Never, you bastard!*), and I don't deny your democratic right to reject my proposition *(Oh, we'll reject it, all right, you posh-spoken looser!)*, you will quickly come to understand how the fruits of my deliberation will benefit us all. If you accept the comprehensive plan I will be proposing, nobody in this Parish will go hungry. I guarantee that I will be able to put food on every table (*And not a single fuckin' table in the Parish?*).

I like very much your approach, Beamer. But can you share with us this plan to get food that you say you have in mind? The SUV Yuppie *dixit*. Proudly displaying his recently laundered Tommy Hilfiger shirt today, with its small red and white flag! Tell us out straight now, he asks, with no humming nor hawing, how you are going to feed this multitude with loaves and fishes, as the Bishop here might say! *(laughter)*

I was hoping someone would ask me that question, says The Beamer, smoothly. And my answer is very simple and to the point: vote me in as Taoiseach and you will see in due course that I have devised an effective and realistic plan to feed you all. You are all witnesses to the fact that I have said this. I have given a lot of thought also to other important aspects of the lamentable state in which we find ourselves. (*For example? For example?*).

Well, let us take for example, the appalling stink to which we are subject as I speak. *(No wonder! No fuckin' wonder! Nothing on what is coming out of your mouth!)*. Together with the related swarms of flies that increase in density with every hour we spend in this appalling traffic hold-up. And the bog around us has become an open sewer. In other words, what is needed urgently is a realistic policy regarding sewage disposal to be enforced immediately. If not, we'll be faced with a battery of diseases, dysentery being the least of the serious problems we'll have to face.

(You seem to know a lot about shite, you scum-bag, hardly surprising since you specialize in verbal diarrhea!)

Ignoring imperiously the scabrous contributions of the numerous hecklers, The Beamer now explains that, with all this toing and froing, many parishioners must already be worried because they are low on petrol. But that he, The Beamer, is putting the finishing touches to a plan that will take care of such a shortfall and ensure that no parishioner will be left stranded in this bog for lack of petrol. *(What sort of plan, you fuckin' chancer? What plan, you fuckin' windbag? Never heard such a mound of poxy dung!).*

And not only that, but as our resources in general become scarcer, and that time is already fast approaching, we are going to need and effective and realistic security policy.

Because, it is then that we will see the emergence of gangs of thugs who, not giving a solitary damn for law and public order, will be found pillaging and burning. The petrol station behind us has already been robbed and burned by such ruffians. We can still see from here, as I speak, the smoke ascending from its ruins. So, unless we establish a strong common defense system, and a strong Taoiseach guiding it, I fear that we are in for some very rough times indeed. We will be crushed unless we organize our defense along effective and disciplined military lines...

At that moment, the deliberations of the Dáil is interrupted by the ear-rending cacophony of car horns to the east. The assembly is indecorously abandoned by its members, who now rush pell-mell towards their cars.

+++++

AS IF THAT, BY NOW, FAMILIAR BLARING SOUND were a signal to draw the hub bub in the Dáil to a close. Maybe all of that verbal jousting we have just heard will, later today be seen, retrospectively, in a Dublin restaurant, to have been just a pointless exercise, now that the Clooneen Jam is a nightmare from the past. This thought enters The Citroën's mind, just before his hearing is assailed by the all too familiar opening and slamming shut of car doors, the starting and revving up of engines…

The dead noonday heat and the emptiness of his stomach are now forgotten. The groundless certainty that that the end of the nightmare of the Clooneen Jam is in the offing fuels a new excitement that promises to expunge all that negativity that has been building up to a crescendo ever since that unpleasant encounter near Glenveal.

He now experiences, imaginatively, the sensuous feel of the hot shower streaming down his naked body, cleansing away the bathing gel suds and this noxious Jam grime. As the lines of traffic accelerate, he joyfully moves from second into third gear.

Yes, he will arrange a date with yonder Ford Escort, if he gets another opportunity to chat her up between here and Dublin. He should have organized such a tryst earlier.

He cannot think of a better choice of person with whom to celebrate release from this miserable Clooneen Jam. Okay, there is the small matter of the not inconsiderable age difference between them! But, thankfully, the 21st century has released us from such ageist prejudices. Thinking of the likes of Silvio Berlusconi, Rudolph Murdoch, etc. Not to mention other grizzled veterans, away older than a middle-aged swinger like himself, and who parade—to put the matter as delicately as possible—with damsels on their arms who have scarcely left their teen years behind them.

Winter marrying Spring, so to speak!

More like late Spring marrying midsummer in my case, giving a little concession to the imagination!

Such couplings rejuvenate old bones, according to the Chinese sages, on whose authority he would joyfully lean in this case. And furthermore, after Maura's final ultimatum this past weekend, his marital status will be, for him, no longer an issue. A hungry animal is seldom concerned about where his food comes from...

He visualizes himself wearing his best suit, the dark grey one. He visualizes himself and The Ford Escort entering the Rawalpindi, a fresh-faced glamorous Spring holding mid-Summer's hand. Jealous looks from the inextricably married herdmen and their wrinkled consorts! But to Hell with them and their likes! Before they consult the menu in the Capital's "premier Asian restaurant" he will order two bottles of ice-cold Cobra, to be poured into chilled glasses. Unless, of course, she would prefer something a little more sophisticated from the choice the bar will offer her: a caipirinha, say, a daiquiri or a mango *mojito*.

As they reach the edge of Clooneen Bog, still in third gear, he glances over at her—her car has kept its position opposite his—just as she was glancing over at him. As their glances meet, she smiles. He imagines that her eyes are smiling also, just like his, both pairs of eyes hidden behind sun glasses. And opines The Citroën, the mutual sympathy that informs her smile is a clear early indicator that she will not turn down his invitation to dine with him in the Rawalpindi.

He absent-mindedly presses the radio button, an automatic response of his to the boredom engendered by long-distance driving. But maybe, in this case, he will hear a piece of music that will harmonize with his new romantic optimism. Or, a report that the obstacle that caused the Clooneen Jam, whatever that may have been, has been removed and traffic is flowing freely again along the East-West Motorway.

Such a hope is doomed to disappointment, however. For the voice on the radio is that of that faux-Yankee Dub, retelling to that garrulous Josie Thornton, the less than riveting tale of her astonishing release from the bondage of fat, thanks to the intercession of the Buddha. And all the *ould* biddies of Ireland, of both sexes or neither, hanging on her words...

The sound of her voice seems to be an ill-omen for the immediate future. For, even before The Citroën manages to silence its jarring tones, the traffic is already slowing down. He moves down again into second gear. And, with the needle dipping down towards zero, the car now groans along in first gear.

The ill-starred chestnut tree comes into view again, standing there triumphantly, as it were, observing the re-emergence of its natural Parish. Its erect candle-like florescence bestowing on it a festive air, as if it were mockingly welcoming a lost tribe back to its native ambit.

The traffic grinds to its predictable halt. The Citroën notes the shadow of the lone tree cast across the road by the setting sun. Once the dusk installs itself, the heat quickly drains out of the day. Drivers and passengers descend from their cars. Loud and angry fucking and blinding is then heard reflecting the total impotence and corresponding fear of the parishioners in the face of a seemingly insoluble predicament.

Night is already falling. The rumor that there will be a hard frost later gains currency.

+++++

THE DAY OF THE HELICOPTERS is destined to establish for itself a firm niche for itself in the folklore of the Parish. Different and variously embroidered versions of the story would be narrated for the purpose of pacifying hyper-excited youngsters or, simply, of providing gossipy entertainment during those long dreary Jam nights. And thanks to the continuous re-percolation of the yarn, and to constant additions to it, it was destined to branch into ten, at least, variants, none of which was destined to be conserved in print...

However, The Citroën is in a position to supply right here the facts, as objectively recorded by him, in this definitive and noncontroversial record of the events of one of the most memorable days in the history of the Parish:

The Citroën is dozing. Drowsily half-listening for the nth time to *Josie Thornton's Morning Show*. As nobody else appears to be astir yet at this early hour, and he has no reading materials to hand believing, before leaving Letterfree that he would have no time to read them), this rehash of Glenawney Sheila's worry about the size of her mammaries is his sole distraction from the anxiety engendered by this inexplicable prolongation of the Clooneen Jam. He has her story off by heart at this point.

Why this modern obsession with breast size? With the miracle of silicone that makes big mountains from small hills? Hollywood booby babes? The influence of pornography? Big is beautiful? The biological desirability of plentiful lactations, with lots of milk for sucklings?

A distant humming noise intrudes on this pointless reverie. As if thousands of bees were on the wing in the distance. The noise continually increases in volume, sounding as if it is coming from the east and from on high.

He descends from the car and looks around him. He is not the only one to have noticed this strange noise. It seems that every parishioner is now standing on the road, their heads craning upwards in an easterly direction from which the hum, now developing into a thunderous roar, appears to be coming.

The Ford Escort is the first to draw The Citroën's attention to the helicopters. Hundreds of them are now coming into view, flying westwards, high in the sky and, seemingly, in the direction of the Parish.

Food is on the way at last, shouts The SUV Hilfiger shirt, in a hoarse excited voice. But will his, and everybody elses, wish be father to the chow?

I hope the hell you are right, retorts The Cortina. Food cannot come fast enough, he says, since the whole bleedin' gang of us are dying from the fuckin' hunger.

It seems that the authorities know at last about our distress, that we are stuck here without food in the back of beyond, says The Ford Escort to The Citroën. Welcoming cheers, greeting the appearance of the helicopters, are heard from the direction of the parishes immediately to the east of us.

Fair play to Wolfie, then, says The SUV, overhearing her comment, if what you are saying is true. (His reference is to the recently appointed Minister of Transport and Commerce, Wolfgang Katzinger.)

Parishioners run back and forth on the bog, waving handkerchiefs, coats, blankets, towels, shirts, panties, vests etc. to draw the attention of the helicopter crews to the location of the Parish. Here, here, they shout, as if the sound of their voices could be heard on high above the thunder of the helicopter motors.

The helicopters are almost directly over the Parish by now. However, they do not seem to be about to descend, still less to dispense food to the hungry parishioners below them, whose entreating upturned faces are probably visible from the cockpits above. However, they stick rigidly to their westwards flight path. The roar of their engines becomes muted, as they draw away westwards from the airspace above the Parish. Curses and swear words replace the previous importunate "here, here"!

Fuck Wolfie, roars Mr. Toyota Starlet, with the full strength of his lungs. Mrs. Toyota Starlet tries in vain to halt her spouse's honest expression of his true feelings. Have we any self-respect left at all, she says, the way we cravenly give the Ministry of Transport and Commerce to a complete eejit of a foreigner who doesn't even live in the country?

Once again, a perceptive Ford Escort is the first to notice that one of the helicopters has detached itself from the main body of the fleet. Look, she says to The Citroën, pointing her right arm towards the sky. He looks and sees a minute spot in the sky, its size gradually increasing along with the roar of its engines. It gives every indication that it is descending with a view to landing in the bog.

Look, says The Fiat 1100 Dub, that bloody whirligig is making right for us. The courage and hope of the parishioners is immediately rekindled. Looks like they're comin' with the grub this time, as sure as eggs are fuckin' eggs, shouts The Peugeot (blue) excitedly. They'd fuckin' better be, shouts The Cortina, before all of us here die from starvation. An egg or two wouldn't go astray, as I hear them mentioned.

Parishioners scamper across the bog towards the spot where the helicopter appears to be about to land. To be the first to receive whatever victuals are to be dispensed when the craft touches down. But, instead of descending, the helicopter remains hovering about 100m above the surface of the bog.

As the hungry eyes of the parishioners, gathered together beneath it, are directed longingly towards it, their cocked ears hear some sort of announcement being read over the craft's loudspeaker. With the racket being created by its engines, however, they find it difficult to decipher its content.

But straining their ears to make out what is being said, some of the parishioners manage to hear the wording of the guttural announcement that now sounds over the bog of Clooneen:

> Im Auftrag Ihrer Herren möchten wir Ihnen, dem irischen Volk, für Ihre Geduld und Opferbereitschaft danken. Wir müssen Ihnen leider mitteilen, dass es auf Grund unvorhergesehener Umstände nicht möglich sein wird, zumindest nicht in absehbarer Zeit, den Verkehr wieder in Gang zu bringen. Wir danken Ihnen nochmals für Ihre außerordentliche Geduld und für Ihre unterwürfige disziplinierte Erfüllung unserer Wünsche. Leben Sie wohl, irische Freunde!

+++++

HAVING DELIVERED ITSELF OF THESE MAGIC WORDS the helicopter begins, noisily, to ascend. Within a few minutes, it is no more than a mere silvery speck in the sky, hurrying westwards to catch up with the rest of its squadron.

The disappointed silence of the parishioners, left empty-handed on the ground beneath is, palpable. It is soon broken, however, by the shouting, keening and general fucking and blinding that drowns the primal silence of the bog.

Was anybody able to make out what in the name of Jaysus that fuckin' cunt in the helicopter was sayin', asks The Mullet of the Mushroom Druid contingent.

Well, that bates bloody Banagher, The Fiat 1100 Dub declares. In all fairness, I've nothing at all against the Irish language as such. My kids are going to a Gaelscoil and they are now attending a summer course at a Gaeltacht college we're just coming back from. But here we are on this God-forsaken bog, dying from hunger and the fuckin' thirst. And what do those bastards in the fuckin' helicopter fuckin' give us? A fuckin' Irish lesson!

But, did anybody here make out what the losers were actually trying to tell us, pipes up The Cortina.

The Citroën decides to sing dumb. No point in sticking out in a crowd like this! The nail that sticks out gets the hammer! The clever word has earned many a broken mouth! So, whatever you say, say nothing! Although he knows quite well that the words descending from the helicopter loudspeaker were anything but Irish!

However, having a genuinely fluent knowledge of that language is anything but an advantage in post-independence Ireland which has abandoned not only its sovereignty but any serious distinguishing cultural trait not valued by the new ringmasters. A *cúpla focal*, a couple of words, for ould time's sake is enough—as long as you don't go over the top with it and actually want to speak the damn thing! These truths The Citroën has well, and ruefully, understood for some time now.

I have Ulster Irish, declares the yellow Anglia veteran. When I was at school, I had a teacher from Donegal. But I'd say that that cunt in the helicopter was speaking Munster Irish, which is all gobbledygook to me. I couldn't make out a word of what the bollix was saying.

Whatever dialect it was, it certainly wasn't Munster Irish, as you say, asserts the Mercedes Benz accountant. My great-grandfather came from Ballingeary down in Cork and he could hardly put two words of English together. But I couldn't understand anything that helicopter nincompoop was saying. I imagine that it must have been Connacht Irish. I once knew a Garda from Aran, and he never...

Well, you've got it wrong there, my friend, I'm afraid, says The Renault 4 Ponytail. One of my grandmothers came from Carna, from Mweenish, if you've ever heard of it. So I'd have no trouble recognizing a Connacht man's Irish anywhere. But I couldn't make out a single word of what that helicopter gent was saying. Not a bloody word! That creep might just have well have been speaking Scottish Gaelic! Or Welsh, for all I know!

So, does anybody here know what sort of fuckin' Irish the helicopter had? Or what in the name of Jaysus he was saying? The questions come from an Hyundai, not a parishioner of ours, driven thither by the hunger. Here you can see, once again, how the fuckers are using Irish to pull the fuckin' wool over our eyes. To keep us just as fuckin' ignorant as a crowd of fuckin' Kerry *culchies*.

I'll tell youse the kind of Irish that helicopter had: a fuckin' mad artificial gobbledygook that was cooked up by civil servants. The speaker this time is another blow-in to the Parish, lured here by the possibility of food. It is a kind of Irish, if you could fuckin' call it that, he says, that even fuckin' Gaeltacht people cannot understand, a fella from Ring I was working with in England once told me!

Well, fuck themselves and their fuckin' gobbledygook, another voice pipes up. I was so fuckin' certain that food was on the way to us that I ate what little food I had left and drank the last drops of water I was keeping in a plastic bottle. I have sweet fuck-all left now.

You are all right, says Mr. Hyundai Pony. I'm in the same fuckin' position as yourself, but you have only yourself to fuckin' look after. Lucky fuckin' you! I have a wife and two infants to feed and water!

+++++

THE BEAMER SINGS DUMB as this linguistic debate rages about him. Standing there in the midst of the parishioners, a reflective look on his face, as he strokes his chin! But, as soon as a lull breaks in the conversation, he enters the fray. He speaks quietly, with a sort of studied *gravitas* that differentiates his contribution from those of the previous speakers. That gives his contribution a certain authority.

You have all been mistaken, fellow parishioners, he says. German was the language chosen by that helicopter crew to deliver their message to us.

That's what I thought, says The Ford Escort And do you yourself know German?

I have a fair knowledge of that language, says The Beamer, though it has got a little rusty for lack of practice.

By now he has gained the attention of the whole parish, which now hangs on his every word.

Did you understand, then, what the helicopter people were saying? asks Ms. Cortina, trying at the same time to restrain little Master Cortina, who is intent on capturing (and probably dismembering) a butterfly he sees fluttering over the bog.

I did not understand every single word that was spoke, says The Beamer. But I certainly got the gist of the message. He pauses, gazing about him to make sure that every ear is attending to his words. He prolongs his pause to give it its full dramatic effect.

Well, aren't you going to tell us what this "message" was, clamor the impatient voices. After all, you weren't the only one to whom that bleedin' message was addressed!

What the helicopter people were saying was that they were flying on an urgent mission to the West. And that mission is: to pick up food and drink for us over there. As they return eastwards later in the day, or maybe tomorrow, they will drop us food supplies. Basic foodstuffs, they said, nothing fancy: bread, butter cheese, ham, cold meats, tinned beans, milk. Enough to keep us alive and well until this Clooneen Jam eventually ends!

About time, says the old lady from the yellow Anglia. Thanks be to God! And fair play to you, Beamer! That is the best news we've heard for some time now, may God bless you, sir! But tell us this: had they anything to say about this awful traffic jam? How long more are we supposed to put up with these primitive conditions? Forever? Or did the helicopter pilot give us any idea as to what has caused this mess in the first place.

He asked us to organize ourselves to help each other, elect a leader, and be patient, says The Beamer. The authorities are working day and night on the solution of the problem, but we must be patient and the green shoots will eventually emerge.

Good news, at last, shouts The SUV Yuppie. But more is the pity that they didn't teach us German at school, instead of fuckin' Peig and her fuckin' Irish!

Hear, hear! agrees the chorus of the assembled starving parishioners.

+++++

THE HELICOPTERS RETURN AT DUSK. Flying eastwards, as The Beamer said they would, high up in the sky, they thunder majestically on their way.

When the Jam folk below hear the throbbing of their engines again, they instantly leave their cars and fan out again on the bog. The wind, which has swung to coming from the north has an icy bite to it, to which they—being famished—are more than susceptible. So they stand there, shivering, patiently awaiting deliverance from the hunger that gnaws at their vitals.

Their eyes on the approaching helicopter fleet are the

eyes of cargo cult folk, those Pacific islanders whose religion was based on the worship of flying machines that would bring them all the goods they would ever need. The hopes of these latter day cargo cultists standing in the perishing cold of Clooneen Bog are doomed to disappointment, however. For this time, anyhow! Not a single helicopter breaks formation as that majestic fleet, high in the sky, thunders eastwards.

The Clooneen Jam folk remain eyeing silently and glumly the formation flying of this cavalcade on high, still illuminated by the setting sun, without a single craft breaking formation. Until they can no longer hear the distant throb of helicopter engines!

Recriminations surge forth instantly. What was the Taoiseach, as The Beamer is now increasingly referred to by parishioners, what the hell was he talking about when he told us that we could expect succor from these helicopters? Bread and milk and so forth!

An angry crowd confronts The Beamer later with these questions.

Standing beside his car, he pulls his collar up as he considers the most appropriate form of words to respond to a query he wished he didn't have to answer.

Things don't always work out as one would wish, he says slowly, measuring his words. I have just found out that when the helicopters reached Galway, their crews discovered that the storage facilities, where emergency food supplies are kept, were completely empty. What they could never have suspected was that these same facilities had been ransacked by non-nationals. By those, who along with their children, come to this country to batten on our social services!

But how in the hell did you find that out? Given that every fuckin' means of communication in this bleedin' Parish is on the fuckin' blink? asks The Fiat 1100 Dub, the timbre of his voice reflecting the general anger that this latest disappointment has caused the starving

Jam people.

I have my own ways to access information, says The Beamer quietly, seemingly unruffled by the other's not so thinly veiled hostility.

What sort of "ways" are you talking about?

Fully reliable sources!

A sudden gust of mingled rain and sleet breaks up this discussion group, impelling its participants to run, seeking the shelter of their cars.

A long cold night, cramped in their cars, stretches in front of these cold and famished Jam folk. The story they hear from those who remained in the cars, instead of venturing out on the bog, is that Stacey is not pregnant, after all the speculation. Nobody appears to know where that news has come from!

But the occasional "thanks be to God" can be heard!

+++++

EVERYBODY KNOWS BY NOW that the DAF Mushroom Druids lack neither food nor water, nor other liquid refreshments. So the growing heap of empty water bottles, beer and Coca Cola cans and food wrappers beside their vehicle indicates.

There is a simple explanation for the ability of this collective to wanton in plenty.

The son of the Toyota Starlet couple, he of the combed-over bald patch, informs The Citroën that he has it, on the authority of a friend of his in the next parish, that it was the Mushroom Druid thugs, and their Amazon accomplices, who sent the Mawmeen petrol garage up in flames. They had been seen after the conflagration, their legs bending under the weight of the booty they were carrying away triumphantly from the scene of the outrage to the precincts of their flower-daubed vehicle.

As The Citroën and The Ford Escort, who had come over to pay him a visit, were discussing their mutual insufferable thirst, she suddenly grabbed his arm, interrupting the conversation.

Look over there, she says, indicating the ragged Mushroom Druid, The Mullet, who happened to be walking past as he guzzled the contents of a liter plastic bottle of Ballygown spring water.

Without taking time to think, The Citroën leaps out of his car, followed by The Ford Escort. He grabs the arm of the surprised The Mullet and twists it behind his back. The latter drops his water bottle and The Ford Escort picks it up, losing only a few drops in the process. As The Mullet is about to wriggle free from the grip of The Citroën, she comes to the rescue, giving the former a swift knee in the groin. The Mullet lets out a roar of pain, followed by a list of threats to both the persons and the cars of his attackers.

Hearing the ruction outside, Nose-ring descends from the DAF, roaring out a ferocious war cry. He tries to connect with vicious right hook to The Citroën's head. The latter manages to dodge that one, retreating a couple of steps in the process. Parishioners rush to the battle scene from every direction, howling dire threats and imprecations.

Gaptooth and three other Mushroom Druids, replete with nose and ear rings jump down from the van. They are egged on by the piercingly shrill cries their female companions, the Valkyries, with their creative requests to "kill the bastards", "hang the bastards with their own guts", "leave their fuckin' balls for the pigs", being among the more (barely) printable requests emanating from that angelic chorus.

Things rest so, the two sides measuring their respective strengths and weaknesses, until an unknown giant arrives on the scene. A tall burly tough-looking customer who has never before been seen in this Parish—rumor has it that he comes from the next parish to the east of us—is our new savior. He is an obvious member of the Garda Síochána, his blue shirt and navy blue trousers being the dead give-away. As this exotic new arrival moves threateningly towards the DAF warriors, the latter now deem discretion to be the better part of valor, and retreat headlong into their van, slamming its doors after them.

Take care that your fuckin' *oul'* bangers don't all go up in fuckin' smoke tonight, is their parting pleasantry.

So, the battle is over before it even begins. When The Beamer reaches the scene of the skirmish, The Ford Escort explains the details of the encounter to him omitting, of course, the water bottle incident that initiated the fracas. The DAF Mushroom Druid retinue is the only guilty party, period. The Beamer then talks quietly to the Giant. Ms. Cortina then has her say:

The bastards in that van who caused the whole damn ruckus are threatening to burn all our cars.

What you are saying, Madame, bears out what I have been saying all along: there is an urgent need here for an efficient security system, says The Beamer. In the meantime, I'll go with my friend here, indicating the newly arrived Giant, to have a few words with the DAF people.

The Beamer, along with the Giant, walk together up to the van. He raps briskly on the door of the vehicle with his knuckles. It opens slightly and the scowling countenance of The Mullet is seen, peering out suspiciously.

Who the fuck are you and what the fuck are you lookin' for? is his opening gambit.

You know quite well that I am the Taoiseach of this Parish and that your vehicle comes under my jurisdiction. I wish to have a few words with you and your fellow-passengers!

Will you be by yourself? retorts The Mullet, looking dubiously at the Giant.

By myself, if that is how you want it!

The door opens wide and, the Giant standing aside, The Beamer enters the precincts of the DAF. The Giant joins the throng waiting outside the van, all agog to know if The Beamer will be able to defuse the threat to their cars, themselves and their dependents. The negotiations within the DAF continue for five minutes, ten minutes...

Suddenly, without warning, the car horns to the east start to blare, announcing to all and sundry that the traffic is about to move again. The Beamer hurries out of the DAF and runs like everybody else, but in his own inimitably ungainly fashion, towards his car. The usual shouts, banging of doors, starting of engines ensues.

The manage to cover about 50 meters in the direction of Dublin, before the traffic halts again.

+++++

A FRANTIC KNOCKING ON the door of his car awakens him. The Ford Escort wants to have an urgent word with The Citroën.

He stretches across the passenger seat and opens the door for her. She slides gracefully into the seat. Black is her chosen color for this evening: black miniskirt, black silk blouse and a silver pendant hanging over the unplumbed depths. Make-up applied sparingly but tastefully. He comments on the strength of the perfume she is wearing, which has a most pleasing aroma, by the way. She laughs melodiously and explains to him the purely utilitarian reasons that have led her to apply the perfume so generously.

The complete lack of washing facilities here in the parish, she says, puts me in the same boat as the ladies of the medieval royal courts of Europe who never washed themselves. Did you ever hear of Queen Isabella II of Spain, a canonized saint, of whom it was said that the "odor of sanctity" emanating from her person was such that being near her was a penance in itself.

At least you are honest about it, says The Citroën, his enjoyment of The Ford Escort's fragrance tempered slightly by this unexpected divulgation. He admits that he also is distressed by the absence of washing facilities, and his consequent grimy and sweaty state. But what can a mere male like me do about it? Grin and bear it, until the traffic gets moving again and we leave this thrice-accursed Clooneen Bog forever.

So much for that, says The Ford Escort. But prick up your ears now, Rip Van Winkle. and listen to what I have to tell you. Well, do you notice anything new?

Not a thing!

Well, while you were sleeping we made decisions that have to do with the security of the Parish. The Giant, he drives a Mitsubishi Lancer, has been appointed to see to the necessary arrangements. He'll have a word or two with those DAF bastards, he said.

Nothing new about that!

Well, The Beamer had been talking to them beforehand, as you well know. Well, have you noticed that that damned Trance and Heavy Metal music has stopped? Looks like anarchy rules no longer in this Parish, at least. And we have a Taoiseach, who has appointed a Minister for Justice—or maybe I should have said Minister for Defense—to take care of security: The Mitsubishi Lancer Giant. That quiet lad with the posh accent who drives a Mercedes Benz, the accountant, was selected to manage our resources. And The Saab, who I hardly know at all, was appointed Tánaiste. I would rather be President, to tell you the truth. Travel and lots of formal meals to give me a chance to wear gorgeous evening gowns and suits! Designed by Gucci etc.!

The Citroën feels dizzy. He senses, and not for the first time, that his known universe is rapidly spinning out of control. How could The Beamer be the Parish Taoiseach, when the meeting to elect such a leader broke up before a vote could be taken? Nobody had consulted him on the matter. But it is certainly true that the racket from the DAF has stopped.

You are just joking, of course?

In the matter of gowns and suits, yes! But if you didn't

allow your imagination to soar now and then in this bloody prison, you'd go completely bonkers.

But you said there that The Beamer is now our Taoiseach. I don't remember his appointment being put to our vote. Unless, of course. I missed some meeting or other.

Come to mention it, I don't remember such a vote either. And I haven't missed a single meeting lately. However, you have to admit that he is getting things done. Look, I have to be getting along, I'm afraid. My friends further up the line are expecting me. So look after yourself!

The fragrance of The Ford Escort, which lingers for some time in the car after his departure, sets a thought process in motion that he had little expected. Maura belongs to another life, one that belongs securely to the past tense. The chances that Anna will accept the story of the Clooneen Jam are infinitesimally small except she gets to see the mess with her own eyes on some television news channel.

I may as well face the bitter truth: my life these days is structured by the day-to-day routine of this Parish. The new neighbors, companions in misfortune, with whom I talk every day are my people now! Our thirst and hunger, and how to satisfy them, is all but the one sole topic of our conversations. Our ears are always ready to pounce on some rumor that might give grounds for hope, however forlorn that hope might be. Apart from that nucleus of brittle stability, the universe of The Citroën seems to him to be in the grip of forces that are totally of his control. Things happen without any apparent reason. We all seek relief from the scorching noonday heat in the miniscule shadows cast by our cars. We all seek relief from the bitter night cold, somewhat unsuccessfully, huddled in the interiors of the same vehicles. And all dream of food...

And that is the bare bone to which our Jam lives have been whittled down. The present tense is the only reality. And the corporeal beauty of that Ford Escort has a pristine reality that is denied to all the seductive phantoms of other times, other tenses, other universes.

+++++

THE SUN IS ABOUT TO TOUCH the western horizon. Before it disappears completely from view, however, it is swallowed up by a dense mass of black cloud that hurries towards it from the threatening skies of the South-West. Sudden violent gusts of wind have set the branches of that eternal chestnut tree creaking and writhing in their grasp. Time to batten down the hatches before the storm is upon us!

The Citroën glances into his rear mirror. In the half-light of the gathering dusk, he can make out the deathly pale countenance of The Opel driver behind him. His features seemingly frozen in that look of aloof disdain that repels intimacies. He looks paler than ever, but that illusion, if such it is, could well be just an effect of the fading light. But what if The Opel is really ill or suffering more than most of us from the severe dehydration that afflicts all of us? Remembering the bad vibes of his previous encounter with The Opel, he is loath to investigate further.

However, curiosity gets the better at last of this hesitation. He leaves his own car and walks back to The Opel. He is aghast at what he sees.

For, to look in the face of death is seldom pleasant. That same look of disdain that has configured The Opel's features since early morning has now become his real-life death mask. No, this is no curable illness, other than the result of that terminal illness that is the common fate of all mankind.

Although he is personally disinclined to recognize The Beamer's *de iure* leadership role in the Parish, The Citroën is forced to swallow the *de facto* reality of it. When he reaches the former's car, he is surprised to find him in deep conversation with The Saab, the multi-accented ventriloquist with whom The Citroën has never exchanged a word.

When The Beamer hears the news of The Opel's demise, The Beamer drops his responsible leader mask temporarily, saying some words highly inappropriate to that leadership role and the solemnity of the news. However, at The Citroën's insistence he now addresses himself to the practical arrangements that must be made immediately. The corpse, and the car that contains it, must be excised forthwith from the Parish. He sends The Saab down to the DAF to order the DAFfers to get out there on the bog and dig a grave immediately to accommodate the corpse.

I saw that they have a bunch of new shovels when I was in their van, talking to The Mullet and his buddies, adds The Beamer

What need has that ragged bunch have of shovels?

Stolen shovels, without a doubt! They could sell them to yokels along the route to raise money for drugs!

But do you think that crowd will be willing to go out on such a stormy night to dig a grave out in the bog? asks The Citroën.

I had small conversation with those buckoes a short while ago, says The Beamer. I made the various options open to them very clear. And, believe you me, my friend, I can guarantee that we'll have no more trouble from that crew!

The Citroën would welcome further explanation of this point. But time is pressing.

He himself, An Taoiseach, will inform his Lordship, The Skoda Bishop. And cajole him into leaving the comfort of his car to ensure that the dead parishioner is buried with the full rites of the Church! But, he says, the important thing is to get this damn funeral out of the way as quickly as possible. The traffic could start moving again at any time and we cannot let it be said that this Parish is responsible for holding up all the traffic behind us. Also, we'll have to get that damn Opel off the road. All of these things need to be done immediately. We cannot afford to have a car with a rotting corpse in it right in the middle of the Parish, for Christ's sake!

And it giving off the Lord knows what noxious gases with the Lord knows what results...

You yourself could recruit the men of The Fiat 1100 Dub, The Cortina, and The SUV. Let them know that I say that they, are to help you to open the door of The Opel and take the corpse out to the grave.

While the Bishop is blathering at the burial, I'll order the DAF crowd to push The Opel off the road. After extracting all the petrol from his tank, of course! I'll arrange for that to be stored later in a safe place. Petrol is going to be as valuable as gold in these parts, if this caper doesn't end soon. But, hurry up, for God's sake! There is not a damn second to lose. We could be asked to move again at any moment.

The SUV Yuppie refuses point blank to have hand or part in any of the obsequies of The Opel. I never even met that old bastard, he says. And, in any case, I have always had a fuckin' horror both of fuckin' corpses and fuckin' funerals. So, you can all fuck off with yourselves, so you can!

It is The Fiat 1100 Dub who finally breaks the window of The Opel with a small mallet he keeps in his car—just in case—and opens the handle of the door. The foul smell that wafts from the car interior to the nostrils of the funeral detail lets one know that the decomposition process referred to by The Beamer is already in full swing.

The Cortina says that he feels nauseous. This is going to make me vomit, he warns. Even The Citroën feels his stomach turning over. He covers his moth and his nostril with the scarf he is wearing around his neck. Fighting against their natural impulses, the men of the detail lay their hands on the corpse, that has already stiffened, and lift it out of the car. However, the burial of their dead is an ancient, albeit unpleasant, duty of the living, which they are not at liberty to disobey in spite of the disagreeable nature of the task.

The Citroën grabs one leg and The Fiat 1100 Dub the other one. Between them, they drag behind them the stiffened body of The Opel like a broken wooden doll, the head bumping across the ground, across the road and into the bog. The Fiat 1100 Dub remarks that they had better get a move on; he has already felt some drops of rain in his face.

The shallow grave, already dug by the DAFfers, is about 50 meters in off the motorway. As they reach it, The Skoda Bishop and The Beamer are already waiting for them, just visible in the faint dusk light. The DAF gravediggers stand a short distance away, leaning on their shovels.

Is the poor fellow long dead? asks the Bishop.

The corpse has already stiffened, says The Citroën.

And the whiff from it would make a dog throw up, says The Fiat 1100 Dub.

Does anybody know his name?

We don't, say The Citroën, The Cortina and The Fiat 1100 all at once. If there documents of his in the car, we didn't go looking for them

An unknown Christian, then, if that is the case! Well, if that is how it is, you may as well lay the corpse in the grave immediately, says the Bishop. They all hear clearly the thump of the corpse as it hits the floor of the grave. The Bishop begins to intones his prayer. Just then, words emerge, unbidden and unsought, from The Citroën's repository of the all but forgotten things. He listens to them, amazed that the echoes of his long distant schooldays still haunt the dim recesses of his brain

> *We buried him darkly at dead of night,*
> *The sods with our bayonets turning,*
> *By the struggling moonbeam's misty light*
> *And the lantern dimly burning.*
> *No useless coffin enclosed his breast,*
> *Not in sheet nor in shroud we wound him...*

The Bishop's brief sermon limps on to its conclusion: If the life of this poor creature, eternal rest be his, had little impact on the worldly affairs of the parish, his death—the death of the first of our parishioners—will become an indelible part of our people's folklore. And not too many of us will have that said about them when they pass on to a better life, the life eternal in Jesus Christ. May God have mercy on his soul. And may we all meet together again in the next life, in the divine companionship of Our Lord Jesus Christ. Amen.

And now, he says, beckoning to the DAF gravediggers, close the grave, if you please! And may the sod lie lightly on the remains of this poor creature.

These words have hardly left His Eminence's mouth, when big drops of rain, mixed in with hailstones, begin to pelt the funeral party. In the far distance, to the north, a long streak of blue lightening, briefly illuminates a thickening dusk. The members of the burial party stumble across the bog, and run across the road to their cars to escape an otherwise inevitable drenching.

Safely ensconced in his car, The Citroën is beset again by violent hunger pangs. Slumbering fitfully a little later, with the steady drumming of the downpour on the roof of his car providing musical accompaniment, he dreams that he is a man condemned to walk forever across the hungry grass…

+++++

AT EIGHT O CLOCK IN THE MORNING, on the dot, the women of the Parish take it upon themselves to apportion the remaining food among the starving parishioners.

The boot of the Toyota Starlet is both the common storage and distribution point. Ms. Toyota Starlet had previously reminded the Dáil that her car was the most logical place for such activities. The Minister of Justice, the Giant, has his Mitsubishi Lancer parked directly in front of her. And he is the lad, she says, to batter anyone—the pillagers of petrol stations included—who would make so foolhardy, or stupid, as to try to rob from the Parish's common food store.

The nearby blue Peugeot, should serve as an ancillary storage point, mainly for water and other liquids. When and if such could be found!

The Beamer, adopting the mantle of Foreign Minister, takes it upon himself to initiate talks with the leaders of some of the surrounding parishes, both east and west. Five or six such leaders have already been elected, their parishes taking the lead from our Parish, which is being touted (by The Beamer) as "the ideal democracy". Both The Mitsubishi Lancer Giant, who properly speaking, does not belong to our Parish, and The Saab, usually accompany him on these "diplomatic and trade" missions.

This mission returned triumphantly today, bearing big plastic bags containing liter bottles of Kong Kola and many bags of Taystees potato crisps, "Ireland's Favorite Snack". Along with several bottles of water and—miracles will never cease—two cans of Festivus lager, a German brew that is undercutting and rapidly displacing the native brands on the Irish booze market.

All who want it can have a few sups of lager, says an exultant Beamer. Just to remind ourselves that there is a life other than the boredom and the misery we have to endure, stuck as we are here, in this unprecedented Clooneen Jam.

And that no misery, traffic jams included, can last forever!

+++++

AT A SHORT DÁIL SESSION, organized to welcome back the Parish emissaries, a decision is made to confiscate an air mattress, property of the Mushroom Druid hooligans. This is to be used to add to the comfort of the old lady from the yellow Anglia who complains she is feeling very ill. The Ford Escort, donning her angel of mercy wings, offers her a "genuine" Foxford blanket, bought in a moment of financial carelessness from an importunate huckster in Galway. To compound her distress at the foolishness of this purchase, she later discovered a tiny "Made in China" label on the edge of said article. In an equally careless moment of magnanimity, The Citroën offered the rear seat of his car, roomier than that of the Anglia, to serve as a bed for that elderly patient.

To his horror, his offer was accepted by the husband of the indisposed party. You could sleep in The Opel that lies abandoned at the side of the road, suggests The Beamer. With that smell of putrefying meat to pleasure my nostrils, I think not. Many thanks but no thanks!

The Mitsubishi Lancer Giant returns from the DAF van, carrying a deflated air bed under one arm and a sleeping bag under the other.

Don't tell me that that gang give you that bedding without an argument! remarks Ms. Toyota Starlet.

They did just that, without any problem, replies The Mitsubishi Lancer Giant! And, not only that, but they offered us another air mattress if we need it.

Wonders will never cease, comments a surprised Ms. Toyota Starlet.

What is behind this sudden change of attitude on the part of the Mushroom Druid gang? The Citroën ponders that question, along with the strategy he must adopt to secure a comfortable sleeping place for himself this evening.

+++++

LACKING A PLACE TO SLEEP, The Citroën spends the night playing games of 45 in The Beamer's capacious vehicle, at the latter's invitation. The Saab, an inauspicious individual with a hangdog look, whom he had heard eons ago heckling Ms. Toyota Starlet, makes up the party of three.

The Citroën is at pains to discover the basis of the obvious understanding, if not collusion, between two such disparate personalities, who are as different as chalk from cheese, as the saying goes. The Beamer: loquacious to the point of garrulity, looks you straight in the eye, for example; the watery-eyed Saab seldom ventures beyond monosyllables, always avoiding the eye-contact of his fellow parishioners.

As the game proceeds, the players refresh themselves with *poteen* directly from a bottle obtained by The Beamer, or so he says, from a fellow player—and drinker—in a golf club out west, where they make the best stuff. In which he, The Beamer, had spent most of the last weekend. This bottle is a sort of souvenir of a highly successful golfing foray. Not that he is a great golfer, or drinker, he says with a laugh, but golf clubs are great places to do business. Politicians, captains of industry, bishops: that is where you will find those lads. The fate of countries and counties can be, and bloody-well is—decided at the 19th hole.

Scarcely news to The Citroën!

But I'm no clubhouse bar-fly, avers The Beamer. No sir! Absolutely not! But under the present, shall we say, "extenuating circumstances" his conscience will not prevent him from "breaking out". Without going fully over the top, of course! And as long as this little well-earned relaxation does not hinder the performance of his public duties!

As the level of the colorless liquid in the unlabeled bottle they pass between them falls, The Beamer becomes even more expansive. Yes, he and the Minister are old pals, from a long, long, way back. And he will be talking to him tomorrow about this absolutely scandalous traffic jam. Yes, sir! And, in no way will he be fobbed off with evasive answers. I have information on him that I am sure he wouldn't like to be publicized. A man like me, whose people founded this bloody State, for God's sake, will have, must have a clear and honest explanation of this never-ending Clooneen Jam, or, mark my words, the Minister will know the consequences!

But if all the phones, all the means of communication, are out of order, how do you propose to contact the Minister? asks The Citroën. The old question! But both The Beamer and The Saab looked at him with surprise.

The Beamer then directs a sharp glance over the rim of his spectacles at The Citroën, before allowing a foxy grin to crease his features.

O thou of little faith, he says, I thought I let all of you know that I have my own ways of accessing information. Ways that most people would never suspect. But ways that yield absolutely reliable information.

What do you mean by that? Give us a clue what you mean!

State secret, as they say. I am dead serious. But, leaving that aside, as you appear to be a reliable sort of fellow, there is another secret I can share with you. As my friend here, The Saab, and I traversed the parishes to the east of us, earlier today, we made two exciting discoveries. We came upon a truck laden to the gills with cans of Kong Kola. A little later, in the same parish, we came upon a big van that was full of bags of Taystees potato crisps. To make a long story short, we made a deal with the drivers of these vehicles to supply us with these goods on a daily basis. For as long as the crisps and the coke last of course!

And will we have to pay for these goods, as you call them?

The Beamer gives The Citroën a pitying look.

What we brought back here today we received gratis. As a sort of goodwill sweetener, if you will! But we live in the real world, sir! From now on out we'll have to pay for what we get. 5€ for a tin of coke, 5€ for a bag of Taystees.

But that is highway robbery, Beamer. What happens when the parishioners just don't have the money to shell out for such outrageously expensive coke and crisps?

We discussed that very point with the vendors of these products. There was talk of accepting petrol, in lieu of money, as payment. A bag of Taystees together with a can of Kong Kola for a litre of petrol is the offer on the table.

But how the hell can you expect people to pay for their sustenance with the petrol they need to reach their destination? Parishioners are already afraid that they won't have even enough petrol left to get them as far as Angelbank, never mind Dublin!

The Beamer shrugs his shoulders, then takes a long thoughtful slug out of the bottle, before answering The Citroën.

There is no point in getting upset about the outcome of mere suppositions. This coming day may mark the end of the Clooneen Jam for all we know.

And, if it doesn't?

Every cloud has a silver lining!

Having delivered himself of this mysterious answer, The Beamer turns his attention to the cards in his hands.

The Saab, as is his wont, listens avidly but says not a single word during this conversation. His eyes scrutinized all the while the car ceiling, the cards on the table, the darkness outside, returning again to the ceiling. He nods his head slightly every so often, in agreement with points being made by The Beamer.

The Saab wins all of the card games…

+++++

TRAFFIC IS ON THE MOVE early enough this morning. New hopes are raised as the by now familiar impatient blaring of car horns to the east is now taken up by the horns of the Parish cars.

They are doomed to be dashed, however. By midday, between stopping and starting, the Parish has hardly moved more than 300 meters to the east of its starting point. As the cars groan along in second gear, their drivers can see a small conifer plantation skirting the straight road at some distance ahead of them. They imagine the dark cool shadow that must lie beneath its branches. The Citroën thinks of it as an oasis in the blazing heat of the desert. In which he could lie, protected by the forest cover, from the suffocating heat of a sun now at its zenith.

The prayer on the lips of all the parishioners is that the Parish will reach the imagined seductive coolness of the mini-forest ahead. And, if there are trees there, maybe there will be water there also. Just as in a desert oasis! The heat must be getting at me, thinks The Citroën, to even think of such a crazed comparison.

However, the Parish comes to one of those definitive long halts more than 500m from its coniferous promised land. Engines are switched off. The habitual great oaths and swear words resound across the flat of the bog, shimmering in the heat haze.

The Ford Escort goddess closes her eyes and fantasizes the cold water of a shower raining down on her shoulders. On her breasts. The sensuous feel of it as it streams down her abdomen, her loins. She opens her eyes on the fuel gauge needle, that indicates that she may just have about enough fuel to get to Angelbank.

But from there on, girl?

Taking into account that she has spent almost all of her money on Taystees and Kong Kola, whence the wherewithal to buy petrol. She turns the key in the ignition to turn off the engine. Out of the corner of his eye, The Citroën notices tears glistening on the smooth cheeks of The Ford Escort.

The Beamer is holding court in the "Taoiseach's Office", over by the blue Peugeot. From there goes out the story, relayed by Ms. Toyota Starlet, that the women of the parish are being asked to attend to old lady in the yellow Anglia. She, having returned to the familiar surroundings of her own car has, apparently, taken a turn for the worse.

The leader of one of the parishes to the west of the

Parish had informed The Beamer, in a private meeting that was never reported to the Dáil, that a doctor resided in the vicinity of his fiefdom. He is driving a silver colored VW Passat 1.9, allegedly, the only car of its type in that parish. One cannot but recognize it. The Beamer now beckons to The Saab. Could you head west, and see if you can find that doctor and bring him here.

The Citroën has amused himself, cynically surveying the attempts of The Mushroom Druids to curry favor with the rest of the parishioners. It must be that the last of their water and food—the remains of the booty these ragged hippies carried from the petrol station they consigned to the flames—is now exhausted. So, they are now reduced to cadging Taystees and Kong Kola from their fellow parishioners to keep hunger and thirst from the door of their flower-spattered DAF van.

But, thanking the Gods for small mercies, that loud non-stop concert of rock, heavy metal and trance music that has been annoying the *bejasus* out of the parishioners up to now, has finally ceased. The now-reformed gang covers the yellow Anglia with a large yellow tent they had stored in the DAF. In this way, they seem to have made a cool ambulance of the Anglia, within which the patient rests as she awaits the doctor.

The latter arrives in due course, accompanied by The Saab. A stout bearded young man, carrying the black bag of his trade, a stethoscope dangling from his neck proclaims to all and sundry: "I Am A Doctor". He rapidly diagnoses the condition of the Anglia patient, gives her a spoonful of a dark liquid from a bottle he takes from his bag, and, just as rapidly, takes his leave.

Has she got some sort of infectious disease? asks Ms. Cortina of him as he hurries past that car on his way back to his native heath. She hasn't got any disease, says the doctor, infectious or otherwise. She is weak from the hunger, just like hundreds of others. And the situation is getting worse all the time.

The doctor had asked a tall thin middle-aged woman from the parish to the east, from another Anglia (but blue this time), to look after the patient. Her (alleged) nursing experience qualifies her for the job.

I'm afraid that both of our services are going to be very much in demand shortly, the Doctor tells her. I have closed the eyes of five victims already between here and my own neck of the woods. This Taystees and Kong Kola poison would kill a herd of horses.

+++++

IT IS DUSK ALREADY. The lines of vehicles have been stationary since midday. The conifer plantation and its illusory comforts might just as well be a mirage, seeming to be as far from The Citroën as the fabled *Tír na nÓg* (Land of the Ever Young) of his childhood fantasies.

He has just escaped from the clutches of The Renault 4 Ponytail, who had sought him out, trying to sell him one of his "paintings" for a bag of Taystees (Cheese 'n Onion flavored). The picture was called Triptych Number 7, and seemed to him like a muddy multicolored squish in which he sought form. Any form at all! Or, at least, some sense!

In vain!

When he pointed this failure out to Ponytail, the latter evinced surprise that a person he had presumed to be a cultivated citizen had failed to realize that figurative art was dead and gone; it's with Picasso and Michelangelo, buried deep in the grave. As dead as the damn dodo, Mr. The Citroën! The blatant fascism of form, dimension and color has gone the way of the so-called Enlightenment and all that pretentious blather! No! Present-day artists are more concerned to express their inner landscapes, unshackled by stale tradition or conservative convention. Like lava pouring white-hot out of a volcanic crater, taking whatever form the receptor landscape dictates...

Surveying Triptych Number 7, The Citroën is loath to offer an opinion concerning The Renault 4 Ponytail's anarchic "inner landscape" nor on the "philosophy" that inspired such a "creation". Nor to sacrifice a bag of Taystees, as god-awful as the nutritional value of the latter "food" is, in order to lumber himself with an acquisition of such dubious worth.

Later, boredom impels him to lend an ear to the gossip of the habitual hungry crowd gathered beside the blue Peugeot. The latest rumors from the rumor factory up the road circulate and are greeted with the usual tired cynicism. Ms. Cortina asserts that she knows for a fact that Stacey is pregnant. And that the doctor, Doug, is the father.

I knew from the word go that there was something going on between the pair of them, she says—and you can always trust a woman's intuition (she really said "feelings") in these matters—from the day they met in the Beverley Hills Ashram.

What is an "ashram", when it is at home? And what would they be doing in such a place? asks The Citroën innocently. Boredom has reduced him to asking such cynically idle questions.

Get out of it! says Ms. Cortina. Are you seriously telling me that you don't know what an ashram is?

Not an earthly idea, says The Citroën. You tell me if you know.

Well, says Ms. Cortina, it's a sort of monastery in which they teach spiritual stuff, tantric yoga, power yoga, stuff that comes from India, I think. All of the girls, Susan, Barbara, Beth and Courtney as well as Stacey go to courses there. Both Stacey and Doug were attending some sort of self-esteem course there run by some Shri Sexyrhamda or other. He makes George Clooney look like a troll. That's not his real name, but that's what the girls call him, anyway. Some sort of sex therapy, if you know what I mean, is what he does. Doug was married to Beth at the time, and flirting with Susan as well, but once Stacey and himself saw each other, well, it was love at first sight, as they say.

So Stacey is pregnant now, thanks to Doug's sex therapy?

Are you having me on?

Why would I do that? I'm just trying to make sense of what you are telling me.

Well, that's what I heard from a woman in the next parish back there (her hand points to the west), and she had heard it as gospel truth from another woman who…

Ah, I see, says The Citroën.

And if things keep up like this, Howard will be stuck with Courtney…

+++++

IT STARTS TO BECOME BITTERLY COLD at about 2 am. Those who have blankets and greatcoats thank the Almighty for their foresight and prudence in gearing up for such an unseasonal eventuality.

There is no indication whatsoever that the traffic will move before morning. The Citroën goes over to The Beamer's car. There, before him, are The Mitsubishi Lancer Giant, The BMW Accountant and The Saab. And all of them, with the exception of The Beamer, as grimy and as unshaven as himself!

They are smoking cigarettes, obtained by The Beamer in exchange for Kong Kola in one of the more easterly parishes. Or so he says. The Citroën, who doesn't smoke, is pleased that his companions relax so. The cigarette smoke will help to conceal the stink of human beings who have washed neither themselves nor their clothes for quite a long time now. Not to mention brushing their teeth!

The young doctor from the VW Passat 1.9 parked in one of the western parishes knocks on the door. He looks exhausted and has aged, perceptibly, since he started to do the rounds of our Parish. The Citroën, The Mitsubishi Lancer

Giant and The BMW Accountant bunch together to make room on the back seat for this latest arrival.

I hit the road early in the morning, some time ago now, to reach Dublin in good time. I was to have delivered a paper to a convention of the Medical Faculty of the University there. The subject of my paper was to have been the danger that is being posed to public health by the current obsession with junk food. I have statistics that show the gradual the effects of replacing of the normal eating by this rubbish, which is normally a grazing supplement to a junk food diet. But suppose even junk food is no longer available and a population is reduced to that that grazing supplement alone. In an experiment with laboratory rats, we found their health deteriorated alarmingly when they were fed with Taystees and Kong Kola exclusively.

Little did I think, as I drove along that fine sunny morning, that I would shortly be ministering to a community whose members show many of the alarming symptoms that I was to describe in my presentation.

But that is not what I wanted to say to you.

Unless this so-called Clooneen Jam end soon, he tells his listeners, we will be facing an unimaginable health crisis. And I am not talking about death from hunger only.

He looks steadfastly at The Beamer as he talks.

Unless you here in this Parish adhere rigidly to the sewage disposal guidelines I gave you some time ago, God alone only knows what diseases are going to show up in these parishes. I wouldn't even rule out cholera. The consequences could be catastrophic.

At present, the people are defecating anywhere they wish. You only have to sniff the wind to understand that that is the case. I don't know if you are still digging the sewage latrines I recommended some time ago. I am asking, begging, those in authority to see to it that all of those who, at present, are defecating any old place, are given to understand that they are putting their own lives, and the lives of all in their community, at the most serious risk.

The problem is that the people are too weak now to dig trenches, says The BMW Accountant. But, if we don't manage to get real food shortly, we won't have to be bothered any more with the sewage problem.

And why is that? asks the VW Passat 1.9.

Starving stomachs don't make shit!

If the plan I have in mind comes to fruition, says The Beamer, it won't be long before the people of this Parish have all the food they need.

And sewage latrines that will be used!

+++++

WITH HIS HAND ON THE DOOR HANDLE The Citroën observes a pair of men approaching him.

He is not surprised to see that The Cherokee 4.0 Italian from the next parish is one of them. A man who scarcely ever leaves his jeep, it is said, except to visit our Bishop, a fluent Italian speaker. So, here he is, the fur collar of his leather jacket turned up as far as his ears. And looking for food! He says, The Skoda Bishop, his companion, translating for him from the Italian, that he imagined he detected the smell of roasting meat coming from our Parish.

We are as parched with the thirst and as famished with hunger as you are! The only place you'll find roast meat around here is in our dreams.

The Bishop and The Cherokee 4.0 Italian then proceed to talk animatedly in Italian, with appropriately animated hand gestures, completely ignoring The Citroën.

They continue talking loudly as they walk towards The Skoda.

+++++

MS. TOYOTA STARLET SAYS IT IS A LIVING SHAME that The Beamer cannot put anything better on the table than those bleedin' Taystees, with their artificial tastes of Cheese 'n Onion and Salt 'n Vinegar. The health of the good citizens of the Parish is being undermined by that Kong Kola as the VW Parssat 1.4 doctor says. Which is nothing but donkey's piss, God forgive me.

Where now is the real food on the table, that figured in his election promises.

I wouldn't mind, she said, but I was talking to a woman from another parish who told me that they are having delicious roast pork every second day. And hearty nourishing soup on the other days! There are Taoiseachs, she says, who keep the promises they make to those who elect them. And then, God help us, then there is that other class of Taoiseach...

The members of the Dáil greet these remarks in silence. No one can deny but that Ms. Toyota Starlet has a valid point. Nevertheless, time is needed to assess the relevance of her remarks to the situation in which the Parish now finds itself. This is certainly not the time to upset apple carts, as The Saab remarks quietly, almost to himself, in one of his rare public utterances.

Hmph, says the yellow Anglia veteran, that story we have just heard from the mouth of Ms. Toyota Starlet does not surprise me in the least. I myself sometimes get the whiff of a barbecue when the wind is blowing from the east. I thought at first it was some sort of a mirage, but mirages like that don't be constantly repeating themselves. And I ask myself: if others are enjoying such a feast, why not the fuck us? We have to get our hands on some real food before the crap that we are filling our stomachs with these days fuckin' wrecks our health. My own health is banjaxed, as fucked as fucked can be, by the fact that I have to swallow that fuckin' Taystees poison every day to quiet the rumbling in my stomach. Apart from the fact that I am nearly bankrupted by all that bleedin' Cheese 'n Onion!

The Peugeot, The Cortina, The Citroën and The SUV

Yuppie, now wearing a dirty yellow Lacoste shirt, aver that they themselves have been goaded beyond endurance by that tantalizing aroma of roasting meat. Only they didn't want to to say so for fear of being thought to have gone around the bend. Just as wanderers, lost in the desert and dying from the thirst, are goaded beyond their endurance by the imagined sightings of non-existent pools of clear water, as The BMW Accountant so elegantly puts it! In the same way, I thought that that aroma of roasting pork was some sort of olfactory mirage brought on by the lack of proper food.

Ole fuckin' what? asks The Fiat 1100 Dub!

However, the consensus is with Ms. Toyota Starlet. There is real roast meat out there somewhere. And a Taoiseach who fails to satisfy the needs of his constituents can be replaced.

The Beamer clears his throat and breaks his silence.

I applaud Ms. Toyota Starlet's amazing powers of perception, he says, and am in a position to confirm the accuracy of her observations. Our neighbors to the east have been sacrificing, cooking and eating the various pet animals that were travelling along with their owners. In fact, the parish to the immediate east of us celebrated a festive Black Labrador and Cocker Spaniel Barbecue last night. Hence, the smell of roasting meat that was noticeable here at that time. Unfortunately, as far as I can make out, there are no pets whatsoever travelling along with our parishioners. Unless, of course, some of you are harboring budgerigars, rabbits, pet mice, gerbils and suchlike rodents?...

As he returns to his own car later, The Citroën observes the unexpected presence of The Ford Escort in The Beamer's vehicle. He feels a slight stab of jealousy as he sees the pair of them laughing together. As, doubtlessly, he spins her one of his yarns. In which he compares his own cleverness, doubtlessly, to the stupidity of most of the parishioners whose cooperation he has to tolerate.

+++++

THE CITROËN WRAPS THAT MUCH-READ NEWSPAPER he had borrowed from The Ford Escort, seemingly eons ago, around his body before putting on his shirt and sweater. Mr. Toyota Starlet had told him that newspaper gave great insulation against the cold, especially the Arctic cold that has beset the Parish in recent weeks. He then wraps a blanket he discovered some time back in an abandoned car in the next parish to the west. Sitting there behind the steering wheel, he starts to doze.

In his dream, the body of a dead wild boar, a stake driven through it from mouth to arse, is slowly revolving over a bed of glowing cinders. Drops of liquid fat fall from its body and drop, hissing, on the spit beneath. Thick red Spanish wine is being quaffed from ornate ceramic goblets by his companions, heroes to a man and dressed in the skins of slain forest animals. Their spears are stacked a short distance from them in the middle of the oak forest in which they are roistering. A poet sits on a little hummock, accompanying the long Fenian poem he is reciting with the sweet music he is coaxing from the small harp resting on his knee.

The Ford Escort, wearing a purple silken cloak held in place by an ornate Celtic brooch, is just about to refill his goblet from a great leather wine bottle. But a sudden light rapping of knuckles on the window beside him instantly cuts short his escapist time traveler fantasy.

He has no idea what time it is. Nor how long that dream lasted! The night outside is as black as pitch, not a star to be seen! He would almost swear on a stack of bibles that the aroma of that pork, or roasted dog if The Beamer is to be believed, is still in his nostrils.

The Saab is trying to draw his attention. His urgent message is that The Beamer requests his, The Citroën's, and The Mitsubishi Lancer Giant's presence in his car. As soon as possible!

Sit in, grunts The Beamer, when The Citroën arrives at the door of his car. The Taoiseach is obviously discommoded at having to attend to official business at this hour of night. The Giant has already arrived, and sits uncomfortably cramped, given his bulk, in the back seat. The BMW Accountant arrives and joins him.

The Beamer sets the ball rolling. Our friend here, The Mitsubishi Lancer Giant, has some important news for us, he says.

Well, the story, in a nutshell, is, says the latter, that the yellow Cherokee 4.0 Italian has abandoned both his car and his baggage. And he left his unlocked car behind him.

This news would be of little import to most of our parishioners, as nobody here, apart from The Skoda Bishop, really knew The Cherokee 4.0 Italian. In any case, he had hardly more than two words of English.

As soon as I discovered that he was gone, continues The Mitsubishi Lancer Giant, I notified our Taoiseach that he was missing.

And what did he do?

As you'd expect, he sent out search parties to scour your Parish as well as the parish to the east of us. For all the good that did us! Neither hide nor hair of The Cherokee 4.0 Italian was to be found anywhere. The only person who was in regular communication with that party was your Skoda Bishop. Indeed, we believe that he was a frequent visitor to The Skoda. It could be that he was looking to find out the lay of the land, which the Bishop could well have known as I'm told that he comes from these parts. As well as that, he would have the Italian needed to convey the information to him. So that The Cherokee 4.0 Italian may have been planning to escape on foot from the Clooneen Jam! But, as against that, he did leave his backpack behind him, along with the keys of his car.

And what does your Taoiseach make of all of this? asks The Beamer.

He thinks, on balance, that a sudden onset of despair drove the poor man beyond the limits of what he could take. Lots of cars further to the east of us have been deserted in desperation by people who announced that they were continuing their journey on foot. In fact, the Taoiseach of our parish thinks that the escape of the Italian may very well open the floodgates, unless this traffic jam ends soon.

Yet, there could be another, more complex, interpretation of that story, says The Beamer, affecting the smug expression of he who is about to unveil a mystery.

What do you mean by that? says the instant chorus of four voices.

The Bishop's Skoda, here in this very Parish, has also been abandoned. And, once again, that car was left unlocked and the clerical baggage is still in the boot.

+++++

FURTHERMORE, THE SAAB HERE CAN THROW LIGHT ON certain interesting details of the case of the disappeared Bishop, continues The Beamer. And nobody here is to repeat what they are going to hear in this car.

The Saab coughs to clear his throat before speaking.

I've been keeping my eye on that Skoda ever since I noted a strange thing, he says. That young priest never showed his face at a single one of our Dáil meetings. Nobody ever heard him speaking. Why? It was Ms. Cortina who gave me the clue that that young cleric may not have been what he seemed.

D'ye know what, she said, I've just seen something weird out on the bog. I came upon the young priest having a piss and, d'ye know what, he was squatting like a woman. I said hello to him but, d'ye know what, not only did he not answer me but, with the start I gave him, he took to his heels. And d'ye know what, he was moving like a woman. No man I've ever seen runs like that.

And then I noted something else that was interesting. There is no sign of this "young priest" since yesterday. Like The Cherokee 4.0 Italian. Like the Bishop who abandoned his Skoda this morning, leaving the key of the car and all his baggage behind him.

And, what sense do you make of this story? asks The Beamer.

For starters, I would say that it is certain that the Bishop was traveling with a woman. One of the abandoned bags was full of women's clothes, anyway. I've seen The Cherokee 4.0 Italian sniffing around The Skoda often enough. Putting two and two together, I would say that he had a thing for the Bishop's woman. And that the pair of the decided to elope together to escape from the Bishop and this bloody traffic jam! And that pure bloody jealousy sent the Bishop scooting after them to reclaim his woman, if indeed a woman she is.

The Citroën is about to make his contribution to this story of a most unlikely *menage a trois*. But, just then, the silence of this wintry night is rent by a thousand car horns.

Having delivered himself of a mouthful of expletives, The Beamer sends The Saab down to the DAF, to order one of The Mushroom Druids to drive The Skoda, once the traffic starts moving.

As The Citroën twists the key in his ignition, his thoughts are in a whirl. Inexplicable things are happening beyond the range of his explicatory powers. What possessed The Saab to relate that crazy yarn about The Skoda crew and The Cherokee 4.0 Italian, for example? Too taken with bad detective stories? An imagination molded by the fantasies of the sensationalist yellow press?

But where could that foreigner from the shores of the Mediterranean be by now. A huddled figure in his leather jacket, stumbling through the chill of an Irish winter's night! Over fields! Over stone fences! Over swampy bogs sucking at his feet! Making for the golden horizon of his wishful thinking?

Or dead? Fuckin'-well dead, drowned in a freezing bog-hole?

Or what prompted those clerics to follow his example? Och, life's manifold mysteries! Those exotic possibilities that lie, buried beneath the grey crust of daily existence!

The cars start to move slowly. They cover about another two kilometers before they halt again. In that short journey, mainly made in second gear, The Citroën notes that may cars of all makes have been abandoned by their owners and have been parked on the grass verge beside the motorway. Because they have exhausted all their petrol? Or because their batteries are so low that they cannot start their engines? Or because their occupants, seeing no end of the Clooneen Jam in sight, have decided to try their luck at reaching Dublin on foot?

In all fairness, said The Fiat 1100 Dub earlier, I don't think we'll live long enough to see the end of this bleedin Clooneen Jam! Whatever fuckin' obstacle that is blocking us is plonked down there for the whole of fuckin' eternity!

Suppose The Fiat 1100 has hit the nail on the head?

+++++

WHERE HAS THAT OPPRESSIVE DEAD HEAT that marked the early weeks of the Clooneen Jam gone? To be replaced by this bitter cold that freezes the very marrow of the bone during these bitter Arctic nights! The lucky ones who are so equipped do not shed their greatcoats, even in the middle of the day. There are rumors of widespread frostbite—and even deaths from hypothermia—affecting the parishioners of some of the neighboring parishes.

Ms. Toyota Starlet draws attention to the scarcity of overcoats and other warm clothing that afflicts a not inconsiderable number of our parishioners. Under the unauthorized scheme she initiates, temporary loans of warm clothes and rugs are to be given to those who badly need them. With an especial emphasis on older parishioners, of course. She herself and her husband set themselves to ascertaining just how many warm clothes can be accessed from among the resources of the Parish. This survey yields seven heavy sweaters, four rugs, three blankets, two heavy raincoats and one duffle coat. Ms. Toyota Starlet makes a list of the elderly parishioners to whom such garments are necessary to combat the current Arctic conditions.

The Beamer, obviously miffed at this initiative having been undertaken by the Toyota Starlet couple, thus undermining his democratically certified absolute authority over the Parish, refuses to offer his trendy mohair coat to the scheme. Her initiative was not authorized, not having been conducted through the appropriate channels he says. Besides, his responsibilities now involve lengthy trips in this bitter cold outside the parish, he says. On important missions! For the benefit of all denizens of the Parish

Take tonight, for example! I will be traveling eastwards in this damn cold and a wind that could cut you in half to see if I can strike a bargain with some crowd over there who have, reputedly, food for sale. That is, if the reports I have heard have any real foundation. If I am not chasing moonbeams, I'll drive a hard bargain over there, you can depend on that. And we shouldn't have to endure Taystees and Kong Kola for much longer.

May God bless all of your efforts on our behalf, sir, says the old lady of the blue Peugeot fervently.

+++++

WATER, WATER NO DAMNWHERE, and not a bleedin' drop to drink intones the Fiat1100, at an emergency meeting of the Dáil. There is no water whatsoever left in the Parish announces The BMW Accountant, somewhat more prosaically, but transmitting the same message. From here, our new position, continues The BMW Accountant, we can see farm houses at some distance from us to the North. There is nothing to be lost by looking for water over there, he says.

He asks The Citroën, The SUV Yuppie and The DAF Mullet to accompany him on a reconnoitering trip to those houses. How could he have known at that time that a virtual state of war exists between the farming community and the famished population of the Clooneen Jam. For reasons that hardly need to be left to the imagination!

For, no sooner does this small reconnoitering detail leave the road, their feet treading one of the small fields beside it, than it is subject to a shower of stones. Together with ball-bearings projected from catapults. The Mullet squeals in pain as a big sharp stone connects with his shoulder. The water foraging expedition beats an ingloriously hasty retreat from the scene.

This incident, however, is far from ending the state of war that now exists between the Jam and farming communities. Very much the contrary!

As dusk fades into night, stones begin to fall out of the darkness, making fearsome noises as they hit the cars. The womenfolk within the vehicles are terrified. Their shrill screams together with the howling of Master Cortina would awaken the very dead. This attack of our unseen assailants intensifies. Is it the forerunner of a full frontal assault?

Somebody out there in the darkness hurls, of all things, a scythe in the direction of the Parish. It falls with a metallic crash on the roof of the DAF, bounces off it and lands on the road between The Saab and The SUV. The noise it makes startles The Mushroom Druids, whose frightened faces appear at the windows of their van. However, they do not emerge from this vehicle, being totally disinclined to face the "fuckin' muck savages" (as they define the attackers) waiting out there, whooping in the darkness like cinema Injuns, for them to emerge.

The mocking loud challenge of the "muck savages" to "come down here, you bastards, and fight like men" is not heeded by the male parishioners, who have no way of assessing the number, physique nor ferocity of their opponents. The stoning of the Parish continues for a while, becomes desultory and, eventually, stops, its propagators seemingly tiring of their pastime.

A pity The Skoda Bishop isn't still with us, says The Ford Escort. Those *cawbogues* out there wouldn't be long in surrendering to his authority.

I wouldn't be so sure about that, answers The SUV Yuppie. Those clerical bucks shot themselves in the foot some time back with all those sex scandals and are now only a part of history. And not only in the cities, mind you! Even in this bloody dunghill of a place, they'd only be laughed at!

The Mercedes Benz accountant, with the aid of his torch, assesses the war damage. The Citroën observes the steam of his breath in the torchlight as he moves from car to car. Apart from the new dings now displayed by almost every vehicle in the Parish—especially the DAF that was a mass of dings, anyhow—windows were broken in the Cortina, the Skoda, the blue Peugeot, the Ford Escort and the Volkswagen. The roof of the DAF, of course, sports a huge new ding and a long scratch in the paintwork caused, presumably, by the blade of the scythe that struck it. The external rear mirrors of the Saab, the DAF, the Beamer and the Ford Escort are either so broken or twisted, as to be effectively non-functioning. The Citroën is pleased that his car escaped with only a few superficial dings.

We'll have some fuckin' problem, I'm afraid, if we try to make claims on our insurance, remarks The Renault 4 Ponytail, drily.

Fuck this for a lark! My teeth are chattering with the fuckin' cold, says The Fiat 1100 Dub. We should all get the fuck into our cars or we'll catch our death from *hypobleedinthermia!*

They all hurry to their cars.

+++++

COULD I PLEASE STAY IN YOUR CAR TONIGHT, asks The Ford Escort of The Citroën. A big stone—a bloody rock is more like it—smashed through my windshield. If I slept in my own car tonight, I doubt if I'd ever wake up. What with this damn cold!

This unexpected request generates a sense of pleasant surprise in The Citroën. This woman, for God's sake, is growing more beautiful by the day. And, thanks to this diet, made obligatory by our extreme circumstances, she has shed some spare kilos to the benefit of her appearance.

The conditions under which we are now living are, undeniably, primitive. This is made abundantly evident by the filthy ragged—and stinking—clothes worn by most of the parishioners.

Nevertheless, in a miracle of feminine resourcefulness, The Ford Escort has managed to keep herself attired neatly and attractively at all times...

+++++

NEITHER THE CITROËN NOR ANYBODY ELSE is keeping an accurate estimate of the progress, or its converse, that the Parish has been making since that first ill-fated day on Clooneen bog.

Given the endless number of advances and retreats that have made since then, there are those who believe that we have yet to cross the boundaries of the seemingly interminable Clooneen Bog. The bog that surrounds us now, they say, is still that fuckin' ill-omened bog on which our cars got stuck in the first place!

That is the sort of talk The Citroën hears from those who now seem to have given themselves over to the darkest despair. It can hardly be based on the true reality of the situation, he reasons. One must take the following into account: as drivers leave the Jam to try their luck with making way to their destinations on foot, commit suicide or simply die from hunger or exposure, their abandoned cars are pushed aside to the verge of the motorway. The car behind them moves ahead to occupy the vacant space and so on, right down the line! In this way, the line of vehicles is constantly shortening, thus reducing the distance between the remaining drivers and their destinations. And from this logic arises the myth, re-broadcast by The BMW Accountant, that whatever obstacle there is to the free movement of traffic is being gradually dismantled.

Yet, the irreducible fact is that the Parish is still surrounded on all sides by Clooneen bog. The Citroën considers his options. Abandoning one's vehicle in the dead of Winter, as so many others are considering, is not a decision to be taken lightly. Nor is the decision to try to reach one's distant destination on foot, which verges on the insane. But, in certain cases, what else can one do? Supposing my petrol tank was empty, for example, and the battery was flat with no jump leads to be had in the vicinity, then? Or, if that minor dysfunction of the engine at the beginning of the journey had now developed into some major problem that issues in a "the fuckin' engine won't start." Not to mention the refusal of neighbors, the once friendly fellow parishioners to accept me into their cars, the latter not wishing to jeopardize their own survival prospects by having one more mouth to feed, by burning more petrol as their vehicles have to shift the increased weight on board. Furthermore, our contemporary "Greed is Good and Altruism is for Losers" belief is alive and well, even in the extreme conditions of the Clooneen Jam.

Be that as it may, why would a starving motorist, with a car that refuses to budge, hang around until that same car become his, or her, fuckin' coffin? as The Fiat 1100 Dub so memorably put it at the most recent meeting of the Dáil.

Other good reasons for leaving his, now, not so cozy car suggest themselves to The Citroën. Frustration at this abysmal lack of progress! The complete uncertainty that attends the future of this mother of all traffic jams, for starters! Then, dissatisfaction with the abominable and corrupt administration of the affairs of the particular part of the Jam in which he is stuck! Or, simply, his outlier's profound distaste for the habits of these unsought new neighbors, for their incoherent *weltanschauung*, for their magical core beliefs, for their *de rigeur* narrowness.

Or a confused *gemisch* of all of these perceptions!

But whether he decides to bail out or not, whatever decision he makes cannot be for himself alone! It must take a new reality into account: The Citroën and The Ford Escort are now an item.

Fulfilling the dream of that butterfly whose flight first united their glances?

+++++

THEY HAD MADE A SENSIBLE DECISION on the "Night of the Stones", (as the night of the attack of the peasants on the Parish came to be known as in parishioner folklore). The Ford Escort told The Citroën that she had hardly enough petrol to take her as far as Angelbank. But, with a broken windshield she would not be able to survive another night in her car. The cold would surely kill her.

But, if she abandoned her own vehicle and transferred what is left of her petrol into his tank? The Citroën briefly considers this proposition. He himself has not enough petrol to get him as far as Angelbank. He should have refilled his spare can at the Maumeen petrol station. But, he didn't think that such a precaution would have been necessary at that time and he could hardly have foretold the jam, literally speaking in which they now find themselves. But now, supposing the two of them pooled their energy resources? Then they would have more than enough to bring them as far as Angelbank, and for some distance beyond that now unreachable Shangri-La!

What you are proposing makes very good sense, he says,

turning his head to face The Ford Escort, who is sitting in the back seat.

She says nothing, but reaching forward, grasps his head between her hands and plant a long kiss on the top of his head.

Will we do it right now? she says.

Right away!

He then has her remove her bags, a big leather case and a smaller one, with her "personal effects" (as she says) from the stricken Escort. He places them in the boot of his own car. Together, under the light of a frosty moon, they push her car on to the grass verge of the motorway.

Tomorrow morning he will siphon the petrol in her tank through a plastic tube into his own tank.

Hoping against hope that the lines of traffic do not move in during this operation!

+++++

THERE ARE GOOD INDICATIONS that a change in the weather is on the cards.

A soft southerly breeze replaces the piercing northerly wind that has left the parishioners exhausted, frozen and more gloomy than usual. However, the raindrops that are swept towards the Parish by this breeze are merely the harbingers of a mingled sleet and rain downpour that, by midday, has left a layer of slush under foot. This, together with the gale-force wind that has suddenly veered around and is now blowing from the north again, makes communication between the various cars of the parish more difficult than usual.

The Beamer announces that all sessions of the Dáil have been cancelled until such time as weather conditions improve. The days that follow, when the wind quiets down, are cool enough but, for the most part, sunny.

There are those who say that Spring has come at last. Insofar as there are distinct seasons anymore! The Ford Escort says she can hardly wait for the sound of the cuckoo.

Taking advantage of this welcome respite, the parishioners

desert their cars and greet their neighbors, intent on renewing old relationships, friendships, even. Almost as if their fellow-parishioners were long-lost relatives. Some, when their strength permits it, even venture beyond the parish boundary to fraternize with their acquaintances there and pick up the latest rumors that are doing the rounds.

There is much to be discussed. However, the latest diversion, they discover, has to do, not surprisingly, with food. Or rather, with talking about food! Detailed accounts of past, and future, meals are lovingly given. The Citroën is horrified by the appearance of the gaunt, pale and squalid specters who relate these stories. They describe fried eggs, bacon, sausages, black and white puddings, mushrooms, hamburgers, Kentucky Fried Chicken, take-outs, egg foo yung, chop suey, prawn madras, papadams, roast pork, fillet steaks, roast lamb, cod 'n chips, apple tart, bacon and cabbage, fajitas, fried ants, burritos, bratwurst, spaghetti bolognese, haggis, gumbo, pastrami ham, coquilles San Jacques, Spanish mountain ham, hamcoddle, the full Irish breakfast, frankfurters, botifarras, seafood paella, sushi, sashimi, camembert, roquefort, emmenthal, brie, gorgonzola, apple pie, twenty flavors of ice cream, rhubarb crumble...

Until the teeth of the parishioners are swimming in their mouths and their empty innards groan pitifully...

The makers and suppliers of Taystee crisps and Kong Kola come in for some vigorous cursing on the part of participants in these (purely verbal) feasts. But, as The BMW Accountant points out, it is these products that are keeping body and soul together, just about, in this Parish.

Nevertheless, many believe that it is that very nutrition that is responsible for the diarrhea and the many stomach ailments that now afflict so many of our parishioners.

This negative assessment of the value of Taystees and Kong Kola, as dietary components, coincides with that of the VW Passat 1.9 doctor. He asserted, one day while attending the elderly Morris Minor matron that, as a medical doctor, he wouldn't feed "such crap even to pigs"...

+++++

THE BIG STORY THAT EXERCISES the imagination of the parishioners this morning is that The Renault 4 Ponytail has abandoned the Parish.

Like The Cherokee 4.0 Italian before him, and The Skoda clerics (if such they were), he left his baggage and his "Triptychs" squish "paintings" behind him. Nor did he, like the other "refugees", discuss his plan, assuming he had such, to leave the Parish with any other parishioner.

Did he abscond so suddenly, so mysteriously, of his own free will? Likewise, wild rumors concerning a possible link between the disappearance of The Skoda clerics, and the Italian, and that of Ponytail, abound.

These questions without answers cannot be avoided. Nor the groundless speculation that takes the place of answers. Every parishioner, it seems has his, or her, opinion concerning the mysterious disappearance of the Parish artist. And all clamor to be heard.

The Volkswagen, a mild-spoken teacher, is ordinarily quite reticent when it comes to offering an opinion. He is parked right behind the Renault 4 and claims that he heard violent shouting in the middle of the night coming, more or less, from the direction of that vehicle. He didn't think to interfere in the ruction however. He thought, at the time, that such a nocturnal disturbance could only be due to the Mushroom Druid mob whooping it up.

At daybreak, however, he noted that the driver's door of the Renault 4 was swinging open and that Ponytail was nowhere to be seen. However, later on, he discovered the latter's broken spectacles lying in a pool of water a short distance from the car. And, later again, he chanced on a trail of blood leading from the car across to the opposite verge of the motorway.

The Fiat 1100 Dub wants to get in his speak. He says that he finds it "fuckin' weird" that he is hearing the same sort of story in the surrounding parishes he is accustomed to visit. But that non-nationals are the most numerous among the disappeared. And that their vehicles are usually torched by their kidnappers if, indeed, such they are.

To tell you all the God's honest truth, he says, I saw a sight in one of the other parishes that would put the heart across anybody. A long line of vehicles—twenty, at least—and every shagging one of them burnt out! And they tell me that there are away more horrifying sights to be seen further east…

The Fiat 1100 Dub's story is discussed *ad nauseam*. Some opine that he has his facts baw-ways. Others—less optimistic—seem to take a masochistic satisfaction in opining that it is a sign of nasty things to come. Our parish can never have the luxury of ignoring universal trends, they say.

The Beamer, who has been silent up to now, then speaks. The strange story of Renault 4—added to what The Fiat 1100 had to tell us—underlines what he has been saying all along about the Parish's need for an adequate security and defense system.

And, by God, fellow parishioners, you'll shortly see me put flesh on those words!

+++++

IT IS BECOMING INCREASINGLY DIFFICULT to organize meetings of the Dáil beside the blue Peugeot. For, the bitter wind that is blowing from those Atlantic storms these days pierces to the very marrow of the bone.

And, given the greatly deteriorated general state of health in the Parish, few are willing to risk their life by leaving whatever sparse comfort afforded them by their cars, unless summoned by an emergency call.

Given these conditions, the Dáil pushes through legislation to the effect of reducing its quorum to a mere three deputies. Until the weather picks up again, of course! In the meantime, it is decided that Dáil meetings can now be held in the more hospitable environment of The Beamer's vehicle.

As the batteries of most of the cars in the parish are now just about exhausted, the use of car heaters is out of the question. Parishioners remain sitting, or lying, in their cars throughout most of the day. Wrapped up in their blankets, when they are lucky enough to have such! All windows and doors are shut to conserve within the cars the pitiable amounts of heat generated by their occupant's bodies and breath.

Do your utmost to keep warm, advises the VW Passat 1.9. doctor. Quite a number of people in the other parishes have died from hypothermia.

Have died from hypo-what? asks Ms. Cortina. What sort of bleedin' disease is that?

Death from the cold, says VW Passat 1.9 curtly.

And why didn't you say that in the first place? This is neither time nor place for posh talk!

Cars whose windows were broken on the Night of the Stones have difficulty in keeping out the bitter cold. Necessity being the mother of invention, their occupants stuff the gaps that are allowing the frosty air to enter their vehicles with anything that comes to hand: old newspapers, cardboard, dirty underwear and the towels that are hardly needed here, there being no water available for washing. The luxury of personal hygiene seems to belong to another universe.

The Mushroom Druids stole empty potato sacks from a barn (or so they proudly claim). The female members of that ragged tribe fashioned rough clothing—cloaks and monkish habits—from this booty. With the beards they now sport, and wearing this Clooneen Jam Chic, these ruffians resemble, for all the world, members of some medieval monastic mendicant order. That is to say, for a person innocent enough not to understand that the Mountjoy Jail in Dublin's fair city will be the much more likely permanent lodging place of these hooligans than some cloistered monastery in picturesque Tuscany.

The Citroën idles away the time, of which there is no shortage here, lazily observing the new sartorial style of the Druids. Suddenly, The Ford Escort, who has been sleeping in the back seat, awakens. Looking out the window, she tells him that she can see the lights of a city, as plain as daylight, close enough to The Parish and over there to the left. The Citroën looks in the direction she indicates, but sees nothing but the flat bog stretching for a short distance northwards before losing itself in a grey mist.

She insists that she can see a city. You could be right, he says, placatingly, but with this frosty haze that has been surrounding us for some days now, visibility is down to about 30 meters. You must have seen some sort of a mirage. Or, maybe, your imagination is playing tricks on you.

She starts to weep. Through tears, she claims that the city she has seen is a real city. Hadn't she seen with her own eyes the lights of its streets and houses and vehicles moving along its streets. And people walking about!

He soothes her, telling her that he is sure she has seen a real city. He doesn't mention to her that he had read somewhere that hunger is a great instigator of illusion; the angels and Virgins "seen" by fasting monks and nuns being a matter of ecclesiastical record.

The Ford Escort is by no means the only famished visionary in the Parish. The demented ravings of The Morris Minor Veteran are driving his wife out of her mind, on her own admission. He shouts, foaming at the mouth, that the vengeance of God is nigh (as evidenced by the Clooneen Jam), and that this disaster has been forecast by Columbanus, Nostradamus, Old Moore's Almanac and the Aztecs. Hadn't he himself seen the Angel of Death at the gates of Hell announcing the Day of the Final Judgment with blasts on his crooked trumpet? The souls of the damned behind him, were swimming helplessly about in liquid fire, he says. And that, says Ms. Morris Minor is only a small sample of the damn nonsense I have to put up with.

It takes some time for the VW Passat 1.9 doctor to reach that Morris Minor. Because he has to make his way through the snow that has been falling since midday and has blanketed the Parish and its environs. It now lies about 20cm deep in the Parish itself. But, unfortunately, he is unable to administer a sedating injection to the old-timer. The huge demand has exhausted his very limited supply of injectable sedative. I'm afraid that there is nothing for it, he tells Ms. Morris Minor, given that you have no food to give him. Just let him go on spouting. He'll tire out eventually and fall asleep.

In fact, such is the extents of this totally unexpected demand for medicaments in general that the small supply he normally keeps in his car has been almost fully depleted for some time now.

On his return trip to his own parish, the VW Passat 1.9 stops at The Beamer's vehicle, when the latter lowers his window and beckons towards him.

+++++

ANY NEWS, DOCTOR, enquires The Beamer, avid always for any piece of news that might illuminate the hidden corners of his constituency. Sit in here for a few minutes, man, till we discuss a few matters of common concern.

He himself has just returned from a foraging expedition in the eastern parishes, he says. Business matters! The doctor is surprised at the warmth of the air within The Beamer's car. How do some people, in the midst of such misery, manage to have such comfortable nests for themselves? While the majority without are both dying with the hunger and perished with the cold?

I am afraid that I have only the bleakest of reports to give you, says the doctor, in response to The Beamer's question.

It is simply that starving people are unable stand the cold. Many of them are already driven around the bend. I am afraid that we will faced shortly with death on a large scale, unless we can find some way to meet the nutritional needs of the parishioners. For some of them, who have gone for too long with no food, it is already far too late. Likewise, I cannot hold out much hope for veterans who lack the stamina of the young. As I say, we are on the eve of an unprecedented disaster unless food can be sourced immediately. Have you yourself any idea as to how such a certain tragedy can be averted?

I can only speak with authority concerning the feeding of my own parish, says The Beamer, lowering his voice. An what I am going to tell you, Doctor, is strictly confidential. Can I trust in your absolute discretion?

But of course!

+++++

FOR SOME DAYS NOW I have been at my wit's end trying to solve this food and drink problem. My sense of duty, and of responsibility towards the people who elected me, impels me to travel far from the Parish to see if I can find the solution of their difficulties.

And I am not talking here about sourcing the likes of Taystees and Kong Kola, which are no longer acceptable here. As an old woman told me earlier today, she would prefer—she said—to die of the hunger rather than contaminate her mouth ever again with such filth. Her own words, doctor!

She had every right to say that, Beamer, says the VW Passat 1.9 medic. But tell me this, did your travels yield any sign of hope for her and her likes?

They certainly did just that, Doctor. About 6 kilometers to the east of here, I located a refrigerated truck that is stuck, just like us, in this infernal traffic jam. It is filled to bursting point with a cargo of frozen pork destined for some of the more top-ranking hotels in the Capital. Or so the crew who is managing this consignment tell me. Since they, just like us, haven't the remotest clue when this nightmare is going to end, they have decided to sell off their valuable cargo. Contacts I have made in the parishes between here and the Smilin' Porkys, the name of the company that owns the truck, assure me that the meat they are selling is simply delicious.

But, is it expensive?

The venders, Doctor, and believe you me, have nothing at all in common with Mother Theresa of Calcutta or her ilk. I recognize them for what they are: hard-nosed business types. And they would be more than pleased to do a deal with this Parish that would be fair to both sides, they told me. On condition, of course, that we will be satisfied to play the game according to their rules! In my negotiations with these Smilin' Porkys, I did my utmost to ensure that the best interests of the Parish were safeguarded.

Necessity knows no laws, said their negotiators. It is its own law! And you, along with the people you represent are powerless, by yourselves, to eliminate that necessity. But we have that power! And never forget that we are the only game in town! If you refuse to play it, death will be your lot...

And?

Well, to make a long story short, they will supply us all the meat and soup we are able to consume!

But what conditions does the Parish have to satisfy in order to ensure the continuity of such an arrangement? asks the doctor. When the gun is put to your head you are hardly left with much choice.

Well said, Doctor! But this is a serious matter that I must first discuss with my own constituents. You can understand that protocol. And I am far from being 100% certain that they will want to row in behind my proposals to link up with the Smilin' Porkys. Especially when they understand the long-term implications of that relationship.

But the parishioners have no second choice!

Not a fucking one, saving your presence, Doctor. That is exactly what I will be telling them. But I will have to discuss the whole package with my constituents, as soon as I can. While there are still some of them standing. And put such a grave and far-reaching decision to a vote. Do you accept the proposals of the Smilin' Porkys. Yes or No?

I will make sure, Doctor, that they understand clearly that

a "No" vote is a vote for certain death.

+++++

IT IS LATE AS THE VW PASSAT 1.9 TAKES HIS LEAVE of The Beamer. Snow is falling heavily outside. Cold flakes whirl in the beam of his torch and brush his face as he trudges on muffled footsteps on a thick carpet of snow. As he passes The Citroën he slips and falls heavily on his backside.

The Citroën himself is outside his car at this late hour, busily wiping a layer of snow off the front windshield of his car. He hears the doctor falling and runs to assist him.

On his feet again, with the aid of The Citroën, the doctor opines that it would be useless, and foolish, for him—with the snow falling faster than ever—to attempt to reach his own car under these conditions. The way is too slippery, with a frozen layer of old snow lying under the softer snow whose height continues to mount. Apart from that, the night is pitch dark. Not a solitary star to be seen!

He asks The Citroën if he knows of a car in the Parish in which he could spend the rest of the night until morning. You are most welcome to stay in my car, says The Citroën, as long as you are willing to share it with The Ford Escort and me. The doctor accepts this offer gratefully.

Within an hour, the mysterious offer of the Smilin' Porkys is being discussed in all cars of the Parish.

As heatedly as the debilitated state of the parishioners will allow!

+++++

A conspicuous gap in the narrative occurs here. It isn't clear that any meeting of the Dáil was convened to analyze in serious depth the offer of the Smilin' Porkys. Nor, if indeed there were such a meeting, how many parishioners were present, or understood the full implications of what was on offer. Sections of the original text, not published here, give us clearly to indicate that a not inconsiderable portion of the population of the Parish was either ill or at the point of death at that time. Two, The Volkswagen and The Morris Minor Veteran, had died from the hunger just recently. One or two sentences in the original text, not reproduced here, give us to understand that their dead bodies were cannibalized by the starving parishioners. There is a somewhat obscure reference to such anthropophagy following the funeral of The Volkswagen, an insurance salesperson, by all accounts. In another section of the original text, however he is referred to as a "fish merchant".

(The Editors.)

+++++

A GOOD RELIABLE SOURCE OF FOOD that will enable us to survive this drawn-out emergency was what I sought to access over there in the east, says The Beamer. For, as we have seen just this very morning, unless that source is located quickly, I am afraid that there will be very few of us left with even the strength to drive a car when the traffic starts to move again. Therefore, listen very carefully to all I have to tell you.

A couple of days ago, I came upon a huge consignment of frozen pork belonging to a company called the Smilin' Porkys. They were on their way to deliver this cargo to the classiest hotels in Dublin when they were caught, just like us, in this miserable never-ending traffic jam. Other parishes, nearer the truck, have done deals with the Smilin' Porkys, which work out to the satisfaction of all, as far as I can make out. Anyway, the reps of these communities tell me that it is the best pork they have ever eaten.

Will we get potatoes and vegetables along with this meat, asks The Blue Peugeot Veteran, in a weak and faltering voice. In all fairness, though, I'd prefer a bit of fish to meat any day. Meat can be very tough. A nice tasty bit of salmon, you know what I mean...

If you are looking a menu with a broad range of

choice, with salmon or cod 'n chips, I'd advise you try some restaurant other than that of the Smilin' Porkys, answers The Beamer. But if there is such a restaurant in this Jam, I or anybody else have yet to find it.

How are we going to eat this pork? asks The Ford Escort, if we have no cooking utensils nor facilities. Don't tell us that we're going to eat raw pork, which is known to harbor worms. Isn't that the very reason why Jews and Muslims refuse to eat it!

You need have no worries at all on that score, says The Beamer. The Smilin' Porkys themselves cook all their meat before serving it to their customers. They operate like a food take-out; they send whatever meal you order by messenger right to your door. You could order a grilled pork steak from the Porkys, for example. Or pork stew! Or roast pork! Or pork chops! Or pork goulash! Or a pork chop suey! Or minced pork. Or pork sausages! Or black pudding! Or white pudding! Or pork soup, even!...

So that we'd never want to see the sight of a bit of pork again as long as we live!, commented Ms. Cortina. Although, in all fairness, one of Beth's favorite dishes is roast pork, done Caribbean style. Remember the time that she made it for Stacey! Just before they headed off to Shri Sexynanda's class at the Beverley Hills Ashram. With rice and black beans, d'ye remember. Stacey said she couldn't get enough of it...

You may never want to see pork again, and that is your democratic right, says the Mercedes Benz accountant to Ms. Cortina. But it's either pork or death!

The Porkys have us over a fuckin' barrel, then, opines Mr. Cortina

Your account of the various pork meals you can get from these Porkys makes my mouth water, says The Ford Escort. But a nasty little question occurs to me. Tell us, Beamer, will these delicious treats cost us parishioners an arm and a leg? Or are these Smilin' Porkys going to offer their pork to us free gratis?

I'm happy that you ask that last question, Ms. Ford Escort, says The Beamer. You don't get anything for nothing these days. Consumer goods, services, even personal services: all have their price. You hardly have to be a Milton Friedman to understand that price and profit are of the essence of the free market, that very foundation stone of real democracy. You could hardly expect businessmen to the manner born, like the Smilin' Porkys, to manage their meat market in any other way.

+++++

CAN YOU GIVE US SOME IDEA, THEN, of what exactly, then, the Smilin' Porkys would charge us to take the edge off our appetite, asks The Fiat 1100 Dub.

I spent a long time at the bargaining table with them, putting all my effort in to getting them to lower the price they are demanding for their pork. To no avail! They wouldn't budge. It's up to you, they said, to accept our terms. Or not to accept! The choice is entirely yours! Whether you accept our meat, or not, is of no great concern to us. The line of potential customers is a long one.

You still haven't answered my question, says The Fiat 1100 Dub.

Okay, then, says The Beamer. Somewhat sharply, having hoped—very obviously—that the minutiae if his deal with the Porkys would not be exposed to the light of day.

They will accept cash on the nail, he says, but no checks or credit cards. They will also accept petrol, gold, jewelry, cameras, watches, fur coats, fashionable clothes, cars, even. Or title deeds to properties for those who want to assure themselves of a continuing supply of meat. I have a leaflet here on which the Porkys have outlined the prices they charge for the various cuts of meat. You can pass it around from person to person. But take into account also, before you gag, that this is very much a seller's market.

But what do you, or they, mean by the "services" that is mentioned here, asks a ragged emaciated Ms. Toyota Starlet, waving the Porkys' leaflet.

That's a good question, says The Fiat 1100 Dub. We are all strapped both for cash and petrol by this time. So strapped, in fact, that you'd have to take either cash or petrol from us by force. Only a fuckin' half-wit would surrender his house or his car to these fuckin' bloodsuckers, or the Smilin' Porkys, as you call them . Especially when, as far as we know, this bleedin' traffic jam could end at any time!

There is no way I'd let them put their greasy trotters on my car. Nor on my apartment either, shouts The SUV Yuppie.

Therefore, as I see it, nearly all of us will be paying for our pork with "services", whatever the hell that is supposed to mean, continues The Fiat 1100 Dub. What I am saying, therefore, is that the people of this Parish, those of us that are left, are entitled to know exactly what these Porkys mean by "services".

Murmurs of support and "Good Man Yerself" are heard coming from the ragged skeletal figures that are assembled in the freezing cold at this Dáil meeting. But The Beamer gets no opportunity to answer The Fiat 1100 Dub's question.

For, the proceedings of the Dáil are suddenly interrupted by a loud explosion, not far from the Parish, that startles the members present. This blast is followed by a staccato rattle that sounds as if it could be a machine gun and, then, a series of smaller explosions.

The parishioners look at each other quizzically, fear and curiosity vying with each other in their eyes.

I once did a stint in the army, says The Fiat 1100 Dub. And I'd swear on a heaped stack of bibles that there is either a battle simulation exercise, or even a battle itself, going on over there to the east of The Parish.

In any case, whether a mock battle or the real thing, this totally unexpected intervention puts an end to the Dáil debate. The members do not return immediately to their cars, however. They linger there in the cold, their faces to the north-east, in the direction of this "battle".

The echoing thunder of the discharge of heavy weaponry is carried to their ears as they see ominously big puffs of black smoke over ascending slowly towards the sky.

Like Armafuckingeddon, murmurs Mr. Toyota Starlet.

Like Armafucking what? asks The Cortina.

+++++

THE HABITUAL TUNELESS CACOPHONY of hundreds, maybe thousands, of car horns to the east of the Parish announces yet another movement of those interminably long metal lines. Parishioners plod, leaden-footed, to their cars, the energy and enthusiasm needed to race to them, as during the early days of the Clooneen Jam, having been eroded by malnutrition and repeated disappointments. Car doors close. Engines splutter into action. And now, at last, the lines are moving. A weak chorus of groans of disappointment and shouts of impotent rage is heard from the occupants of the cars.

For, once again, the lines of cars are retreating backwards, towards the west...

The Citroën is now behind the steering wheel, The Ford Escort in the front passenger seat beside him. Suddenly, the driver's door of the red Cortina in front of him opens. The track-suited Mr. Cortina himself emerges and runs back to The Citroën.

My bleedin' car won't fuckin' budge, he shouts. A trifle hysterically.

The horns of the cars immediately to the front of him are sounding angrily. They cannot drive in reverse with this damn Cortina blocking the way. The Skoda that belonged to the disappeared Bishop, directly in front of the Cortina, is now driven by one of the Mushroom Druid mob. He appears to derive some sadistic satisfaction from beeping nonstop for all his worth.

The Citroën and The Ford Escort quickly get out of their car and run back towards the Cortina. While the women hurriedly transfer the contents of the boot of the Cortina to that of The Citroën, and the noxious brat to the back seat of the latter, their menfolk push the vehicle, now in reverse gear, in one last vain effort to get the battery to spark and so start the Cortina.

The battery is well and truly fucked, says The Cortina, tersely, after some minutes of vain effort. All that listenin' to Fuckface Thornton has banjaxed it...

Both he himself and The Citroën are too weakened by hunger to push against the resistance of the reverse gear and so generate the magic spark. So, with the assistance of The Fiat 1100 Dub, who crosses the divide between the two lines of cars to help them, they just about manage to park the Cortina on the grass verge of the motorway.

All of that sudden physical effort makes The Citroën dizzy. He feels himself almost falling out of his standing. But—with the proud stoicism of the true manly man—he shrugs away that unpleasant sensation, gives the fingers to The Skoda Druid, and returns to his own car.

Once re-installed there, both he and The Ford Escort occupy the front seats. The Cortina couple sit on the rear seat behind them, their offspring lodged between them. No sooner has the car been started than this menace starts to emit loud ear-splitting screams. This behavior must be habitual to the little bastard, thinks The Citroën, since his parents make little or no effort to quiet down their offspring.

Now, now, stop being so bold, my little rogue, croons Ms. Cortina, somewhat half-heartedly. The little darling is angry because we left his electronic game behind us in the car. Now, now, now, my little rogue...

The Citroën feels like his head is being pierced by an electric drill every time Master Cortina screams. On top of that, there is now an evil smell in the air. And no bloody wonder! He understands clearly that parishioners have had no opportunity to wash themselves nor their clothes since this horrible misadventure began. That is a given that every parishioner understands. Every drop of water that the parishioners manage to get hold of must be used for the purpose of slaking thirst. And only that!

Up to now, The Citroën developed the habit of never standing on the downwind side of his fellow parishioners. But now there are five of them crammed into the limited space of his car. As the windows are closed to keep out the cold, this stink is a hundred times worse, a hundred times more foul than he ever imagined it could be. Could it be... shite?

His question is quickly answered by Ms. Cortina.

I'm afraid the poor little darling has diarrhea, she says. All that screaming is because he pooped into his trousers, God love him. Those damn Taystees always give him the runs. But there is damn-all else for him or the other children—or for us ourselves—to eat. In any case, I'll try and clean up this mess the next time we halt. Although, without water... In the meantime, I suppose we'll just have to get used to the smell. I'm really sorry about all of this!

A silence followed this revelation, as the knowledge was digested slowly by the now grim-faced Ford Escort and The Citroën.

What do you think that gunfire we heard earlier was all about, asks The Cortina. In an obvious attempt to break this awkward silence and deflect the attention of all from the fouled trousers of Master Cortina.

When there was no answer to his question, he continued his monologue.

And, then, that smoke cloud we saw just afterwards? what was set on fire? I hope to hell that those terrorists we always see on the television, Al Quaeda or what ever they call themselves, or Talibans, haven't come as far as this country!

As this suggestion fails to elicit any comment, good

bad or indifferent, and The Cortina is emboldened to continue in similar vein:

With the number of non-nationals, foreigners, who come here to scrounge off our social welfare system, we're going to have to pay for our stupid generosity. And it has started already. You all heard The Beamer talking about the non-nationals who raided the food storage depot in Galway, making off with the food the helicopters were going to bring to us.

And you see the state we are in now: starving here in our own country, while bleedin non-nationals make off with our food! Somethin' will have to be done!

+++++

THE CARS GROAN PAINFULLY, RETREATING BACKWARDS in reverse gear. If this doesn't stop soon, The Citroën tells himself, the little that is left of our petrol will soon be all used up. What do we do then?

Glancing out through the windshield, lines of deserted cars are to be seen lining the side of the road. Some of them are burnt-out shells. The Cortina is proud to be able to name them all: the Honda Civic VTI, the C180 Esprit Sport, the Mazda XSEDOS 6, the Nissan Micra, the Hyundai, the Daihatsu Terrios, the Fiat Punto 55SX, the Ford Mondeo, and many others...

Where are their owners now? Trying on foot to find some secure sanctuary, if such there is! Many, obviously, do not succeed in this quest. If the roughly hewn crosses that stand there bleakly in the cold over these new *ad hoc* graves, in a little bit from the road, are any indication!

Well, what did you think of The Beamer's recommendations regarding the Porky's offer, is The Ford Escort's conversational icebreaker during a brief respite from the brat's caterwauling—though not, alas, from the foul smell emanating from the said party—which gives the adults a chance to talk.

But what choice have we got, woman? answers The Cortina. Here we are reversing for the umpteenth time. We haven't a fuckin' clue where we're going or when we'll be able to reach our journey's end. In the meantime, keeping fuckin' alive— if that's the word—depends on those fuckin' Taystees and Kong fuckin' Kola, whose supply is just about used up. Or, so The Beamer tells us! We'll all fuckin' croak from starvation unless we accept the Smilin' Porkys' offer!

But we're not talking about a gift here, says The Ford Escort. Gifts don't come with a string of conditions. But who gave the Porkys the authority to lay down their own self-serving conditions for the sale of their pork?

They own the bloody pork! Isn't that enough authority for you?

Hardly so, given the hordes of starving people that surround them! If they had even the slightest spark of humanity and social conscience in them, that fact alone should impel them to share out their hoard of pork equally to all who need it to stay alive. The only valid condition they have the moral right to lay down is that the recipient be starving and have no other means of obtaining sustenance.

In all fairness, I've not the slightest idea what you mean by "moral right". This is the 21st. century, unless I've gone completely fuckin' gaga. All I know is that if owners were denied the right to sell off their goods in whatever way they see fit, the bottom would fall out of life as we know it!

Life as we know it seems to many to be just the playground of celebrities and scam artists, says The Ford Escort, somewhat heatedly. But there is another way, if the men of this Clooneen Jam had any backbone at all, and the faintest glimmer of understanding, they would organize, seize the pork hoard of the Porkys, and distribute the lot in a fair-minded way among their starving neighbors.

Are you seriously telling me, girl, that the Porkys would meekly surrender their pork distribution rights to a bunch of fuckin' communist yobbos? says The Cortina. Are you telling me that they are such fuckin' *eejits* that they never ever imagined that the hungry horde around them might try to grab their pork for free? And do you think that they haven't by now built up an alliance of friends?

Friends?

Gunmen! You know from earlier that there are guns around.

Another bout of screaming, courtesy of Master Cortina, ends this exchange of views. The Citroën monitors the petrol gauge anxiously. The needle hovers at zero and he is afraid that they have scarcely enough left in the tank to carry them more than another kilometer in reverse gear. As luck would have it, the long line of traffic is beginning to slow down. Then it stops. As the car engines around him are being switched off, he quickly descends to the road. With an urgent wish to expel the foul air of the car interior from his lungs and fill them with the clean fresh air of the country side.

His wish is not destined to be fulfilled.

The stink of raw sewage outside is too strong.

+++++

MEN LOVE TO BE ALWAYS SOUNDING OFF about politics, says Ms. Cortina to The Ford Escort. The women are by themselves in The Citroën.

And, as far as I am concerned, they are like the barber's cat: all wind and piss. But, I myself couldn't give a tinker's curse for politics and politicians. They are all the same, the whole fuckin' bunch of them! Robbers, cute-arses, all out for themselves! I wouldn't waste my time listening to any one of them. Not even for a second! Not even to the likes of The Beamer, who seems to be a respectable man, though I don't understand what he is saying half of the time. But if somebody like Josie Thornton turned his hand to politics, well, that would be another story. I might even give politics another chance.

Another story is right!, comments The Ford Escort.

Would you like me to tell you now what is really

getting to me?

Fire ahead, says The Ford Escort, steeling herself to hear the lurid details of Master Cortina's diarrhea. Or worse!

But no!

What I really cannot stand, says Ms. Cortina, is the fact that half the country knows already whether Stacey is pregnant. Or not! Only *gaums* like us, stuck here in this damn traffic jam, haven't a fuckin' clue about Stacey's condition. I myself believe that she is in the family way. And I now firmly believe that it was that bastard, may God forgive me, Howard who put her up the pole. Wasn't it that sneaky little prick that came between Barbara and Brad? What do you yourself think about the question. Do you think she looks as if she might be pregnant?

It'd take a wise woman to answer that question, answers The Ford Escort, as diplomatically as she can manage.

Standing on the grass verge of the motorway, carefully avoiding the excrements that have been deposited there, The Citroën looks around him. He notices the sinister shape of that eternal chestnut tree, a bare 50 meters from where he is standing.

+++++

I CAN WELL UNDERSTAND YOUR FEARS, The Beamer is saying. And I myself put the selfsame question to the Porkys. They tell me that "service" is a word that cannot easily be defined, as it encompasses a number of functions, some of which have yet to be clarified.

The Smilin' Porkys themselves are the ones who will decide, in a given context, what service is needed. A man or two might be needed to shovel snow from the motorway, for example. Or to remove trees blown down by the storms or burnt-out cars that impede the traffic. Women are needed to take care of the sick, children or babies. And, especially, the growing numbers of orphans that are left after their parents die from the hunger or commit suicide.

Nobody who had the slightest respect for themselves could accept such an agreement, Beamer, says Ms. Toyota Starlet. How do we know what other services these Smilin 'Porkys may have in mind? Use your bloody imaginations, for God's sake, fellow parishioners!

I must say that I resent the implications of the final remark of the last speaker, says The Beamer. The Porkys I deal with are neither lechers nor bloodsuckers. They are plain honest people, just like ourselves. People who told me that they are eager to help us! If we had difficulties with the administration of Parish affairs, for example, they say they would be ready and willing to come to our aid. The difficulty of one will be the difficulty of us all, as they say.

So, cutting through all this bullshit, you are saying that we should make an agreement with the Porkys, on their terms? says The Fiat 1100 Dub. Isn't that what you are really trying to tell us? Even though we don't know yet what they really mean by "services"?

Correct! I, as Taoiseach, will be strongly opting for that course of action. I have an absolute trust in the honesty and integrity of the Smilin' Porkys. But, of course, it will be up to you, with your votes, to mandate such a decision.

Look, says Ms. Toyota Starlet, the sarcastic undertone of her voice indicating that she is about to go on the offensive. If these Smilin' Porkys are unwilling to give us a full account of the services they demand, or may demand in the future, as payment for food, accepting their offer, as it stands, would be the height of irresponsibility. I propose that you return to the negotiating board to tell these Porkys, out straight, that this is the stance of this Parish. And, if such a complete and comprehensive list is not forthcoming, then no agreement with the Porkys will ever be possible. Full stop!

Silence follows this proposal, that is broken by the Mid-Atlantic accented voice of The Beamer, who is also acting as Chairperson for this session In the absence of the usual Beamer II, who vanished recently under mysterious circumstances.

Everybody here has the right to speak, he says, and that right will be respected here as we are justly proud of our democratic tradition. But, one would sincerely hope that the tongues all who are disposed to exercise that right are firmly connected somehow to feet on the ground.

What in the hell do you mean by that sort of a remark, asks The Fiat 1100 Dub.

I now give the floor to The BMW Accountant, says The Beamer, completely ignoring The Fiat 1100 Dub's truculent intervention.

Well, I don't know to what extent Ms. Toyota Starlet is aware of the true situation today in our Parish, says The BMW Accountant quietly. But let me give her, and all of us, a few facts to chew on! That was an unfortunate choice of a word, I admit. Sorry! Anyway, I guarantee that a full disclosure of the facts of our situation will help this assembly to make the correct choice, when the time comes to do just that. Let us take the question that most concerns us: the question of food. Right now, we are down to one meal a day. That is, if a bag of Taystees and a can of Kong Kola can rightly be called a meal.

Even pigs would turn up their fuckin' snouts at such muck as that, as the doctor said. The Citroën cannot make out who exactly in the assembly made that remark. The Mitsubishi Lancer Giant, maybe; that individual, in his capacity as director of security, has become a *de facto* honorary parishioner.

Well, I might not express it quite like that, answers The BMW Accountant, but I am at one with the spirit in which the remark was made. In any case, it is common knowledge by now that the stock of Taystees and Kong Kola is well nigh exhausted. In keeping with a well-known law of economics, as resources become more scarce, they cost more. So, the substantial price hikes regarding these products will place them beyond the reach of most of our parishioners. We all know, to our cost, that their need for these products has already brought most of us here to a state of near penury, along with gravely depleting our petrol reserves. The reality is that we have no alternative food source. An early death from hunger will be our lot unless we accept the offer of the Smilin' Porkys. It is our only lifeline!

Well, I have to say that I agree with Ms. Toyota Starlet, says The Fiat 1100 Dub. Would anyone, apart from a raving lunatic, sign an agreement unless all the conditions that went along with that agreement were crystal clear? Let us have a bit of common sense, for God's sake! We should wait a few days before being railroaded into making a rash decision. Even if we have to go completely hungry! There are persistent rumors in the parishes to the east and the west of us that the Clooneen Jam is to end shortly. I propose that we stay patient for the time being and not make a rash decision that may give us much cause for regret later on!

Fair play to you Fiat 1100, shouts Ms. Toyota Starlet. I second that.

Would anybody else like to speak before we take a vote ? asks The Beamer.

The show of hands indicates that almost all surviving parishioners wish to have their voices heard.

I call upon The BMW Accountant to speak, says The Beamer.

But he has already had his say, indicates a chorus of protesting voices.

But I didn't get a chance to say what still needs to be said, retorts The BMW Accountant. I was going to give you all the lowdown on the real petrol situation. The Fiat 1100 Dub spoke about a rumored end to the Clooneen Jam. Would that that were true! However, I have surveyed the amount of petrol that remains in the Parish. And, let me tell you, if the cars started to move this very day, most of us would be unable to reach even Angelbank, not to mention Dublin, for lack of petrol. Furthermore it is certain that every petrol pump between here and Dublin is as dry as a bone.

Therefore, fellow parishioners, we will be stuck, unable to move, even if the traffic becomes unjammed.

All of you, bear that in mind when you come to consider the advisability, or not, of signing a contract with the Smilin' Porkys!

+++++

I NEED TO CLARIFY A FEW POINTS, says The Beamer.

There is another aspect of this proposed agreement with the Smilin' Porkys that I have not yet described and that would work very much to our advantage. And, in a nutshell, it is this: they would be willing to pay for services rendered with petrol. In other words, they would fill out tanks as long as we fulfill whatever services they require. Quite frankly, we would be cutting our own throats if we refused to avail of this offer.

And, with not a drop of petrol to be had anywhere, where, in the name of God Almighty, do these Smilin' Porkys manage to get a surplus of the stuff? asks The Ford Escort.

That is easily answered, Madam, says The Beamer. The Porkys made bargains with some large petrol trucks in the Jam to the east of them. Their crews pay in petrol for the food with which they are supplied by the Porkys. The result of this exchange is that the Porkys are swimming in petrol, so to speak.

And now, to conclude, let me mention another interesting aspect of the package that is being offered to us by the Smilin' Porkys. Once we indicate that we intend to take a decision on the deal with the Porkys, they will start to deliver cooked meat to us on the following day. Not only that but, on ratifying the agreement, they will deliver a whole week's supply of meat to us, absolutely free of charge, not costing us either a drop of petrol nor time spent rendering a service. Think about it: your stomachs filled with prime meat for a whole week without any cost whatsoever to you.

Having said that, The Beamer looks every participant in this Dáil session right in the eye, a look of triumph on his face.

I believe it will not be necessary to take a vote, he says, in a soft quiet voice.

Nobody answers him.

+++++

THE DEATH OF THE OLD LADY in the yellow Anglia is the latest in a series that has been ravaging the surrounding parishes. Malnutrition was the cause of her death, in other words: hunger, said the VW Passat 1.9 doctor, who arrived too late on the scene to do much more than certify the cause of death. He announces the smallpox and scarlet fever have made their unwelcome appearance in his own parish and to be on the lookout for them here.

The Citroën and The Cortina are chosen to take part in the detail that The Beamer is putting together to dig the grave out on the bog. It is a shallow grave—the detail simply hasn't got the energy needed to dig it to its appropriate dimensions. As they are throwing the sods down the body of Ms. Yellow Anglia, wrapped in a black plastic rubbish sack, The Cortina remarks that rumor has it that corpses are being dug up and devoured by packs of dogs, driven wild by the hunger.

Later, exhausted by the effort of digging the grave, The Citroën feels dizzy. His body needs a long rest. However, he is unwilling to return to his own car. That squalid stinking den with its complement of unwashed bodies is the last place he would choose for a nap. In spite of an early morning chill in the air, his upper body is covered by a thin shirt. His sweater is being used as a blanket by the odiferous Master Cortina...

His greatest worry this morning is the certain knowledge that he is almost out of petrol. On top of that, almost all his money has been spent on Taystee crisps and Kong Kola. The Ford Escort is just as broke as he is. Not wishing to be under a complement to his "guests", The Cortinas, he has yet to broach the question of money with them. But he understands, from the occasional hint they have let drop, that they are as poor as he himself is. He must let them know of the desperate plight all of them are in, almost penniless and the petrol tank empty.

The only ray of hope he sees is the possibility of filling his tank again in return for service to the Smilin' Porkys. If he were away from the parish on such service, there would be at least one other driver, The Cortina, who would be able to take his place behind the steering wheel. Assuming he had already earned some petrol.

But, of course, if the Porkys accepted his proposition, their offer of petrol would cancel their offer of meat. Which is the more important to him: a full stomach or a functioning car? Such mental gyrations only compound his dizziness!

+++++

THE CITROËN REMEMBERS THE WORDS spoken by The Beamer at the last Dáil session. While enjoying the clean quasi-opulence of the latter's car, he cannot help but compare it to the noisy squalor of his own. The Beamer does not accept refugees in his car as such would distract him from the work he performs on behalf of the Parish.

The Porkys would fill my tank if I offered them a service, says The Citroën. That is what you gave us to understand recently. Well, I am ready to perform such a service, as long I am paid in petrol. What sort of service do the Porkys have in mind these days?

By happy coincidence, we have a gentleman here in the back seat who can answer that question for you, answers The Beamer.

While The Citroën is shaking hands with this stranger to the Parish, a swarthy middle-aged male, sporting dark blue glasses with a thick black frame. Being clean-shaven, he could easily be singled out readily from the male parishioners, all of whom without exception, including The Beamer, now sport long dense beards.

Then, The Beamer, in obvious self-congratulatory mood, continues:

I thought, if I may say so myself, that my conclusion to the debate yesterday was highly satisfactory. A vote just wasn't necessary, as the correct way to alleviate our distress here was so abundantly obvious. Or so I thought! However, there are certain people—and you yourself would have no difficulty in naming them—who are so intent on upsetting the applecart that nothing would satisfy them but to invite a Smilin' Porky to come here to answer their questions.

And this is why I am here, completely at your disposition, says the stranger, now revealing himself to The Citroën to be one of the Porkys.

Quite frankly, I have no idea what the real agenda of those spoilers is, says The Beamer. But our friend here is ready and willing to answer any question that arises from the offer of his company. I have sent The Saab around the Parish to announce that a special meeting of the Dáil will be held in a half-hour's time and at which we will finally be afforded the petty details that some people want to know.

So, if you have a question to put to our friend here, we have time for such. I'm sure he won't mind answering it.

The Porky smiles his assent.

The Citroën rapidly explains his case. He is responsible for the transport of five people. He has no petrol left. Not a drop! But he is willing to place himself in the Porky's service if that will ensure that his tank is filled.

The Porky answers, speaking smoothly and rapidly, with a slight foreign accent. Only women are required for service at this time, he explains. But when the times comes, as it most certainly will, for men to perform heavy labor, I will certainly keep you very much in mind. Minding babies, orphans and old people are the services that are in most demand these days.

Will you be requiring a woman to work tomorrow? asks The Citroën.

Yes! To take care of a woman who is seriously ill! I was

going to announce this shortly at this special session of your Dáil, as you call your council. But if you can guarantee to me that you can find such a woman, then I will certainly give her priority.

I'll investigate that possibility immediately, says The Citroën. And I'll come back to you with a definite answer before the meeting commences. What sort of recompense will she get? The women I have in mind are certain to ask me that question.

Recompense? What is that?

Payment!

Ah, I see. Five liters of petrol and a pork meal! That's our standard payment for that sort of service.

A little later, The Citroën discusses this proposition with the two women of his car, Ms. Ford Escort and Ms. Cortina. Both of them say they are ready and willing to accept the responsibility described by the Porky. Their level of excitement at the prospect would give anyone to think that they were in competition for some plum position.

If I don't go, this car will never be able to move from this spot, both of them say, enthusiastically and almost at the same time.

I'll go then says Ms. Ford Escort. Looking after Master Cortina is going to keep you busy here, she says to Ms. Cortina.

The latter says, however, that she'd pay a fortune just to be able to escape for one day from this prison. Just to be able to speak to other people than the parishioners. People who might be able to tell her what became of Stacey. And, she would put some of the meat into her handbag for her child, who hasn't been looking at all well, lately. And no bloody wonder, with nothing else to eat now for an eternity, it seems, but those bloody Taystees. He's losing weight, and as for that bloody diarrhea… And, in any case, I'm sure you wouldn't mind looking after him while I'm gone?

Ms. Ford Escort eventually accedes to this plea...

+++++

HERE IS HOW OUR RECEIPT SYSTEM WORKS. As soon as a person performs a service for us, we give them receipts.

It is a fine warm afternoon. Swallows, high in the sky, swoop back and forth in pursuit of flying insects. Far beneath them, a plump obviously well-fed Smilin' Porky, is talking to a ragged, starving group of parishioners.

But, as we have been given to understand, services are to paid for with petrol, says The SUV Yuppie, addressing the Porky.

Correct! The Beamer here, has kept you accurately informed. We pay with receipts and each receipt we issue is worth a liter of petrol.

But, how much does a person have to do to gain a receipt? asks The Cortina.

Well, that depends on the kind of service performed!

For example?

For example, say a man was working for us for a whole day. Distributing petrol for us, for example. In that case, we would give him five receipt stamps at the end of his workday. That would be the equivalent of 5 liters of petrol. He simply surrenders the receipts and we bring the petrol to his car. It is a very simple system and it works well in the other parishes that have opted to become our customers.

Five liters of petrol per day is the salary you are offering, then? asks The BMW Accountant.

Well, not exactly! Not all forms of work are valued equally. If a woman were taking care of a baby or an old person for a whole day, say, she would only earn three receipts. That is to say, three liters of petrol!

What you are saying there is that the work a woman performs does not compare with male labor. Don't you think that is a wee bit discriminatory? asks Ms. Toyota Starlet. Not to say scandalous?

I am glad you mentioned that point, Madam. But that is the heritage that has been left to us by history, the habit of hundreds, maybe thousands, of years, so to speak. We are constantly reviewing this policy, of course. And when the policy is modified, be assured that you in this parish will be the first to know of whatever changes are made to it!

Regarding these services, asks Ms. Toyota Starlet again, to whom do you offer the most work, women or men?

That is a very good question, Madam; I'm glad you asked it. Given the number of orphans, children in weakened conditions in our own, and the surrounding, parishes, the demand for female labor, far exceeds, at present, the demand for male labor. In this context, it would be worth your while to consider our bonus system. The woman who contributes three full days of her labor earns our bonus for so doing.

What sort of bonus? clamors a chorus of female voices.

As I have explained, the basic wage for three days of women's work is nine liters of petrol. But we add a bonus of one liter to that payment. Which is to say, a woman would return to her car, after such a 3-day stint, ten liters of petrol the richer. Or, with its equivalent in pork products, if she would prefer to be paid that way!

Here's another question that puzzles us here in this parish: why don't you pay directly with petrol rather than going through this complicated business of the vouchers, or receipts, as you call them. The Fiat 1100 Dub asks this question.

The reason is simple, sir! We do not have petrol storage tanks. But we do have a big reserve of pork. We depend on our petrol distributors, with whom we have already developed an extensive network. We buy petrol with pork. Our distributors have no interest in small orders: a liter here, a liter there! This would entail a waste of time and, more importantly, such increased transport would entail a waste of petrol on their part.

Their policy encourages customers to store their receipts until such time as they are able to make substantial orders. I think you should all be able to appreciate that.

Still, receipts don't fill, petrol tanks. So when the traffic starts to move again and you find yourself with an empty tanks and a stack of receipts?

That would be absolutely no cause for worry, says the Porky. Before the traffic is due to move, we arrange for the distributors to gather receipts and distribute petrol correspondingly. Apart from that, we arrange to resurrect dead batteries with jump leads.

That is all very fine! Normally, we have only a couple of minutes after hearing car horns blaring to the east of us to get into our cars and get them started. How in those few minutes can you supply hundreds of car simultaneously with petrol?

We know two hours before the traffic moves in this area that traffic movement is impending.

What! How? Magic?

Not quite! Movement begins always at the head of the traffic columns. We are in regular contact with another truck of ours that is located near the head of the columns. Along with other Smilin' Porky trucks between here and there! They keep us informed continually regarding the movement of the columns. So that we are never caught unawares! So that, as I said, we know approximately two hours beforehand that traffic movement is impending here. Which gives us lots of time to ensure that all holders of receipts receive their petrol in good time!

This is a bit incredible, comments The SUV Yuppie. Everybody knows that all public communication networks are completely banjaxed ever since the day this goddam traffic jam started.

We never use public communication systems. We Smilin' Porkys have our own private internal system which, I am pleased to report, functions perfectly, and is never subject to the inefficiency of the public system. Therefore, I can solemnly promise you all that we will be easily able to distribute petrol under all the conditions you mention, when the agreement with us is signed on your behalf, I hope, by your good friend and ours, The Beamer.

I can guarantee, says The Beamer that our good friend here is telling you the truth, and nothing but the truth. I have had the opportunity to discuss this matter with leaders of other parishes nearby who have signed agreements with the Smilin' Porkys. And I have not heard a single complaint—apart from the usual mad vaporings from the usual cranks—from the plain people of those parishes.

And what had those "cranks" got to say? asks The BMW Accountant.

I'm not saying that we haven't heard somewhat similar claptrap from people who should know better and who dwell much closer to home, says The Beamer.

People would swear later that he was looking out of the corner of his eye at Ms. Toyota Starlet and The Fiat 1100 Dub as he spoke those words.

Be that as it may, says the Smilin' Porky, I think I have little else to say to you concerning this matter. It is up to you now to discuss the contract that is on the table among yourselves and arrive at a democratic decision as soon as possible.

I stress this "as soon as possible", my friends. Because, and I don't want to sound alarmist here, from observing some of you, I would have to say that a visit (perhaps I should have said "multiple visits") is due any day now in this famine-stricken parish from that most unwelcome of visitors, Death. But always remember, as you discuss this life or death issue, that the Smilin' Porkys are here always to help keep that grim specter away from haunting your doors.

I would ask you all now, says The Beamer, to show your appreciation of this most distinguished representative of the Smilin' Porkys, for having taken the trouble to come all this way to clarify lucidly for us the steps we must take on the only road that is still open to us.

A sudden thunder shower ends the faint ripple of faint applause that follows The Beamer's request. The parishioners, half-drenched, stumble towards their cars.

+++++

From occasional scattered, sometimes confused, references on pages that do not form part of the current text, it seems the Master Cortina died from hunger or fever. Ms. Ford Escort opines that the Cortina couple ceased speaking to each other a few days after his death. It seems that the only interests they share in common are jogging and looking at television. And since they are too weak to jog and television is a distant memory, an icy silence reigns between them.

The following pages coincide with this reading of the history of the Parish.

They are of interest also in that the account they give of the solution of the petrol question is not as described heretofore. This raises questions about the correspondence of the original Das Citroensche Tagebuch *to the real facts of the Clooneen Jam. Is it a compendium of the contributions of more than one author, as some researchers suggest. Or is it a work of the imagination, from start to finish? as suggested by others. The majority suspect, however, that sections of the* Tagebuch *may have benefited from some creative input.*

Still, the archaeological evidence shows incontrovertibly that The Cloneen Jam did in fact happen. Whether the description of it in the Tagebuch *corresponds to its terrible reality is still a moot point among scholars.*

(The Editors.)

+++++

IT OCCURS TO THE CITROËN that they have spent a week, at least, in this place, under the most squalid conditions. Without moving a single centimeter. And always with that accursed chestnut tree in full sight.

Four days chattering to the neighbors, tantalizing ourselves with description of the magnificent spreads we enjoyed before the Clooneen Jam loomed on our mental horizons. And enjoying, the word is incontrovertibly excessive, the new rumors carried by our new neighbors from the west, whose cars now occupy slots made vacant by the decease, or flight, of the original parishioners. Yet, such wild and scary flights of fancy, engendered by the boredom that enforced inactivity produces, is our sole entertainment.

The traffic cannot budge because there is a war raging in Ireland, for example. Can't you hear the gunfire that keeps me, for one, wide awake all night, says a Ferrari that is now parked just behind the accountant's BMW.

Warfare that is intensifying, one would think, judging by those heavy nocturnal explosions that are enough to awaken the very dead! But if there is a war, who might the contending parties be? What are they fighting over?

Ancient prophecies, that The Citroën never heard tell of, are quoted extensively. To tell the truth, he only half-listens to the sensational products of such romantic inventiveness which, occasionally, have some entertainment value. The real truth is that he remains listening to such fanciful guff out of a lack of desire to return to the squalor of his own car.

A continuing thorn in his flesh is the emptiness of his petrol tank. The seemingly insoluble problem that must be faced is: how in the name of Jesus is he going to annul that lack. Didn't The Beamer say (or was it the Smilin' Porky? Even his memory is being unbalanced by the hunger) that petrol could be bought with a "service", whatever the fuck that really means. If he offered to perform a "service", then, surely he would be entitled to have his tank filled with petrol. If that is really the case, he says to himself, I must discuss that possibility forthwith with The Beamer.

He parts company, accordingly, with the bunch of habitual

loiterers that hang about the vicinity of the blue Peugeot. As he draws near The Beamer's car, however, he is beset by a sudden attack of dizziness and he falls to the ground. As he lies there, unable to rise, he fancies he hears the familiar blare of car horns in the distance, signaling that the traffic is about to move again.

He is now behind the steering wheel of his own car, but turning the key in the ignition produces only a dull click. Not only is his petrol tank as good as empty, but his battery seems to be as lifeless as those parishioners whose corpses lie in those shallow hastily-dug graves out there on the bog. Repeated efforts to get a spark out of the battery are rewarded only with a dull clunking sound. But get real, Mr. Citroen! Even if that lifeless battery could generate a single spark, there would hardly be enough petrol in the tank to produce anything more than a fleeting combustion. He sees the cars of the parish in front of him gliding away eastwards from him. And he hears the angry horn blasts and roaring of the drivers behind him.

Thus, he is reminded forcefully that he is parked in the way of God knows how many vehicles behind him whose drivers are hell-bent on joining the free-flowing east-bound traffic whose materialization signals the end of the Jam.

Release your fuckin' brakes, you bastard, screeches The Mullet, and we'll push you to one fuckin' side.

The Citroën does just that and The Mushroom Druids from the DAF, with their astonishingly creative repertoire of swear words, push his car over to the grass verge of the road, barely out of the way of oncoming traffic. Sitting there, he sees a long line of cars skim past him. Until the tail-end of the Jam is reached! He is alone now, sitting in a car without petrol or functioning battery, night falling, the occasional star winking into view, weak with the hunger. And not another human being, dog or any living thing in sight. A silvery frost mist covers the bog, like a magical blanket glittering under the light of the full moon.

When The Citroën awakes, he senses that the very marrow of his bones is frost-bound. It is night already. But, with a sense of relief, he notes that his own parish is still around him. He had been dreaming, then: a horrible nightmare in which his known universe was no more. He remembers, vaguely, that he was making for The Beamer's vehicle when he fainted from the hunger. Then he suddenly remembers the purpose that had impelled him to desert the company of his fellow parishioners.

Standing now, he stretches himself and yawns before continuing on his mission. It is now or never...

+++++

AS THE CITROËN ARRIVES AT THE BEAMER'S VEHICLE a stranger, identified to him by The Beamer as a representative of the Smilin' Porkys, is conversing in the back seat with the self-designated Parish Taoiseach. He sits in the front passenger seat. He explains his case: battery as dead as the dodo, petrol tank and wallet all but empty! He receives a patient and courteous hearing, even in his own estimation, from the Smilin' Porky.

I'm afraid that there is very little we can do for you right now, says the latter. Hundreds of men have offered their services to us; our list of names would stretch, exaggerating a little, from here to the end of this Jam. And most of them come to us with the same story of desperate privation as you yourself.

But The Citroën does have young women in his car, interjects The Beamer, addressing the Porky.

Ah, you should have told me before; that is another story altogether, says the Smilin' Porky. Women are always needed to look after children and old people, even to teach the surviving youngsters of school-going age. How many women are there in his car, he asks The Beamer.

Two, says The Beamer. One single woman and one married with a small child.

But, would they be willing to offer us their services? The Smilin' Porky addresses his question to The Citroën this time.

We have yet to discuss that question in our car!

Well, if that is how it is, Mr. Citroen, I would advise you to return to your car immediately and put the Smilin' Porky's question to your womenfolk there. Would they be willing to buy petrol this vey night with their services.

Exactly, says the Smilin' Porky. Come back to us as quickly as possible when you have the answer. There is only one service on offer tonight. I'm not saying that there aren't hundreds of women in this Jam who would take us up on that offer. But, given that this is my first visit to this Parish, let us say that I am in a position to dispense with the first-come-first-served obligation. You can tell your womenfolk that the service in question has to do with looking after two orphans whose mother died from the hunger a couple of weeks ago.

And don't forget to announce to them that our first order of pork will be arriving at lunch time tomorrow, said The Beamer.

And tell them also that the lady who performs that service for us tonight is guaranteed a fine pork meal with wine, adds the Smilin' Porky. Bring one of them back with you, if she is satisfied with our offer.

+++++

AS HE MAKES FOR HIS OWN CAR The Citroën notices that the DAF Mushroom Druids are lounging around outside their van. As is usual? Not quite! The difference this time, however, is that are fondling guns that resemble AK-47s- They look frightenly like the real thing. Both the Druids themselves and their female retinue are so equipped. Some of them carry these weapons slung over their shoulders. Others paw them lovingly, for all the world like children for whom Santa has just brought new toys.

The Mullet holds a Glock pistol in his right hand, its empty holster dangling from his belt. The smirk on the features of this lout resembles that of a precocious brat who has received a Christmas present that bests those of his playmates!

How in the hell did those thugs arm themselves with that dangerous hardware? Hardly from the Clooneen Garage shop they looted and destroyed! Here's hoping to the Gods, The Citroën prays, that they have no ammunition to go with their new toys!

This question is followed by another unconnected one: since no formal vote was taken by the Dáil on the matter of signing a contract with the Smilin' Porkys, whence the authority of The Beamer to sign such a contract?

Both questions take their place in the line behind the question that immediately matters: would either of the two women in his car be willing to look after those orphans mentioned by the Smilin' Porky rep. All in a good cause: putting some petrol in a well-nigh empty tank! So that The Citroën "household" will not be left behind, abandoned, when, and if, the traffic begins to move away from the shadow of that sinister chestnut tree.

When he reaches his own car, Ms. Cortina and Ms. Ford Escort are waiting there for him. He is struck once again by their pallid features and the fact that their clothes hang loosely from their bones.

Skeletons, for God's sake.

The Citroën finds it difficult to imagine that this is the same buxom young Ford Escort that he introduced himself, a seeming aeon ago, not a thousand miles from this spot, when they were both annoyed at this "temporary" traffic jam. The Cortina is reported as scavenging in the neighboring parishes, hoping that he can, miraculously, scrounge a crust somewhere or other. He'll be lucky: hundreds, if not thousands, are up to the same trick.

The Citroën explains the Porky's proposition, briefly,

to the two women. They listen to him carefully. Making up their minds!

All three are startled by a sudden burst of gunfire in the very environs of the Parish. Are they coming to kill us, Ms. Cortina asks anxiously. Hopefully not, says The Citroën; I think it's just that the Mushroom Druids are trying out some new toys they probably robbed somewhere recently. Or that Santa brought them! Probably having a bit of target practice! I had hoped they wouldn't have any ammunition. I'd better ask The Beamer later about how the hell this new twist to the life of the Parish happened.

Both of the ladies sounded for their willingness to look after orphans for the Smilin' Porkys give an immediate and positive response. Especially when they hear that a pork meal, with wine, is being offered for their services on top of the petrol coupons that will guarantee their vehicle's mobility when this traffic jam ends. And, of course, because they are both dying of hunger and thirst, as they say, their gaunt looks not giving the lie to this assertion. But which of them is to make the long journey to the east to take up the Smilin` Porky's offer?

Ms. Cortina gives to understand that such a duty would be, for her, a sort of psychological therapy. Looking after orphans might, who knows, help to lift that black despair and low self-esteem that has clouded her spirit since the recent death of her own child. Ms. Ford Escort, in a spirit of sympathy and female solidarity, agrees to stand down…

I'd love to go. But when I hear you say that, she says, I know that I haven't it in my heart to oppose you.

And, who knows, but maybe somebody over in those parts knows for certain whether Stacey is pregnant or not!

The Citroën wonders if this nonsense from the mouth of Ms. Cortina is not some sort of sick joke! Can it be that this floozy is serious? But, no! It seems that she does not see the black humor of this remark…

By the time he accompanies her, made up to the

nines, over to The Beamer's car her husband has not yet returned from his scavenging mission. She has doused herself generously with Ms. Ford Escort's perfume to conceal the natural perfume of a body that has probably not seen a drop of water since the Clooneen Jam began.

Although it is night, the surrounding bog and the bare limbs of the chestnut tree are bathed in the silvery light of a full moon. The armed Mushroom Druid band is nowhere to be seen. Can it be that its members are asleep?

Or have they decamped to some other parish in search of booty?

+++++

LET ME HAVE A GOOD LOOK AT YOU, says the Smilin' Porky, when The Citroën introduces her to him and The Beamer. She stands, pirouetting like a fashion model, in the light of The Beamer's car, the only car in the Parish to be still so equipped. The Porky's eyes sweep her body from head to toe, as he strokes his chin.

You'll do just fine, he says after the briefest of intervals. But let's get moving quickly. We've a long way to go! We'll leave her back here at the same time tomorrow evening, he tells The Beamer and The Citroën. And to Ms. Cortina: you must be proud that you are the first person from this Parish to offer us a service!

As soon as the Porky and Ms. Cortina are out of sight, The Citroën seizes the opportunity to ask The Beamer some direct questions. Why, for example, is the contract with the Smilin' Porkys a done deal, although it was never the subject of a vote?

The Beamer breathes a long sigh, before he answers.

Lookit, you are old enough to know that not every Tom, Dick or Harry knows what's best for the society of which they are a part. And the democratic process does not always yield decisions that are in the best interests of the public good. Indeed, it often gives a platform to windbags whose sole talent is to confuse the public with ridiculous fancies and plain irrelevancies. So that those who have a vocation for leadership, real leadership, must give precedence to this instinct, must strike out and do what they think is best for the society they lead.

In the case of our Parish, the way forward is clear. Parishioners are dying from hunger. The Smilin' Porkys have the resource, food, to defeat this famine. As always, this resource comes with a price tag, a fundamental law of human existence. It would be the height of irresponsibility for a public administrator like me, to allow crackpot rhetoric to stand between me and my clear duty, which is: to advance the general interest of the Parish. Remember also, that the Porkys wanted a quick, clear decision. We simply had no time to waste on a long drawn-out debate that was always bound to be fruitless.

I see! We could argue that question in the abstract, but I have now a very different and somewhat more concrete question for you, Taoiseach. How come that that DAF mob, the bloody Mushroom druids, is armed to the teeth?

That can be easily answered. The Smilin' Porkys made the arms available to them. I myself was a little perturbed at introducing arms into our Parish until the Porkys explained their rationale to me. They told me that it is their policy to arm every parish that enters into a food contract with them. Such parishes, just like ours, are surrounded by famine-stricken parishes that are increasingly resorting to violence in order to rob the food that is supplied by the Smilin' Porkys.

So that is why we sometimes hear gunfire and explosions at night?

There you have it, says The Beamer! He lets out another long sigh before continuing: Unfortunately, we do not live in the best of all possible worlds. And it is a fact of life that we will always have the weak and the strong with us. And that the strong will always trample shamelessly on the weak who neglect to counter them with adequate defense systems. My responsibilities lie with this Parish; for the parishes without who will be seeking to rob our food, I have not a single solitary responsibility. And, in the matter of arming ourselves to withstand the onslaught of the hungry hordes without, I have absolutely no scruples. Not a one!

But you know quite well that the Mushroom Druids are criminals. It was they who robbed and burned that petrol station at Clooneen in the early days of this long drawn-out Jam. What possessed you to let the Smilin' Porkys arm that mob, without so much as a squeak of protest from us

Now here, don't get the idea, Mr. Citroen, that I was solely responsible for that decision! You should know that there is a paragraph in the contract with the Porkys, signed by me on behalf of all of us, that gives them the right to arm whatever group of parishioners they see fit. We have an advisory role regarding that matter, but final decisions in that connection are made by the Porkys. Like yourself, I am not entirely happy with that state of affairs, but beggars cannot be choosers. And where would we ever get guns?

So, what you are really saying is that the Smilin' Porkys are our masters?

The Beamer lets out another long sigh before he answers.

Do you know what, Citroen! Sometimes you disappoint me greatly. That is the sort of guff I would expect to hear from the mouth of a Ms. Toyota Starlet, say. From the mouth of some *ingénue* who has yet to twig on to life's basic truths.

Basic truths?

Exactly! I think I told you before that the weak must accept the patronage of the strong these days or allow himself to be swept, as so much rubbish, off the face of the earth. That is a basic truth: the necessary dependence of the weak on the strong. I admit that I didn't pay very much attention, at first, to that paragraph in the Agreement. Nor to a lot of the small typeface print on the Contract, if it comes to that. But, looking at the bigger picture, if you seriously think that "negligence" shames me, then you really have another think coming...

But yet, you must know that the devil is in the detail, in that same small print?

Well, let me reiterate that one basic truth for you: the strong, in this case the Smilin' Porkys, have food, lots of it. And we, the weak, are dying from the hunger. The situation, if you don't mind me saying so, doesn't allow for rhetorical niceties. For it is they who hold the trump card in this game. Real bargaining never really occurs when the strong are dealing with the weak. The person who cannot understand that basic truth cannot understand life itself. Do I make myself fully clear?

If you don't like the conditions we have laid down, the Porkys said, there are many other hungry parishes in the Clooneen Jam. Where does that leave your niggling concerns about the small print? Apart from which, I have full confidence in the experience the Porkys have in dealing with military and other affairs in their dealings with other parishes. Your parishioner's fear of the DAF thugs we have armed is groundless, they told me. The food we provide them with regularly keeps them healthy and nourished. And as well disciplined as the Praetorian Guard.

+++++

WHEN THE CITROËN REACHES HIS OWN CAR he finds The Ford Escort sleeping in the back seat. The Cortina has yet to return from his wanderings, although it is long after midnight. So, for the first time in what seems like nine eternities, the lovers are now alone.

The Ford Escort wakes up as he enters the car. She asks him, sleepily, to come and sit in the back seat and hold her. As he does so, she drops her bombshell: the "great secret she has been carrying in her heart", as she phrases it. She is carrying his, The Citroën's child, in her womb. She had asked the VW Passat 1.9 to examine her, as she had felt that those morning nauseas she had been experiencing recently were more than just hunger pangs.

The Citroën is stunned momentarily. Yes, they had made love more than once! But how could this Ford Escort know that her being pregnant with his child was a physical impossibility. It is as if that dark secret that he never had the courage to reveal to Maura had come back to haunt him in this totally unexpected way. He doubted that he would have the courage to broach the matter with The Ford Escort under these trying circumstances. The Gaelic description of lived human life as "the way of lies" is now thrice underlined.

His treachery is visited on the traitor: a Gaelic proverb now murmured silently to himself by The Citroën.

A stranger's fetus in the womb of his true love is the cruel price he must pay.

Who was this stranger? The Beamer?

That proverb was never bested!

+++++

IF THIS PARISH LASTS LONG ENOUGH to develop its own folklore, myths and historical referents it is certain that today will be known to future generations as "Parochial Meat Day".

The exhausted famished appearance of the assembled parishioners waiting there for their ration of pork, alarms The Citroën. They remind him of of images of the Great Famine in the schoolbooks of his early schooldays. Skeletal women! Bearded spectral faces! With hardly the energy to raise their heads as a volley of shots rings out to the west of the Parish!

The Cortina is nowhere to be seen. He failed tp return last night from his wanderings. Did he manage to find a place in this Clooneen Jam where food is more readily available than in The Parish? Could it be that taking to his heels would afford him a better chance of surviving this extended tragedy?

He thinks again of The Skoda Bishop, of his clerical assistant (if, indeed he/she was a cleric), of The Cherokee 1.4 Italian, of The Renault 4 Ponytail and of many others who abandoned this accursed Jam. People who were never seen again! And without any explanations for their disappearances other than the speculative flights of fancy parishioners indulge themselves in order to blind themselves temporarily to the squalid details of their circumstances.

The VW Passat 1.9 Doctor is speaking now to the parishioners, who are clustered, as usual, near the blue Peugeot:

Remember: this is going to be your first full meal for some time now. You'll all tend, at first, to eat too much pork, he warns. But, believe me, if you gorge yourselves on it, you'll only succeed in making yourselves as sick as dogs. Your digestive systems are not accustomed to such an intake of rich food. I advise you to drink the soup at first. That will accustom your innards to the quality of the food you are about to eat. But take it easy after that! Only a small quantity of meat should be eaten on the first day, no matter how big, and how tempting, your plate looks. I implore you not to go beyond a few morsels, no matter what the temptation. A good tip is to eat only sufficient to take the edge off your hunger.

Put the remainder in your pockets to eat later when you feel hunger coming on. It is a pity that we won't have vegetables and potatoes along with the meat; a balanced meal would be preferable to a feast of just meat alone. But that is how it is. Beggars can't be choosers. Let us make the best of what we will have!

This should be a joyful occasion, one would think. But joy involves expenditure of energy, a commodity in which the ragged pallid crowd listening to the doctor is notably lacking. The armed Mushroom Druid mob is on sentry duty on the Parish borders. To repel any attempt on the part of the starvelings without, who attracted by the aroma of pork, might be tempted to invade our precincts!

+++++

THE PORKY'S WHITE VAN ARRIVES at last. Its sides displaying the characteristic Smilin' Porkys' logo: a dancing smiling pig on a blue background, his head encircled by a halo of stars. The staff that came with the van, readily identifiable as such by their clean-shaven faces, quickly open its back doors and proceed briskly to distribute tin mugs and plates to the expectant diners. They then remove a foldable table from the back of the van and place on it what looks like a tall metal milk churn.

We are going to serve you soup, at first, shouts one of the Porky operatives, a short rotund individual topped by a large chef's hat. The Citroën is unable to relate his accent to that of any particular nationality. Just a sort of universal European! The Beamer stands beside him, his features creased by a self-satisfied grin.

Porky, he of the dark blue spectacles, who is now known in the Parish by that name, and now wearing a dapper grey suit, and standing beside the "chef" now proceeds to address the multitude, assembled before him in the hope that they are about to participate in this contemporary variant of the miracle of the loaves and fishes:

We of the Smilin' Porkys are both pleased and honored that the good people of this Parish have opted to sign a comprehensive nutritional agreement with us. I would ask you all to stand in an orderly line, women and children to the front. And then come here (indicating the churn), one by one, extending your mugs in order to receive your soup. We will move anyone we detect skipping their place to the back of the line. Just for today! In the future, any body who tries to skip his, or her, place in the line will be automatically disqualified from further meals. We must ensure an orderly distribution of our products so that nobody from this Parish goes away from here hungry. When you have drunk your soup, please bring with you the plates we have issued you with and form a new line, as orderly as the previous one, and we will serve you the meat. We have a pork stew for you today, which our dedicated chefs have prepared and which I am sure you will enjoy. But, please, we do ask you for your co-operation, which will make possible the orderly distribution of our delicacies and which would be to our mutual advantage. In the meantime, as the French say, *Bon Appétit!*

The Citroën thinks. Apart from the courteous gloss put on the proceedings by Porky, the present scenario is basically a throwback to the days of the Great Hunger, as the starving peasantry lined up in the Poorhouse for thin gruel to be ladled into their empty bowls.

+++++

HAVING GULPED DOWN THEIR SOUP, the morale of the parishioners improves notably. What was, up to now merely words will now shortly be made flesh. Pork, to be exact! Praise for the tastiness and richness of the soup is heard on all sides. A great "pick-me-up" is the judgment of the green Hyundai, a new car in the parish. The arrival of the meat, however, moves the praise index up a couple of notches. Large pieces of beautifully cooked meat, accompanied by a thin gravy or soup, draws ecstatic responses from the parishioners. For people whose enjoyment of meat is a distant memory, this is nothing less than a regal banquet.

As The Morris Minor Veteran proclaims, through belches: I could be totally wrong, it's so long since I enjoyed a steak or a chop or any other sort of meat! But, in all fairness, this bit of pork is the best meat I have ever tasted in my life. The chorus of voices around him indicates that he is not alone in his judgment. Never ate better! No less than *cuisine de luxe*, me oul' segotioner! These are two among the many positive comments regarding the pork stew heard by

The Citroën from the mouths of these guests of the Smilin' Porkys.

The SUV Yuppie claims that this pork is better than any other pork he has tasted in his whole life up to now. In fact, he wonders if it is really pork. Its taste is more or less the same as pork, but not the consistency. It is certainly neither beef nor mutton. Could it possibly be deer?

Having delivered himself of such notions, he belches loudly. This followed by a gale of belches from the diners. And a gale of laughter after that. The debate about the nature of the meat continues:

Still, although its tastiness is undeniable, I maintain that it is still not pork. It has a certain gamey taste that the pig fed on animal food lacks, opines The BMW Accountant.

There is every possibility that people like us, whose taste buds have grown unaccustomed to meat, are no longer able to discriminate between the different kinds of meat to which people are ordinarily accustomed, says the VW Passat 1.9 doctor, who is The Beamer's banquet guest.

Why don't we ask Porky himself? He is sitting over there, reading a book, in The Beamer's car.

The SUV Yuppie stands up and, goaded by curiosity (his *haute cuisine* pretensions being well known in the Parish), walks over to where the Porky is sitting.

As he does so, The Fiat 1100 Dub agrees that, although the meat is, admittedly, first class, he would like to know, exactly, what services are going to be demanded in order to pay for it. There's no such bleedin' thing as a free lunch, he says.

Nobody listens to him.

The SUV Yuppie returns shortly, a self-satisfied smirk on his face.

I wasn't far off the mark, he gloats. Porky explained to me over yonder that these pigs were not pigs fattened with the conventional fare—pig nuts, and such like—that are used to fatten your common or garden pig in Ireland. The meat we are eating is gourmet pork that comes from free-range pigs who forage for themselves in woodlands. Their diet is supplemented by truffles and acorns, he told me. This natural feeding affects both the taste and consistency of the meat, which is akin to that of the wild boar. Therefore, there is a high demand for this gourmet pork in Dublin's most exclusive restaurants and hotels.

Having delivered that short lecture, The SUV Yuppie receives a round of hearty applause from the assembled diners.

+++++

AS THEIR STOMACHS FILL WITH PORK the parishioners become increasingly lively. Exhibiting an energy they have not expressed The Citroën is delighted to note the return of a trace of red to the pallid cheeks of The Ford Escort, that treacherous lady with whom he is in love, in spite of her infidelity, on her journey along this "way of lies". But who is he to speak thus? Sitting down beside her on the grass verge of the motorway, he understands all too clearly that there is nothing left of his life with Maura, not to mention Anna, but some rapidly fading images, the broken shards of dreams—or nightmares—whose promise could never be fulfilled.

Which are you hoping for, a boy or a girl? he asks. Diffidently! Why, in the first place, would he bother asking her such a question? What way has he of knowing whether the fetus growing in The Ford Escort's womb is, or is not, the result of a careless dalliance with The Beamer? In any case, this bounty of the Porkys cannot last for ever. And, after all, if hunger returns to haunt the Parish, a miscarriage is the most likely outcome of this unwanted pregnancy.

She glances shyly at him out of the corner of her eye as she answers him:

A fine healthy baby, without any defects, is all I want, darling, she answers. Full stop! That is, if we ever manage to escape from this damn Clooneen Jam. A boy or a girl? Why should I really don't care which! Only that, he or she, whichever the baby turns out to be, is recognizably yours!

Recognizably mine!

How much longer will I have to endure this pantomime? The Citroën asks himself. Only that, he or she, whichever the baby turns out to be, is recognizably mine! Yet another comic note added to life's tragic symphony!

And if the choice were yours? The Ford Escort asks.

It is all the same to me, love. I'll just go with the flow of life's symphony!

+++++

PLATES ARE NOW BEING GREEDILY LICKED by many of the parishioners. Hardly a single soul pays any attention to the doctor's advice not to overeat. They'll pay for this heedlessness later, thinks The Citroën. He places a portion of the meat, partly dried by licking it with his tongue, in his pocket. The Ford Escort will be bound to be ravenous later. No harm in having a tasty tidbit with which to feed her!

As the licking and scraping of plates abates, The BMW Accountant, stands up and clears his throat before addressing the Smilin' Porkys and the assembled guests:

I know that I am speaking on behalf of everybody here, he says, when I propose a vote of thanks to the distinguished representatives of the Smilin' Porkys who are here with us. (*A loud "Hear, hear!" and the occasional belch bursts spontaneously from the parishioners*). But for the fact that you so kindly came to our rescue, when our need was the greatest, God alone knows where we would be today. In fact, but for your generous aid, I am afraid that we were fated to die miserably in this desolate place far from kith and kin. Indeed, some of our dear friends and neighbors have already passed away from this vale of tears. Would that they had been here with us on this joyous occasion! May the good Lord have mercy on their souls (*a massed "Amen" from the parishioners.*) Therefore, my heartfelt thanks—and not only from my heart—for the loving and neighborly way you

Porkys have helped the Parish to survive its worst days. You have, with your generosity, helped us to draw back from the very mouth of the grave! A thousand, thousand, thousand thanks!

I would like to formally second this vote of this vote of thanks, says The Beamer. A raucous cheer bursts from the parishioners, interspersed with shouts of "good man yerself". "Fair play to you" and "no better man"! And then, they shout, addressing the Porky, still sitting in The Beamers car: speech, speech!

As if awaiting his cue, Porky leaves the car, walks over to the assembled parishioners and raises his hand to call for silence. From the liveliness of their present behavior, an observer might conclude that his audience was drunk. Drunk on pork, who would ever have believed it! They gradually quieted down. When the Porky is satisfied that he has their full attention, he begins his speech:

I am delighted to be here in your midst on this historic occasion. I have always heard that nothing can beat a real Irish welcome—a hundred thousand welcomes is how you express it, I gather—and that is surely what you are giving to me here. I am more than honored. A long life to you all! (*loud applause*). And now I would like to mention a few points that are of some importance to all of us.

Since our mutual agreement has been signed here by your Taoiseach (he glances over his shoulder at a smiling self-satisfied Taoiseach), I am happy to announce that today's meal, tomorrow's meal and the meal of the day after are yours, free gratis, with the compliments of the Smilin' Porkys.

The Beamer starts to clap his hands and the assembled guests follow his example. The Citroën notices however that neither The Fiat 1100 Dub nor Ms. Toyota Starlet join in this almost general applause. Are they asking the same questions of themselves as those of The Citroën? Free meat for three days promised by the Porky, when The Beamer had announced that the Parish would be receiving one week's free supply of pork! He himself, by moving his arms and hands, simulates the action of clapping without bringing his hands together. This silent action of revolt is perceived by nobody, thanks to the noise of the handclapping around him. The Saab looks sharply at him, but seems to detect nothing.

The Porky raises his hand again to silence the applause and bring the proceedings to a close.

My thanks to you all, dear people, he says. And a thousand thanks. Please, there is no need for all this applause, he says, in what could be a slightly irritated tone of voice. The assembly quiets down gradually and, eventually, the Porky gets his opportunity to speak without interruption:

I have to tell you now that, once these three days of grace are over and have become a part of history, it will be incumbent on all of you to pay for your food. Your Taoiseach here tells me that he has explained all of that in detail to you, so I need not repeat what he has told you. Therefore, I would advise you now to assemble all those items that we regard as valid currency, money, watches, jewels, gold items, so as to have them ready when the time comes to pay. It was probably explained to you also that we accept petrol, which we can siphon from your vehicles as payment. As I am reliably informed that little of that commodity remains in your beloved Parish, you have been informed that there exists an alternative method of payment, namely, the performance of a service that will be specified by us Smilin' Porkys.

I just wanted to remind you of these details before asking you to return all the mugs and plates to us before we leave. The cook, wearing a white coat, will accept them at the rear door of our van and will carefully count the eating utensils as you return them. A word of warning! The number of items you return to us must correspond exactly to the number of meals supplied. A single item missing means a single meal less for your Parish tomorrow. I hope that that point is clearly understood.

So, tomorrow you will have soup, together with black

and white puddings. Free of charge, as I have said, dear friends.

With these honeyed words resounding in their ear, the parishioners produce a long burst of spontaneous applause. Which continues long after the white van of the Smilin' Porkys disappears from sight…

+++++

WE HAVE JUST BOUGHT A PIG IN A POKE says The Fiat 1100 Dub to Ms. Toyota Starlet. But to celebrate such an insane step? I often wonder whether our fellow parishioners are fuckin' naïve! Or just plain bonkers?

Do you remember Alice Glenn, that grand ould TD in the old days? asks Ms. Toyota Starlet.

Refresh my memory, answers The Fiat 1100 Dub.

Well, she was the one who compared gobhaws who vote to do themselves harm to turkeys voting for Christmas…

+++++

WHEN THE CITROËN AND THE FORD ESCORT reach their car, Ms. Cortina is installed therein before them. She is laughingly good-humored, her pork meal obviously agreeing pleasantly with her.

The Citroën was just about to inform her of the disappearance of her husband, but stalled himself just in time. Such unpleasant reports are best left until later. He notes that the residual foul smell of the car, part of the legacy of the unfortunate Master Cortina, has been almost eclipsed by the strong perfume that is now being worn by his mother. It is probably a memento of her service with the Porkys.

Did you find out over there if Stacey is pregnant? The Citroën asks Ms. Cortina, who fails completely to note the undercurrent of sarcasm in his question.

I wish I was able to tell you, but unfortunately I'm just as wise now as before I left, she says. I asked the Smilin' Porkys, of course, but they didn't seem to know what the hell I was talking about. To tell you the God's honest truth, they seemed not to be able to understand the half of what I was saying. In any case, they just looked as me like donkeys when I asked them the question.

And why was that, do you think? asks the Ford Escort.

Well, unlike you and me, these Smilin' Porkys are non-nationals. They were muttering some language among themselves that I couldn't make head nor tail of. German or French or Polish. Some gibberish like that!

How did you manage with the orphans? asks The Ford Escort.

Well, when I reached their base, they told me they had already got somebody else to look after the creatures. So, they told me that they'd have to find some sort of alternative service for me to perform…

Which was?

The pallid features of Ms. Cortina are illuminated by a sudden blush. She hesitates before answering;

Oh, another type of service altogether! But, I'd rather not talk about it now. But, in any case, when I had performed my service for them they gave me your petrol coupons.

And she hands what look like big stamps over to The Citroën. He looks quizzically at The Ford Escort as he accepts them. He then scrutinizes the stamps. They show the face of a pig, smiling from ear to ear, over which is printed the words *"Ein Liter Benzin"* on each of the stamps.

So, you won't tell us what you did to earn those stamps, says The Ford Escort.

Lookit! All I need to tell you, love, is that they treated me well. They gave me a beautiful meal, all the pork I could eat, the best pork I have ever eaten, and Hungarian wine to wash it down, after my service was completed. The Smilin' Porkys said they would be happy to have me any time in the future. They gave me a bottle of perfume when I was leaving. They told me it was from their own country.

The Citroën and The Ford Escort exchange a long

look. But they say nothing.

I was going to ask you for a favor, says Ms. Cortina. At home or in the car, I always listened to Josie Thornton. Every morning without fail. Like all the rest of the country! I don't exaggerate when I say that Josie and Stacey are just like members of the family. Did I ever tell you that before? Like a brother and sister! And I miss them, just like I'd miss my own flesh and blood, you know what I mean. Now, if you'd just turn the radio on, I'm certain I'd get to hear his voice. It'd mean so much to me. Would you mind doing that for me?

The Citroën groans inwardly. The thought of hearing once again the interminable inane patter of Thornton would be bad enough. Not to mention the waste of valuable electricity on such senseless babble. Fighting against his will, he presses the radio button. The response to this act is instantaneous:

You know, or should know, that this program welcomes free and open discussion of questions that were taboo up to now in Ireland. No hot potato is too hot for Josie Thornton. We want our Morning Show to be the breath of fresh air that is needed to sweep out all that stale air that has stifled free debate for far too long in the dark and fetid corners of Mother Ireland's kitchen. Fresh light on dark corners, as the fella says. For far too long, the women of Ireland have been smothering under a pile of meaningless superstitions that have no basis in fact.

And let you all of you listeners out there who are listening to me, the women of Ireland, realize that the Josie Thornton that Sheila is talking to is a married man. Yes sirree! Your sympathetic host for whom tits, breasts and other private parts not usually given an outing over the air waves, are far from being a mystery. Things that are as natural as... Are you still on the line, Sheila?

Why wouldn't I be Josie! In all fairness...

Fair play to you, Sheila! The beauty queen of Glenawney is still with us.

The Citroën and The Ford Escort listen to this patter

for as long as The Citroën can stand it.

I think we have heard all of that guff before, he says roughly, as he turns the radio off. And more than once! Seems the air waves are jammed just like the motorways.

Once again, Ms. Cortina fails to detect the sarcasm in The Citroën's voice.

Well, I could listen to him all day, she says. What he says doesn't really matter to me. What I love is the sound of Josie's voice. And with the sound of that voice in your ear, you'd imagine that things were normal again. Instead of being like we are here now, waiting for the next blow to fall...

+++++

THE CITROËN IS ABOUT TO RESPOND SHARPLY to Ms. Cortina's musings regarding Josie fuckin' Thornton, his blather, psycho-babble and other works and pomps, when he detects a light tapping on the window beside him. The Saab, The Beamer's right hand man, is standing outside. He lowers the window.

The Taoiseach would like to see you, he says, as soon as possible.

The Citroën descends from his car and makes for The Beamer's, accompanied by The Saab, as silent as usual. It is a clear crisp night, the Milky Way above stretching like a silent starry mist from horizon to horizon. Moonlight sparkles on the metal roofs of vehicles, the lines of which stretch eastwards until they are lost in darkness. He has no time, however, to enjoy the beauty of a night whose beauty hides so much suffering.

He greets The Beamer, who is pacing impatiently up and down on the south-facing side of his car.

You wanted to see me urgently?

The Beamer removes a lighted cigarette from his mouth. Throws it on the ground and stamps on it before speaking! (A quiet question The Citroën asks himself: where does the Taoiseach get all his cigarettes when a tobacco famine, as The Mitsubishi Lancer Giant calls it, has been raging for a long time now throughout the entire Clooneen Jam?)

I have an urgent matter to discuss with you, says The Beamer. The Smilin' Porkys communicated a message to me a short while ago. According to them, an old woman in their parish is quite ill. And they need a woman from our Parish to look after her. Seems to me that the ideal woman for the job would be your Ford Escort. I would be beholden to you if you would encourage her to prepare herself to make the journey to the east. And to get herself ready as soon as possible!

Suppose she doesn't want to make this journey at this hour of night?

Tell her that she has no choice in the matter. You have got to understand that this emergency cancels the free will of us Jam folk. The imperative is the form of the verb to which we, as we circle about in the orbit of the Smilin' Porkys, will have to become accustomed from now on out. Therefore, go and tell her that she must be here within 20 minutes. The Saab will take her as far as the parish where the Porkys have their base. He has a great sense of direction. That Saab could, by now, find his way to that base blindfolded.

Persuading The Ford Escort to obey the Porky's bidding and journey with The Saab through alien parishes is easier than The Citroën thought. The spirit of adventure and a strong desire to change her surroundings, even temporarily, fires a suppressed spirit of adventure that lies dormant beneath the dreadful sameness of the Jam days. So he didn't need to explain to her that the sovereignty of the Parish had been sold for a mess of pork.

Enjoy your service, love, says Ms. Cortina, as The Ford Escort gets ready to leave. With a low suggestive laugh accompanying this pleasantry.

The Ford Escort, together with The Citroën, present themselves at the door of The Beamer's vehicle, within 15 minutes of the issuing of the latter's order.

There is a possibility that you may be needed over there for a couple of days, remarks The Beamer. But never fear! The Porkys assure me that they will feed you well. They were highly satisfied with the previous woman we sent over to them. Ms. Cortina, wasn't it? They'll certainly be requesting her again. And if you hear any rumor or news over there, that might be of use to us in the Parish, please don't hesitate to let me know.

The eyes of The Citroën follow her shape as she and The Saab walk eastwards, away from him. The woman who is carrying child. The woman who thinks that he, The Citroën, thinks that the child is his. The woman who is fated to be his companion until either, or both of them, merges with the graveyard clay.

The couple are swallowed up by the darkness of Clooneen. He turns on his heel and returns to his car.

+++++

I THOUGHT YOU'D NEVER SHOW UP, says Ms. Cortina, as The Citroën eases himself into the driver's seat. She herself reclines on the rear seat. The sweet heavy scent of the perfume she is wearing surprises him. The sort of aroma he imagines to be more appropriate to a Mid-Eastern harem than to the interior of a vehicle stranded in the Clooneen Jam.

Now that we are by ourselves, why don't you sit back here with me. To keep me company and to keep me warm! You don't have to be afraid of me. And no-one will see us here!

Do you know that I have my eye on you ever since that day you asked me a question, all innocent like, about *Cougars?* Letting on that you had never heard of Stacey and the girls, if you remember! That was very funny. You nearly took me in, but I like men with a sense of humor.

And, to tell you God's honest truth, you always remind me of Doug, Stacey's favorite lover. I'm not joking; you are the spitting image of Doug. And you letting on that you had never heard of Stacey! But you didn't pull the wool over my eyes. I'd say that you are just as gamey as the Smilin' Porkys, even. Do you like the perfume they gave me!

The death of her child and the fact that her husband has gone missing have driven this woman around the bend, says The

Citroën to himself.

I know the way you feel, he says. Without moving from his seat.

My God! Aren't you the shy one, she says. Come over here, Doug! Stacey wants to play with you. Let's break the ice into teeny little bits!

What sort of "play" have you in mind? asks The Citroën.

Cougars!

Cougars?

There you have it, darling. I am Stacey. You are Doug. And the pair of us are attending a course in the Beverley Hills Ashram.

Just make yourself comfortable!

+++++

AN EXPLOSIVE CRACKLE OF GUNFIRE awakens The Citroën and Ms. Cortina this morning. Bursts being fired from AK-47s, accompanied by shouting and screaming. As they rub the sleep from their eyes, and wipe the condensation from the windshield, they can see more clearly what is happening. A sight that fills them with horror.

For, they are just in time to see Ms. Toyota Starlet and The Fiat 1100 Dub, blindfolded, their mouths taped shut and their hands tied behind their backs with wire, being frog-marched eastwards. An armed group of Mushroom Druids escort them to...where?

Instinctively, The Citroën alights from his car and runs after the group.

What the hell are you people up to, he shouts. Let these people go immediately. You have no authority to arrest them.

You shut your fuckin' mouth, you fuckin' bastard, shouts The Mullet, or our mots'll have your guts for garters. And he points his Glock pistol directly at The Citroën.

Tell the fucker to ask The Beamer, if he's asking about what fuckin' authority we have, says another Druid, fondling an

UZI submachine gun. That'll fuckin' cure his fuckin' curiosity!

The Mullet startles The Citroën by emitting a savage whoop and firing a shot into the air. Now, if you don't fuck off outa here, the next bullet is for you. His fellow druids find that remark hilariously funny.

That'll set the shit shakin' inside him, says one of the Valkyries, with an AK-47 slung over her shoulder.

There is renewed laughter, before this sinister party, with its bound captives, continues on its trek eastwards.

The Citroën understands that there is not a thing he can do against such a heavily-armed band. He is left alone on the road, staring after them until the Parish's "security force", along with its prisoners, disappears from sight.

Cowed parishioners emerge gradually from their cars.

A new parishioner, the Hyundai, an agricultural instructor from Carlow, according to himself, asks: does anyone here have any control over that mob from the DAF, the ones you call The Mushroom Druids? The only person who has some kind of hold over those hooligan, says The Citroën, appears to be The Beamer.

If that is the case, then he should come here immediately to explain what is happening. If he doesn't exercise this supposed authority of his immediately, I'd fear for the lives of The Fiat 1100 Dub and Ms. Toyota Starlet.

I'll notify him immediately, says The Saab, who has been listening to all that has been said, without expressing any opinion himself. However, there is no need for him to call the Parish Taoiseach, for The Beamer himself now walks from his car to the usual meeting place near the blue Peugeot.

There is absolutely no cause for worry, he assures the shocked parishioners. The faint relaxed smile he permits himself indicates that he himself is not worried, as if inviting others to share his relaxed view of the latest turn of events.

I admit that our security force could have exercised a little more delicacy in the difficult situation in which they found themselves. But when over-enthusiasm is allied to lack of experience...I think you can understand what I mean! I'll give them a talking-to a little later on. But, let me explain the context of this morning's arrests to you in more detail. As you will plainly see, you have absolutely no cause for worry. The story is not all that complex!

As part of my responsibilities, under the terms of our contract with the Smilin' Porkys, I have to compile and send a regular report to the contractor. This I do, scrupulously.

To avoid misunderstanding, let me say clearly at this point, that I was in conscience bound to explain to the Porkys that Ms. Toyota Starlet and The Fiat 1100 Dub disagreed with certain articles of the contract. I specified, based on their contributions, the nature of their disagreements (which you were all witness to), in particular as related to the question of "service".

And, although I explained to you all the precise, though flexible, meaning the Porkys attach to the word "service", the pair in question were still not satisfied. Acceptance of this contract was equivalent, according to them—and you all heard them say it—"buying a pig in a poke". Their own description, mark you!

Has anybody any question about what I have said so far?

The gloomy silence of the parishioners is his answer. Somewhere in the distance a crow caws.

The Citroën has never seen the fine print of this contract, or treaty, with the Porkys. Nor has anybody else, except The BMW Accountant, it is rumored. Does such a document exist? Or, are provisions being composed, *a la carta*, by the Porkys? He is on the point of asking a few pointed questions, but—with the way the wind appears to be blowing these days—he decides that discretion is the better part of valor. How often clever words have harvested broken teeth! Or worse!

The Beamer is in full flight, once again.

Therefore, you can imagine my surprise this morning at receiving this missive from the Porkys. Ordering me to send The Fiat 1100 Dub and Ms. Toyota Starlet over to them, so that they, the Porkys, could teach them the precise meaning of the word "service"! Re-education, they call this process.

But when I sent The Saab to these parties to inform them that they were required to accompany him to the Porky's base of operations, both of them refused point blank to do so. A refusal coming, no less, from people who enjoyed Porky hospitality yesterday without a murmur. Leaving me with no other option than to have recourse to our security force to ensure that the Parish honored it obligations!

To be clear about all of this, I would like now to draw your attention to Article 187 of our contract. It states that the supply of meat to a contracted party shall cease immediately when a summons issued by the Smilin' Porky authority is ignored. I think all of you can now understand the grave implications for our parish if the two parishioners I have named refused to obey that summons. It would be, literally, a question of life or death for us all.

Therefore I think you can all understand now why I had no other option but to call upon our security force to detain the two culprits and bring them to the Smilin' Porkys. I am very sorry that neither of them was willing, peacefully, to put the interest of the Parish before their own selfish prejudices.

+++++

THE SILENCE THAT FOLLOWS THE TAOISEACH'S speech is rent by a sudden burst of gunfire nearby. Upwards of six shots! And then, after a short interval of a few seconds, two more shots. The unexpected intrusion of the sounds of violence startles the assembly. People look quizzically at each other. Their eyes reflect fearfully the same question that arises spontaneously in The Citroën's mind. Were the two shots in that final volley the sound of a *coup de grace* being administered to the Parish dissidents, Ms. Toyota Starlet and The Fiat 1100 Dub?

He imagines the brutal satisfaction of The Mullet at such an outcome of these early morning arrests. A gentleman who desires nothing more than an opportunity to test the effectiveness of his Glock pistol on a human target!

No-one dares to question the "security force" when they return to the Parish environs a little later. The Citroën observes their self-satisfied arrogant swagger. Their guns, cradled in their arms, an unspoken threat to all.

They make immediately for the Fiat 1100, and smash in its windows with their rifle butts. The Mullet brings a can of petrol from the DAF, and pours it on the ground under that empty vehicle. The Queen of the Valkyries, a fearsome creature with an impressive display of nose, lip and ear rings, casts a lighted cigarette butt on to the petrol. The Mushroom Druids emit a long barbaric howl when a small explosion is heard as the Fiat 1100 takes fire. *Whoomph!* Suddenly the car is totally ablaze, and billows of choking thick black smoke waft through the Parish

The Toyota Starlet is given the same treatment. But, not before the youthful driver of that car and his elderly father are forced to run the gauntlet of the rifle butts of the Mushroom Druids, an experience that leaves them bloodied and vowing revenge.

The Druids desist finally from their violent rampage later when The Beamer arrives on the scene, and orders them quietly to retire to the DAF. The Citroën draws his own lesson from these incidents. It occurs to him that all other spectators of this gratuitous pyromania must have drawn the same conclusions as he has from the grim events of the day.

But have they?

+++++

WHEN HE RETURNS TO HIS OWN CAR, Ms. Cortina is there waiting for him. Her ear glued to *Josie Thornton's Morning Show*. The faux-Yankee *Meditate Your Fat Away* lady expounds her nonsense for the umpteenth time. Ms. Cortina turns off the radio as soon as The Citroën appears on the scene. She explains, with a guilty look, to him that she only turned on the radio to see if they'd say anything about Stacey and that lady's possible pregnancy.

More's the pity that The Ford Escort is absent, says The Citroën to himself. At least, one could rationally discuss the disturbing events of the morning with a person of her ilk. But this brain-dead zombie lives her whole fucking life inside the vacuity of some trivial soap opera. She'll exhaust the little that is left of power in the battery with her fucking *Morning Show* obsession. Just as she exhausted the battery of her own Cortina, which is now rusting away on the verge of the motorway somewhere to the east of here. How do I break this communication logjam?

Well, what did you think of the morning's events?

To be honest with you, and in all fairness, I hadn't a fuckin' clue about the half of what The Beamer was going on about! All those posh words! But he was dead right. When you think of the insult that pair gave to the Smilin' Porkys, and they doin' their level best to help us! But for their pork, we'd all be fuckin' dead, you know what I mean, Doug. But to be honest with you, *Josie Thornton's Morning Show* is much more fun than all this fuckin' boring Jam talk. That's where you'll find people's—especially women's—real problems discussed openly and honestly. Self-esteem problems! That sort of thing!

And you don't think that the problems that beset us here, how we're stuck in this god-awful Clooneen Jam, for example, are really "real" for you? Life or death are what are at stake here, after all…

Ah, there you go again, always tryin' to take the mickey outa me!

+++++

THE RUCTION OUTSIDE—doors opening, shouting—give The Citroën and Ms. Cortina to understand that the soup and pork chops, supplied by the Smilin' Porkys, will shortly be distributed again to the famished inhabitants of the Parish.

As he and Ms. Cortina head for the Dáil assembly area, where the food is to be distributed, The Beamer beckons to The Citroën.

Come over here for a second or two, he says, I have a few things to discuss with you. You can go on ahead, he says to Ms. Cortina.

Things that have to do with the services demanded by the Porkys?

The Beamer looks sharply at The Citroën before he answers.

More or less. In fact your guess is correct, one hundred per cent. Congratulations. But, for starters, The Ford Escort sends a message to you to say that she plans to stay a few more days to fully complete her service to the Smilin' Porkys. She asks you to be patient with her.

Okay! I get that! But you gave me to understand that the Porkys have some business with me?

Exactly. I received a message from them this morning. Unfortunately, the Fiat 1100 Dub had an accident. He is so indisposed that he is unable to perform the service that the Porkys demand of him. They need another man to take his place. And you are the man best qualified to do just that.

What sort of service are they asking for?

A service which, if performed, will fill you tank with petrol and your belly with prime pork!

But, what do I have to do?

That is something I am not authorized to tell you. Suffice it to say that I am convinced that your journalistic background has something to do with the service. My friend, The Saab, will be your guide, when you have eaten this meal. He could, by now, lead you blindfolded to the Porky's base of operations.

And, supposing I didn't want to commit myself to such a service? The Citroën is thinking of The Fiat 1100 Dub's "accident" and the terrifying events of earlier in the day. And of those two dull pistol reports that followed that burst of rifle fire.

The Mullet happens to be passing by just then, the Glock pistol dangling from his hand, an AK-47 slung over his shoulder. The two of them, The Citroën and The Beamer, observe this phenomenon. Then they look at each other. The Beamer shrugs his shoulders.

You're no fool, says The Beamer. And you probably realize by now that this game is bigger than either of us. And I would hope that you have the good sense to take the road I am suggesting to you.

He shrugs his shoulders again, allowing a short interval to let the impact of his words to sink into The Citroën's brain.

The Saab will be waiting for you when you finish this meal. But hurry up, or all of the meat will have been distributed by the Porkys.

+++++

THE CITROËN STANDS AT FIRST in the soup line. His thoughts are in a whirl. What should he do? Not allow himself to be guided eastwards by The Saab? To ignore the summons of the Porkys? The echoes of the shots he heard earlier are still bouncing around in his skull. And the voice of The Ford Escort! As if she were saying: for God's sake, love, don't go near the den of the Porkys! A strange nightmare, and he fully awake, his consciousness as clear as a bell.

A mug of soup is extended towards him. He grasps it mechanically and takes a sip of it as he moves towards the grass verge of the motorway. The rich meaty taste of the soup reminds him of what used to be on offer in those banquets in the times of yore before the Clooneen Jam initiated a sequence of events that seem to be drifting to their conclusion with the clear inevitability of a Greek tragedy.

Ms. Cortina is sitting on the grass some distance from him. He would prefer to enjoy his soup without the company of that vacuous ninny, but she has already caught his eye.

More blather about Stacey and her fuckin' pregnancy will interfere with his internal deliberations regarding the mortal danger he now believes himself to be in. She appears to be excited. He walks slowly towards her and sits down beside her.

Well?

There's something weird here in my soup I want to show you!

What do you mean weird?

Come here till you see it. It looks like a piece of skin in the bottom of my mug. I almost ate it. There's some sort of pattern on it that I think I've seen somewhere before. But I don't know quite where. What do you think it is?

Let me see it, says The Citroën.

She passes the mug over to him.

What The Citroën sees in that mug, that Celtic design, *a la* The Book of Kells, sets the faces of Ms. Toyota Starlet, The Fiat 1100 Dub, The Renault 4 Ponytail, The Cherokee 1.4 Italian, The Skoda Bishop and his companion, The Cortina and many others swirling around in a hellish bloody whirlpool constructed for their own benefit by the Smilin' Porkys. And now, good God above, please don't tell me that even my Ford Escort has been sucked into that bloody maelstrom.

> *Tattoo on a strip of white skin:*
> *Design, wrought by monkish hands,*
> *I once kissed so lovingly*
> *Tell me now, O God*
> *who hath hidden Thy Face from man*
> *That this is the stuff of nightmare*
> *From which I will soon awaken*

+++++

With this verse The Citroën's account of the Clooneen Jam comes to a sudden end. We have no idea why the chronicler brought it to a close at this point, if indeed he did so, unless overcome by personal distress. Various scholars have offered their opinions regarding this point, but the reader's opinion is as good as any. Many scholars have attempted to access recorded or printed versions of Cougars, an apparent obsession of many citizens at the time of the Clooneen Jam. All these efforts came to naught. Therefore, we are unable to let the reader know whether "Stacey" was pregnant or not.

In any case, the story of the Clooneen Jam, and the results of the adventures of The Citroën, do not end here. We are beholden to the dedicated work of a legion of researchers whose effort enable us now to draw the tragic story of the Clooneen Jam to its logical conclusion.

(The Editors.)

+++++

THE TEXT OF *IS STACEY PREGNANT?* which you have just read is an abridged—and edited—version of a much longer text. *The Citroën Notebook*. The discovery of what remains of the latter text, and how we in the *Müllingarische Institut zur Erforschung der Weltgeschichte* came to possess it, is a story in itself.

It was discovered quite by accident when one of the few known, and probably the last, survivor of the Clooneen Jam (though this is pure guesswork) tried to sell the handwritten original of *The Citroën Notebook* to a bookshop in Düsseldorf, many years after memories of the Jam had dwindled to a vague folk memory. This mysterious individual, of quite advanced years, reputedly, was never identified and carried no identification papers, official or otherwise.

According to the latest research (Priebschke and O'Rourke 2499), this potential vender of *The Citroën Notebook* was unable to give a coherent answer to even the simplest of questions posed to him by the bookstore personnel. He couldn't recall his name or his place of origin. Such confusion is almost unimaginable to our citizens of today, who know that the authorities can always extract all the data they need from the microchip that is embedded from birth in all human bodies. Chan (2506) surmises that this man may not have even been able to understand the questions put to him. (It should be noted here, however, that neither the *Eurareich Polizei* nor appropriately appointed officials of the *Die Deutsche Gesellschaft für das Studium der Ölkrise* never had the opportunity to question this strange vagabond. This could never have happened if current universally binding legislation had been in place then).

His apparent inability to understand German is puzzling. However, although it may seem incredible to us today, substantial non-German-speaking minorities survived in many parts of Europe even beyond the middle of the first century of our Millennium (Himmler, Hanley and Srb, 2438). The reader of *Is Stacey Pregnant?* is bound recall the helicopter incident in the text and the inability of ordinary citizens of the then Republic of Ireland to understand the simple message addressed to them, *auf Deutsch*, by the helicopter crew.

What is glaringly obvious, however, is that this would-be vender of *The Citroën Notebook* was an escapee from the Clooneen Jam. He is recorded as being one of the worst cases of Jam Psychosis, ever recorded, displaying all the physical and psychological symptoms of the rare condition according to the fragmentary medical evidence now available (Beck and Coll, 2405). An autopsy on his body indicated overwhelmingly the presence of the physiological trauma that inevitably accompanies advanced Jam Psychosis: physical emaciation, fatigue, hunger and, above all, elevated levels of carbon monoxide in his blood.

Given the poor state of his health, it is hardly surprisingly that he took a bad turn in the bookshop and was removed from there it in a condition adjudged to be critical. We now know that he was placed in an ambulance (a specialized automobile used in the 20th and early 21st centuries to transport patients to hospitals) which became ensnared in a routine 5-day traffic jam, during which he, most unfortunately, died. Thus, it seems highly unlikely that we will ever know definitively the relation the deceased might have had to the author of *The Citroën Notebook*. Or how he came to be in possession of said document, in the first place.

Many (including the editors of *Is Stacey Pregnant?*) are strongly convinced that *The Citroën Notebook* may have been snatched from the lifeless fingers of The Citroën himself. Some even hold that the deceased Jam escapee may himself have been The Citroën. This begs a question: if this, in fact, was the case, why was he carrying only a part of his writings, and these in a highly disorganized state? In spite of many assertions to the contrary, it is now held generally that the man who tried to sell *The Citroën Notebook* in Düsseldorf was, in fact, a jam escapee, possibly a fellow parishioner of The Citroën. In any case, this unfortunate Clooneen Jam veteran—not appreciating, in all probability, the historical value of the document in this possession and the strict legal requirements that apply to such materials, even in that distant era—failed to bring it to the attention of the relevant authorities.

Parenthetically, it is ironic to note that had a desperate man not needed money to buy food, the world today would not be in a position to read the scarcely credible, but historically valuable chronicle, even its incomplete condition, that is *The Citroën Notebook*. And, thence, a new, valuable and unsuspected window is opened on aspects of life as it was lived in one allegedly developed European country in the years immediately preceding that nodal Peak Oil Crisis that initiated the termination of the Automobile Age as the Great Disaster loomed.

Luckily for mankind, this starving benefactor took great care of what remained of *The Citroën Notebook*. It was almost as if he sensed the unique value of his acquisition, however he had acquired it. When he presented it at the Düsseldorf bookshop, he had carefully placed its pages, in no particular order, in a self-sealing plastic folder. Only a few pages were damaged but, even though rainsoaked, they were still partially legible.

However, the vast bulk of The Citroën Notebook was never recovered. When The Citroën decided finally, together with some companions, to abandon their stranded vehicles and undertake the long hazardous journey on foot eastwards to their original destinations, he seems to have left or, possibly, had been forced the leave, most of his writings behind in Clooneen. And, unfortunately for us, he seems to have set out on this, his last, journey with neither pen nor paper, so his adventures after leaving the precincts of his „Parish" can ony be a cause for speculation.

As fortune would have it, the librarian then in charge of the bookstore, Doktor Hans-Dieter Rasmussen, who was left holding the document as its owner was being removed in the ambulance, was an avid connoisseur of genuine historical documentation. Thus, he understood immediately the importance of that untidy collection of papers wrapped in their plastic envelope. He placed it for safe keeping, along with other valuable documents in his possession, in his private safe.

And it is there, to make a long story short, that they were discovered hundreds of years later by a lineal descendant of Hans-Dieter, a certain Eva Rasmussen, in an excellent state of preservation, on the date recorded by her, 19th February 2438.

She instantly contacted the Ministry of Cultural Marketing in Mönchengladbach for the purpose of maximizing the cultural benefit that might accrue to historical scholarship and society in general, were this document to be examined by experts in the field of ancient manuscript exegesis.

Doctor Graciela Schultz, a former student of ours, was appointed Minister for Cultural Marketing in 2492. She almost instantly charged us at the Müllingarische Institut zur Erforschung der Weltgeschichte with editing The Citroën Notebook as well as gauging the possible significance of its contents of in relation to the subsequent Great Disaster, the center of much contemporary historical controversy.

We found that the landscape sketched in The Citroën

Notebook seldom transgresses the physical boundaries of "The Parish", a tiny section of that massive traffic jam in which stranded motorists got to know each other and organized in order to confront the daunting challenges posed by the radical uncertainty of their future.

Did the unpalatable truths of existence beyond the pale of his own „Parish" inhibit the desire of The Citroën, a journalist, to capture them in words? Especially, when the ghastly „truth" of the same Parish impelled him to desert his automobile and „take to his heels", as Wycliffe (2511) opines. Who really knows! All we can do is regret that The Citroën failed to bring his journalistic talents to bear on the adventures that lay in store for him subsequent to his escape from the nightmarish horror of his situation. For, as such travails must have been the lot of the lucky few who managed to escape from the nightmare of The Clooneen Jam.

Nightmare? The word is hardly excessive in this context when we consider an oral deposition made by a long-dead survivor of the Clooneen Jam to the Peak Oil Crisis Historical Society (POCHS), as consulted by us in the preparation of this text. According to him, the immediate grouping of cars in which The Citroën and his companions resided—known to him as The Parish—seems to have been one of the few parts of the Clooneen Jam to boast some semblance of order and civilization. Stretching ahead of the ragged hungry group (an estimated quarter of the population of The Parish), who decided to desert their automobiles at the same time as The Citroën were about 150km of dangerous Jamland stretching eastwards all the way across the Central Plain of Ireland as far as Dublin, where law and order had ceased to exist.

Wild and starving bands roamed this territory, preying on equally savage other sections of the Clooneen Jam together with towns that had the misfortune to be located in the hinterland of the Great Jam. Swords, machetes, guns, even rocket launchers, emerged as if from nowhere. Pitched battles ensued. Towns such as Loughrea, Athlone, Müllingar and Kilcock were burned to the ground. As is evidenced by The Citroën's manuscript, cannibalism became endemic in the Jam zone.

Some idea as to the hazards that The Citroën and his famished band must have encountered may be gleaned from a transcribed deposition of another contemporary source (OCHS, Vol XVI, p1032-3). This witness described the macabre and Dantesque terrain that was undoubtedly traversed by refugees from the Clooneen Jam as follows:

> The areas we passed by then—or skirted—were for the most part total chaos. The nauseating mingled odours of human excrement and the gaseous emanations of decaying corpses caused us to place neckerchiefs or any available piece of cloth over our noses . Roaming bands of dogs gone wild we tried to avoid, and not always successfully, as some of us fell victim to them. Rusting cars of all descriptions, broken windows, tires and seats missing—for 'bonfires' blocked the road. More ghastly, though, were the skeletons—human skeletons. They were everywhere: in, under and on top of automobiles. The bones of children were particularly pathetic. The sight of dogs, their bellies swollen, obviously sated on human flesh, was sickeningly obscene.

Did The Citroën fall victim to one of these marauding bands? To a bullet or the slash of a machete? To a starving pack of dogs? To his own utter exhaustion? We will probably never know the answer to those questions. However, it has to be mentioned that Professor Hans-Günter O'Sullivan, Müllingar University, has convincingly advanced his thesis that the author of *The Citroën Notebook* escaped from the Clooneen Jam and lived to a ripe old age, operating a chain of florist shops in his native city of Caherciveen or, possibly, in Lucerne, regional capital of the Mittleres Eurareich.

It will be appreciated that centuries of civil, international and interplanetary strife, along with drastic climatic change, have passed since the tragic events of the Clooneen Jam were recorded by The Citroën. Thence, the vast majority of the documentary evidence and other records needed to complete the definitive story of the tragedy—and, most particularly, its immediate aftermath—are no longer available to us. In fact, it is not likely that the Clooneen Jam story will ever be completed.

The most we can do here is give thanks that this modest, self-effacing and unlikely author has given us an unique insight into a deeply disturbing period of human history from which all of us can extract those universal lessons which the human race always forgets to its cost.

AFTERWORD

What follows is a series of four epilogs, in which reflections on *Das Citroensche Tagebuch*, the original source of *Is Stacey Pregnant?*, are presented. They are by-products of ongoing historical research being conducted currently by staff members of the *Müllingarische Institut zur Erforschung der Weltgeschichte*. They may, hopefully, enable the reader to better appreciate the historical context and significance of the unspeakably grim events recorded in *Is Stacey Pregnant?*.

EPILOG ONE

Is Stacey Pregnant? is a popularized—and imaginatively edited—version of a much longer text in Irish Gaelic, referred to by linguistic scholars and historical researchers as *The Citroën Notebook (Das Citroensche Tagebuch,* Diesel, Kelly und Fromm, Müllingar, 2497).

Recent surveys show that few of our fellow citizens are aware of the notorious traffic snarl "The Clooneen Jam", now known to have occurred half a millennium ago in the then Republic of Ireland, and which is described by *The Citroën Notebook* from within. Our own research indicates that this event happened shortly before the so-called Peak Oil Crisis irremediably altered the history of mankind. That is to say, slightly before chronic flooding due to rising sea levels and increasing rainfall levels, together with dangerous radioactivity levels due to the Great Windscale Disaster, led to the mass abandonment of Dublin, together with low-lying sections of the country's Atlantic coast, and the re-location of the country's capital in Müllingar (now about 75m over sea level), near the island's geographical center.

Likewise, few denizens of the former Republic of Ireland will have heard of The Citroën, the anonymous, not to say eponymous, scribe of the aforementioned traffic jam that stretched all the way from the remote boggy townland of Clooneen (the present Klühneberger Heide) all the way to Dublin, paralyzing all traffic movement in the then Republic of Ireland. Yet, the diary of this journalist is one of the very few surviving historical documents of from that turbulent era. It is an indispensable account of the interests, hopes, concerns—and the grim desperation—of ordinary men and women who found themselves setting out on a seemingly normal spring day to confront an unspeakably horrible disaster, grim fruit of the savage mores of those primitive times.

We are forever grateful that The Citroën had both

pens and paper (primitive materials employed in the act of writing), together with the will and patience needed to record the day to day happenings as the epic of the Clooneen Jam gradually unfolded. One importance of this little-known text resides in the fact that it involves us personally in the interaction of those unlucky enough to be trapped, innocently and unintentionally, in this traffic jam, thus enabling us to relive, imaginatively and graphically, the ambience of that tragic event.

Is Stacey Pregnant? situates us on a key historical nodal point, when small self-governing entities (nation-states), such as the Republic of Ireland (ROI), were enthusiastically shedding their national sovereignties and merging to form multinational entities! Some idea as to the dynamic involved in this process is of interest in this connection. The "Western Eurareich" Island (WEI), the successor of the ROI, was integrated with the Eastern Eurareich Island (EEI), the administrative descendant of the United Kingdom (UK) to form the Eurareich Archipelago (EA). This merger was propitiated by a more or less common media exposure that unified the language, values, interests and tastes of the populations of the two islands. The AE, in its turn, with other European states, in the Eurareich, which was eventually swallowed up by World Government Incorporated (WGI), whose banner now flies proudly among the other regional flags of the Solar System.

But was the Clooneen Jam really one of history's a nodal points? *The Citroën Notebook* and other fragmentary evidence that supports this assertion, has led us at the Müllingarische Institut zur Erforschung der Weltgeschichte (Müllingar Institute of World History Research) to hypothesize that this disaster initiated that long and often bloody process that culminated in our present World and Interplanetary Order. The soundness of this hypothesis is being continually validated by our researchers.

Thus, we are deeply thankful that the set of unlikely circumstances that culminated in the accidental, but extremely fortuitous, appearance of *Das Citroensche Tagebuch* (and now, in this abridged form, *Is Stacey Pregnant?*) provides our academic—and the wider global and inter-planetary—community with such a fount of unique perspectives, knowledge and tantalizing exoticisms together with an intriguing problematic that will engage the curiosity of historical researchers for many years to come.

Nevertheless, we have, to our shame, allowed the Clooneen Jam, to become a mere footnote in a history which, is the common patrimony of all inhabitants of the still habitable regions of our own treasured planet and beyond. We can only hope that this first edition of *Is Stacey Pregnant?* will serve to make adequate reparation for such a grave sin of cultural omission.

Everybody mentioned in the text of *Is Stacey Pregnant?*, that "open window on the mores of a bygone age"—as it was referred to by Graciela Schultz, our present Regional Minister of Cultural Marketing (Landesrätin für Kultur-Marketing), who from her office in Mönchengladbach has generously supported our project from its beginnings—is identified solely on the basis of the automobile (see Epilog 4, p25) they were driving at the time of the disaster rather than by their personal birth names. Thus, we are almost certain that people of that distant time, unlike those of the tumultuous post-Automobile Era that followed, came to be recognized, and to recognize themselves socially, on the basis of the car they possessed. Hardly ever did they seem to be recognized by their officially validated names, professions or whatever other personal attributes distinguished them from their fellows.

Does this apparent "absorption of the individual by the commodity" (cf *The Civilization that Collapsed*, Mendéz, Grossvogel, Müllingar, 2102), seemingly characteristic of the later Automobile Age, confirm once again a generalized social "de-empathification", the term popularized by many leading contemporary historians and sociologists (such as Fernández, Heilbrunner and O'Malley etc.). Their researches seek to explain the psychological dimension of the social change that followed the end of "The Automobile Era" and the subsequent incorporation of the remains of the European Union (EU), firstly into the Eurareich and, then, into our present World Government Incorporated (WGI)? What light does *Is Stacey Pregnant?* throw on the social and psychological dimensions of that upheaval? Readers of this book should now have their own answers to that question.

EPILOG TWO

The Clooneen Jam: an historical perspective,
by Professor Shivaun Chan

The editors of *Is Stacey Pregnant?* have kindly asked me to delineate my take on the wider socio/historical context within which the tragic events of the Clooneen Jam may have developed, drawing on whatever specialized knowledge I may have acquired of that period. This I do somewhat hesitantly, as the paucity of records pertaining to said period renders whatever we affect to know about it as being speculative, at best.

The story of *Is Stacey Pregnant?* pertains clearly to the Western Eurareich Island (WEI) or, possibly, the 'Republic of Ireland'. The events described in this book occurred, in all probability, sometime in the first half of the 21st. century. As national histories and geographies are no longer studied in the schools of our interplanetary epoch, this context will have little resonance with our contemporary readers. Further elucidation is necessary.

However, and most unfortunately, the catastrophic bloody upheavals of the first century of the current Millennium, before which the events described in *The Citroën Notebook* seem to have occurred, had the effect of destroying most of the documentary evidence we need to fully describe the context of the Clooneen Jam. With that proviso, and a corresponding modicum of modest hesitancy, let us now try to explain briefly the social/political background of the events described in that document.

We are beholden here to the few information sources that survived the disasters of that century. They make it clear that the context in which the appalling events that occurred on Klühneberger Heide (formerly: Clooneen) was fraught with complexities that seem to us to be childish and chaotic. But we must bear in mind that we are dealing here with a mankind still drastically limited by its immature intellectual and emotional infrastructure.

It seems that corruption, greed and bureaucratic inefficiency had ended the reign of one Taoiseach (Tea-shock, Führer, Dear Leader) in the early years of that disaster-plagued century. A parade of successor Taoiseachs followed him. At one point, according to Schreiber and Doherty (2427), the population of the then Republic of Ireland had voted to reject the Federal Europe being proposed to them by Brussels' bureaucrats. However, thanks to the subsequent threats of the said bureaucrats, and their Irish politician collaborators, it was prevailed upon to change its original stance, thus driving a nail into the coffin of the country's hard-won national sovereignty.

Meanwhile, unscrupulous international financiers, aided by Irish accomplices, tightened their stranglehold on the economy of that unfortunate country (O'Reilly and Tannenbaum 2472). Banks, mainly of German, French and British provenance made vast sums of money available to the Irish banks. The latter, in turn, channeled this bounty to Irish entrepreneurs, mainly building developers. Economic experts predicted that this economic boom would never end. Developers, happily taking advantage of this unprecedented El Dorado, constructed building estates all over Ireland, driving supply away beyond demand. Archaeologists still encounter the ruins of so-called "ghost estates", clusters of houses built in that era, but never destined for human occupation. (Betancourt and Kimmel 2431)

Predictably, the bottom fell out of the property market, developers were unable to discharge their bank debts, thus initiating a downward economic spiral from which the country as a whole, major financial operators excepted, was not destined to recover. This was an unexpected turn of events for Ireland's creditors who then bayed menacingly at the doors of Irish banks, clamoring, as such creditors always did, for the return of their pound of flesh, and more.

The Irish political class ran cravenly to the rescue of the banks and their foreign creditors. They ordained that the gaping black holes in Ireland's bank coffers be stuffed with public money extracted from Irish tax-payers. So, all players in this macabre game were happy—Irish and foreign banks, politicians, foreign investors, most developers—all except the unfortunate Irish tax-payer, who subject to an increasingly crushing burden of taxes, would usually have blamed the Government for his plight. However, the latter, in a neat sideways shuffle, caused this blame to be shared with "the men in black" (cf: Grüber and Takahashi, 2434), agents of the then main international monetary agencies, the European Central Bank, the International Monetary Fund and the World Bank, allowed in by the Government to manage its finances and the national economy.

(In many ways, apart from the archaeologically verified factuality of the events described in *Is Stacey Pregnant?*, the said text could well be construed as a metaphor for the initiation of a whole people into a new dimension of a political/economic reality whose true nature will always remain hidden from most of them. But this was hardly the intention of our anonymous author.)

In a nutshell, then, it would seem according to many researchers that national sovereignty was traded for a "solution" of the enormous bank debt problem that entailed saddling the vast majority of the Irish people with the gambling debts of a tiny minority of international investors.

Thus this unfortunate majority was faced with gigantic debts that could never have been paid off in its foreseeable future. Poverty or emigration were the only choices available to large swathes of the population, especially the young.

This picture of the state of Ireland at the time of The Clooneen Jam is contested by many other researchers, however. They claim that it presents an unreal scenario, in that such a fiasco could never have been permitted by a democratically enfranchised majority in a normally functioning republic. The nearby well-documented example of Iceland, which "burned" its foreign investors would have spurred the Irish to a similar response, they claim.

However Yamamoto, Armstrong and Marciano (2475) defend the thesis outlined here. They assert that the erosion of the Irish national morale and moral fiber can be traced as far back as the end of the 17th Century, when the remnants of the Gaelic cultural and administrative order disappeared. Other participants in this debate claim (e.g., Gillespie, McEntaggart and Monks) that the autocratic position of the Roman Catholic Church expedited this erosion of the national fiber. The evidence that a considerable part of the population had come to live at the beginning of the Millennium in a sort of universal media circus, as is intimated by the text of *Is Stacey Pregnant?*, can hardly be discounted as a factor relevant to this steep national decline.

Another current of historical enquiry (Gombrich and McNamara, 2483) hold that the Irish people revenged themselves on the native leaders they felt had betrayed them by refusing to re-elect them. Thus, they elected a series of leaders, who functioned however as de facto Viceroys in an Ireland in which they operated at the behest of the then European Union, banksters and international financial bureaucrats. Meanwhile the wealth of the country continued to drain away through the holes in the coffers of the nation's banks into the pockets of foreign gamblers. The young found employment elsewhere, mainly in Britain, Australia, New Zealand, Canada and the U.S.A.

As, is evident from the text of *Is Stacey Pregnant?*, German had yet to be declared a compulsory subject in all schools of the Republic of Ireland, at the time of the composition of said text. This fact enables us to resolve at least one scholarly dispute. I know that I am on safe ground when I cite textual evidence to prove that the events that constituted the Clooneen Jam occurred when that country was still so named, which corresponds to the first half of the first century of our Millennium.

However, such weighty and complex considerations were very far indeed from the concerns of the anonymous driver, The Citroën, (author of a text now recognized as an undisputed part of mankind's historical heritage) as his automobile hummed along almost silently along dew-wet country lanes that radiant late Spring morning in the West of Ireland. Through the medium of the words he bequeathed to us we can vividly imagine that blue-grey automobile gliding along smoothly beneath his backside towards the awful destiny that lies, thankfully for him, beyond the reach of his imagination…

EPILOG THREE

An Introduction by Herman Grossvogel, The Müllingarische Institut zur Erforschung der Weltgeschichte. May 2497, to *Ein Tagebuch der Katastrophe von Clooneen* (Diesel, Kelly und Fromm, Müllingar, 2503).

"It would be the height of imprudence to ignore the grave lesson inherent to this harrowing true tale." (Siobhán Chan. *Das Citroensche Tagebuch*, Ich. IV-V Diesel, Kelly und Fromm, Müllingar, 2497).

It is a sad reflection on the teaching of history in our schools that few, if any, of our students will have heard of that enormous traffic jam half a millennium ago on the Klühneberger Heide. Clooneen/An Cluainín was how that townland was named in the then Republic of Ireland, a self-governing entity in the short-lived epoch of the nation-state.

The title of *Das Citroensche Tagebuch*, refers to the unknown author of this Late Non-Traditional Irish Gaelic text. The name, or pen name, of this man (his sex is evidenced by the text itself), An (= Der) Citroen, is now a byword among serious students of early 21st century history.

But for the faithfulness with he recorded the gruesome detail of the prolog to that dreadful event, we would be totally bereft of the evidence of a living witness of the Clooneen disaster, and whose account is now an ineradicable part of our contemporary literary canon.

One of the astonishing virtues of *Das Citroensche Tagebuch* is that it holds up a mirror in which mankind sees its own doppelganger, with its "shades of black and white, its images of virtue and decadence" in the words of the distinguished lunar critic, Arlene Sachs (2487). It is not for us here to harp on the destruction and barbarism that were unfortunate concomitants of the First Interplanetary War. The memories of the cannibalism indulged in by allegedly civilized men (and women) on the Martian Plains is still fresh in the memory of all peoples of the Solar System.

However, the recent peaceful incorporation of the Chinese Planets into the Interplanetary Federal System (IFS) gives us grounds for hope that such bloody episodes are, definitively, things of the barbaric past of our ancestors.

Suffice it to say here that contemporary accounts of the Mars Massacre and the bleak landscape of *Das Citroensche Tagebuch*, demonstrate that human nature has not changed to the extent that many of us would like to believe. The wild beast resides within us all, it seems, coded for by our genes, and adroitly camouflaged by the canons of civilized behavior. *Das Citroensche Tagebuch* is a timely reminder of this unpalatable fact.

Therefore, it is not at all surprising that, in spite of its primitively constructed and asynchronic narrative, the reader of *Das Citroensche Tagebuch*, meets within its pages surprisingly recognizable individuals, almost identifiable from their foibles as some of our contemporary citizens.

Then again, that faithful chronicler, The Citroën, affords us a unique glimpse of how ordinary people lived, admittedly in extreme circumstances in a distant epoch when so-called nation-states—such as the Republic of Ireland—were still extant, just before their "democracies", and much else, were finally undermined and destroyed by their anarchic economic system.

It was a world in which separate "races" still existed—Germans, Irish etc.,—years before the forcible miscegenation policies of our WGI outlawed all intra-racial matrimony. Yet, the world of The Citroën is one in which the forms of that public administrative system called "democracy" were still visible, even though its substance was very obviously already corroded, possibly mortally, by the time the Clooneen Jam occurred. In the opinion of Montserrat O'Reilly (2452), the levels of pathological levels of docility and submissiveness displayed by the Parishioners towards the Smilin' Porkys, and the scant evidence of serious socio-political participation displayed by the "parishioners", for example, could never have sustained a vigorously viable democracy. This, of course makes the, as yet unverifiable, assumption that the Clooneen Jam Parish was a representative sample of the now long-defunct Republic of Ireland.

We cannot, in the space afforded us, deal with more than a couple of the many-sided fascinating problematic raised by *Das Citroensche Tagebuch*.

Aaron Sobolev (2485), for example, hypothesizes that the events described by The Citroën (that occurred in 2028, according to his controversial reckoning) signaled the beginning of the Great Disaster, that series of gigantic upheavals that marked the beginning of our Millennium and whose consequence was a gigantic "thinning of the herd" (i.e. greatly reduced populations) and desertification plus oceanification of vast areas of the planet Earth that will not become habitable again for millions of years. Indeed, Sobolev maintains that *Das Citroensche Tagebuch* is a metaphoric account, a sort of microcosm (as he describes it), whether it was intended to be so, or not, of the history and nature of the aforesaid upheavals.

Research being conducted presently at the Müllingarsche Institut zur Erforschung der Weltgeschichte tends to support Sobolev's thesis. And, thereby, to elevate the critical importance of *Das Citroensche Tagebuch* as a necessary key to understanding the dynamic of the troubled epoch in which it was written.

Another aspect of this text that interests us is the reason why The Citroën chose to represent individuals by the names of the cars in which they were wont to travel in rather than in names chosen for them by their parents at birth. Were all of our distant ancestors of 500 years ago recognized by their fellows on the former basis than on the latter? And, if so, why? We remind those of our readers who are unfamiliar with the concept 'car', and that said concept is described directly below in Epilog Four (p. 265).

Or, was this "car-identification" of individuals merely a

personal idiosyncrasy of, our anonymous scribe, The Citroën. We have no yet uncovered evidence that would either confirm, or refute, such an hypothesis.

As Graciela Schultz, our gracious Eurareich Minister for Cultural Marketing, remarked: „the naming procedure practiced by the "cast" of *Das Citroensche Tagebuch* gives us good reason to be grateful that personal identification is now based on a number encoded for in our Universal Identification Document (UID), and acceptable now in all parts of the Solar System. Buttressed by this number, any citizen is entitled the choose a name from the list of names permitted for all for many years now by the WGI."

So, here we have a nameless author! Could we be dealing here with the "cult of depersonalization", a reaction to the earlier narcissistic "Me-Cult" (Srb, 2488) that seems to have been endemic to the Late Automobile Age. (cf: *The Civilization that Commited Suicide*, Colm Mendéz, Grossvogel, Müllingar, 2502)? Or with the "desocialization" with which contemporary sociologists (Ruriko Fernández, Séamas Heilbrunner and Gustavo O'Malley et cetera) seek to illuminate the "psychological dimension" of that multifaceted "Great Disaster', now believed (albeit controversially) by these researchers to have occurred sometime around 2020, give or take ten years.

At that point in history, the dominant economic narrative of the time, an unbridled sociopathic capitalism, collapsed and expired under the weight of its own contradictions, bringing so-called Western Civilization in its train to its gory end. A secondary aspect of this narrative was the conflation of personality with particular commodities, according to both Mendez (2502) and Sobolev (2485). The naming of personalities in the text of *Das Citroensche Tagebuch* demonstrates clearly that this process was at an advanced stage by the time this text was written.

Many researchers draw attention to the involvement of "Psychology" (a failed pre-scientific attempt to make sense of mental phenomena that predated Neurology) and capitalistic magical thinking in this widespread de-empathification. For, incredible as it may seem to us today, there were those in that distant epoch who attributed a scientific character to a cluster of superstitions created ex nihilo by Freud, Jung, Adler and others of their ilk. "Self-help" books followed in their wake, along with faux-Asiatic mysticism and such pseudo-sciences as astrology and crystal healing, all cognitive referents of the de-socialized "me-centered personality" characteristic of the so-called "Age of Narcissism". In this way, gullible, though significant, sectors of "developed world" populations came to believe that ultimate meaning—and happiness—is accessible to mankind, through mystical experiences that transcend the ambit of rational thought.

Certain researchers (Sobolev, Ó Gráinne etc.) hold that this decadent retreat from reason and its replacement by magical thinking played a not inconsiderable part in the genesis of "The Great Collapse", sometimes called "The Great Disaster" the result of which was the incorporation of the remnants of the European Union (EU) into the early primitive version of World Government Incorporated (WGI). At the level of the ordinary citizen, does the interpersonal relating of the players of Das Citroensche Tagebuch bear out the thesis of these researchers? The reader will by now have formed her own answer to that question!

Given these considerations, it is shameful that we have allowed the importance of this event, and the document that describes it in vivid detail, to lie forgotten for hundreds of years. Even today, in spite of its undoubted seminal importance to the subsequent unfolding of human history, this extraordinary *Das Citroensche Tagebuch* seldom merits more than a tiny footnote to the officially approved history of our Planet.

But the undeniable fact is that the Clooneen Jam, together with its complex historical and sociological ramifications, belong to our common human heritage, no matter which planet of the Solar System, colonized by us over the last hundreds of years, now claims our loyalty.

It is to be hoped that this small attempt will be seen as an act of penance, late though it be, through which the unforgivably grave sin of forgetfulness, on the part of our official spokespersons, may be forgiven.

EPILOG FOUR

The Automobile (Car)–A Primitive Means of Transport

It is necessary to draw attention to an aspect of the text you have just read that many contemporary readers will, undoubtedly, have found puzzling. Universally validated research has shown that the "Citroen" was a make of what was referred to as an "automobile", also referred to as "car", a quaint (but ultimately disastrous in its consequences) mode of transport characteristic of what "The Automobile Age" that preceded the Great Disaster.

    The automobile (or car) was, in effect, a metal box or sitting room sitting on four wheels. The rotation of these wheels, and hence the propulsion of automobiles, was obtained by realizing the energy potential of oil or other energy-rich liquids, in a so-called "internal combustion engine", a component part of the automobile itself. Models of this engine, whose widespread utilization for transport purposes preceded the discovery and exploitation of gravitational energy initiated by the researches of Laubsch and O' Growney (and summarized notably in their groundbreaking Die *Energie der Gravitation: ein neuer Anfang für die Menschheit*, 2242), can be observed in science history museums, such as that of Das Staatliche Museum für Antike Technologie, Müllingar, WEI.

    It is now confirmed authoritatively (cf. the works of Sneidorf, Wanamaker, Van der Winkel, etc.) that the gaseous effluent emitted by internal combustion engines, referred to at that time as "exhaust", was an important factor in bringing about that sudden and calamitous climate change that initiated the reconfiguration of human civilization, both on earth and, by extension, on the many other planets since colonized.

TOMÁS MAC SÍOMÓIN

Irish Gaelic novelist, storyteller, poet, and journalist. A doctoral graduate of Cornell University, New York, he has worked as a biological researcher and university lecturer in the Netherlands, USA and Ireland. He was editor of the Irish language newspaper *Anois* and for many years he was editor of the literary and current affairs magazine, *Comhar*. His collection of short stories *Cinn Lae Seangáin* (The Diary of an Ant) won the award for the best short story collection in the Oireachtas 2005 competition, while in the following year his novel *An Tionscadal* (The Project) won the main Oireachtas literary award. His short story *Music in the Bone* was selected by The Dalkey Archive Press for inclusion in Best European Fiction 2013. He has lived and worked in Catalonia since 1998.

ALSO AVAILABLE FROM NUASCÉALTA TEORANTA

The House of Gold by Liam O'Flaherty

A rare perspective on the Irish at a major turning point in their history. Greed, priestly lusts, sexual frustration, alcoholism, and murder are themes woven together in this compelling tale.

Diary of an Ant by Tomás Mac Síomóin

Diary of an Ant is the first English language translation of *Cín Lae Seangáin agus scéalta eile*, the critically acclaimed, award-winning collection of short stories by Dublin-born author Tomás Mac Síomóin. A darkly humorous look at the failure and the innate dishonesty of most inter-human relating against a backdrop of ultimate absurdity that he sees as underlying all human experience.

GiB - A Modest Exposure by Jack Mitchell

An epic poem attacking the system that cloaked the murder of IRA members Daniel McCann, Sean Savage, and Mairéad Farrell by British security forces in Gibraltar. This commemorative edition includes an introduction by Gerry Adams, a preface by Séamus Deane and an afterward by Niall Farrell.

Aran to Africa, An Irishman's Unique Odyssey by Pádraig O'Toole

Starting with an insider's glimpse of a vanished way of life, *Aran to Africa* traces the steps of Pádraig O' Toole from a barefoot Irish-speaking boy to rebellious seminarian. He marries the internationally renowned singer and harpist, Mary O'Hara and retiring to his native Inis Mór, Ireland, sums up reflections inspired by his life.

www.nuascealta.com

Printed in Great Britain
by Amazon